TRINITY'S FALL

P.A. Vasey

Copyright © 2019 P.A.Vasey
All rights reserved.

All characters and events in this novel are fictitious, and any resemblance to real persons, living or dead, is purely coincidental.

This novel is dedicated to Rachael and Lauren.

Never stop making me proud.

What the country needs

is the annihilation of the enemy.

- Lord Horatio Nelson

PROLOGUE

He wakes like he's been plugged into the mains. No sleepiness, no slow warming up. Within seconds his eyes are wide, dreams not just forgotten but erased. He drinks in the feedback of all his senses, but aside from his own noisy breath there is nothing to hear.

The walls around him are a sterile white, gleaming, featureless. He is lying in a bed, but he has no idea where he is. It doesn't look like a hospital. He doesn't know what time it is or even what day it is.

His mind races, and panic begins like a cluster of firecrackers in his abdomen. His heart starts to hammer in his chest and an invisible hand clasps over his mouth.

He doesn't know who he is.

He sits up and pristine white sheets fall away. He's wearing a grey rubber suit, tubes and cables wrapped around his torso. Some of the cables disappear underneath the bed, and pulses of red and green lights travel along them.

He swings his legs over the side and the coldness of the tiled floor through his bare feet gives him a jolt. His hands are tingling and he looks at them, turning them over, checking them out. They look like his. He recognizes the age spots and the plain gold wedding ring is vaguely familiar. He tries to stand and the room spins and the ground feels as if it's melting under him. He collapses onto his hands and knees, his breathing becoming shallow and ragged.

At last you are awake

There's a voice in his head. Is he going mad?

He closes his eyes and tries to slow his breathing.

You need to find out where we are

Alright, he'll go along with this.

Maybe it's a stress response. Amped-up emotions, hormones and the like.

"I've no idea where we are," he says out loud. "Shall we look around?"

There's a slight moment of disorientation and light-headedness that makes him reach out and balance himself with a hand on the bed, but it passes. The cables are still connected to him so he's careful to keep them intact as he walks across the room to where there is a small sink with a mirror. He bends down to see his face and staring back at him is someone he recognizes. White hair combed back, skin pockmarked with old acne scars, three-day stubble. Blue eyes with laughter lines.

His face.

He smiles and leans on the sink, shaking his head.

"It'll all come back soon," he says to his reflection. "You'll be fine. It's over."

A strange disquiet comes over him, an unbidden feeling of restlessness and butterflies in his stomach. A tickling sensation under the skin, like spiders crawling in the dermis, appears. A feeling of pressure behind his eyes.

Then the voice again.

Someone is coming

A doorway swishes open and a girl walks in. Like him, she is wearing a rubber-look suit, slick, like dolphin-skin. She looks young, early twenties, dark hair, quite pretty. Nervous, eyes flitting left and right.

"What's going on?" he hears himself say.

"You're resting," she stammers, and then coughs. "But you're up. You must be feeling better?"

He smiles. "I guess I am." He looks around and makes a sweeping gesture. "Can you tell me where I am? I'm a little confused."

She gives a nervous smile. "You're on the ship. The ship. I'm still getting my head around it."

Ask her what ship

He shakes his head to clear the voice.

Ask her

"What ship?" he says.

"You know what ship," she says. "The alien ship."

Good: we will take it from them

The voice drips with malevolence and the temperature in the room seems to drop below freezing.

"Where are you?" he says, looking around the room.

"Who're you talking to?" the girl says.

Kill her

"What?" He shakes his head, back and forwards, repetitively, frustrated. The girl leans in and he grabs her wrist, pulling her close. He has no free will. He didn't make the move.

"I don't want to hurt you," he grinds out. "But I can't control myself. I can't control …"

Her face changes, and she now has a concerned look, her mouth a tight grimace. She pulls on her arm, but his grip automatically tightens.

"Let go," she says. "You're hurting me."

He continues to squeeze her wrist, and there's a noise as one of her wrist joints cracks, like a knuckle popping.

"I can't," he says, silently pleading with her to understand. "I'm sorry."

She brings her other hand around and grabs his fingers, trying to peel them off her wrist. Then she punches him. Hard. In the face.

Again and again she hits him with her free hand, her face contorted in anger as she gives everything she has. He feels nothing. He hears the impacts but there is no sensation. As she winds up another punch he lets go of her wrist and she jerks back. She rubs her wrists and just stands there, face dark and glowering.

"You're one of them, aren't you?" she says, backing off further, glancing sideways.

He tries to reply but now he cannot move his lips. He feels his throat constricting and a paralysis has come over him.

I am in full control now

Please, no.

Oh yes

He watches the girl reach behind her where he sees what must be his clothes laid out on a shelf.

She scrabbles around in them and pulls out a gun.

A Glock 9mm.

"What have you got there?" he says.

But it is not him talking now.

She shrugs, a gesture laden with surrender. She slowly raises the gun and points it at him and it shakes as if there is an earthquake happening under her feet.

"Are you a gambler?" whispers his voice.

"What?" Her lip twitches and her wide-eyed stare becomes even bigger and wider.

"Do you like to bet?"

She nods. "Sure. Now and again."

He feels himself nodding back, mirroring her. "Do you feel like betting now?"

"What?"

"Do you think you could shoot me before I take the gun from you?"

He wants to scream. To shout out and tell her to unload the whole magazine into his face. But the gun is wavering even more and he can feel his muscles begin to wind up, readying to reach out and grab it in a microsecond, before a single neuronal impulse can travel from her brain to her trigger finger.

"Do it," he says.

Her eyes flicker left and right, before coming back to him. To her credit she backs off a couple of feet until she is against the wall, theoretically out of reach. But he knows better. This isn't going to end well.

"Got every reason to shoot yuh," she whispers, her eyes bulging.

"Yes you do."

She starts to cry and lowers the gun, letting it flop helplessly by her side. He frantically tries to regain control of his body but he has no idea how to do it. He's been locked out. His thoughts echo around his head before fading away to nothing.

"You stand to win," he says, slowly raising his arms in a supplicant fashion. A peaceful gesture, but with no peaceful intent at all.

"Win what?" she sobs.

He hears himself chuckle.

"Everything. Life."

She is wavering; he can see it in her eyes. She is alone, in a nightmare with no way out other than taking the shot. She can see it clearly. See it in his eyes. Knowing that if she doesn't shoot, she's going to die.

She brings the gun up again, points it at him.

"SHOOT!" he yells.

But she crumples to the floor, sobbing, great globs of water pouring from her eyes.

"Get up," he says, with an icy calm.

He feels the contempt. Senses the anger coming from somewhere within him. A strange look passes before the girl's eyes and she rises like a puppet on strings. Her mouth goes slack and her gaze becomes unfocussed.

"Put the gun in your mouth," he says.

He is screaming; silently, passionately, pointlessly. He asks the voice to have mercy, to let her go, to leave, to do anything other than make this young woman shoot herself.

She puts the gun in her mouth. It appears voluntary, but isn't.

"Pull the trigger," he hisses.

He tries to look away but of course he can do no such thing. His head feels like it's going to explode and ice water pours over his body once again. He wants to pull his knees up to his chest and wrap his arms around his shins; if he could just curl up into a ball, he would. Then he's released. He drops his chin to his chest and starts to cry. He reaches backward and grabs the sides of the bed as his whole body starts to shake. He stifles the sobs at first but then, overcome by the wave of emotions he breaks down completely, all his defenses gone. He screams the kind of scream that comes from a person drained of all hope. After what seems like an eternity, his wailing tapers off and his chest stops heaving and he lets go of the sides of the bed. He feels cold; colder than he has ever felt before.

It gnaws at his insides like hungry maggots.

He looks up and the girl is gone.

ONE

There was a biting wind coming off Lake St Clair, and I pulled the collar of my jacket around my neck and tightened my scarf, wishing I'd brought a beanie. The traffic in Detroit at rush hour was hectic, and, despite the chill in the air, tourists were still out and about, heading down to the waterfront. The noise of the city was subdued with sounds from the construction site of a new lecture theatre and education facility at the hospital across the street. The sun was behind me and still bright, so I put my sunglasses on and walked briskly to the junction with Mack Avenue where the bus stop was. There was a metal seat and I sat down, grateful to be out of the wind.

My phone rang, and I rummaged around in my bag, eventually finding it hidden in the detritus of my disorganized life. The strident *whoop-whoop* of an emergency vehicle siren started up, a red fire truck rounding the corner and heading my way. I keyed the answer button on the phone.

"Hello?"

"Is that you, Kate?" A male voice: no one I recognized.

"This is Dr. Sara Clarke. Can I help you?"

There was a pause, then: "I don't want you to freak out."

"Why would I freak out? Who's this?"

The sound of the siren increased, and now it was audible on the phone as well. I waited until the fire truck crossed the junction in front of me, turning right and heading back up into the city.

"Waiting," I said. "Speak now or never."

The voice at the other end had also waited until the siren decrescendo had become inaudible. I looked up and down the street, checking out pedestrians, none of whom were talking on their phones. The cars passing had their windows up, and none were slowing as they passed me.

"I'm over here," said the voice. "Straight across the road."

Toward the side entrance of the Medical Research Centre was a figure standing in the shadow of the overhang by the closed doors. He raised a hand and moved forward into the daylight, giving a glimpse of a buzz cut and a tweed jacket.

"I only want to talk to you."

"Who are you?"

"Pete, Pete Navarro. Remember me?"

I squinted into the sun, but the face didn't ring any bells. "I don't think so."

He started to vigorously nod his head. "Yes, you do. Very well in fact."

"I think you're one of my patients," I said, trying to get a rise out of him.

"No, no. I can prove it. How do you think I got your number?"

"Hmmm, let me think, the hospital switchboard?"

There was silence for a few beats, then: "Who're you hiding from, Kate?"

"Who the fuck is Kate?" I said.

"You are. Who the fuck is Sara Clarke?"

I took a deep breath and hung up.

I pulled out a packet of Marlboro Lights, cupped my hands around my mouth and lit up. A long drag allowed the acrid smoke to wash around my throat and lungs, and the hit kicked in as the chemicals percolated into my brain. Four thousand chemicals, and at least fifty were carcinogenic. I'd started smoking a few months ago, despite my job as an Oncology Fellow exposing me daily to the horrors of cigarettes and the toll they placed on human life. I hid my new addiction from my patients and colleagues fairly well, and if I was ever discovered, I planned to respond 'Do as I say, not as I do.' I also reckoned it was either going to be cigarettes or alcohol, and I hated how the latter made me feel.

The phone rang again. The figure hadn't moved, but he was staring at me, cellphone stuck to the side of his head. I stubbed the cigarette out on the sidewalk and crossed my knees against the cold.

"Can't you take a hint, asshole?" I muttered to myself, picking up my phone once more.

"Please listen," came the voice. "This is really important. Let me come over there and show you."

He looked harmless enough, not a big man. He was wearing eyeglasses of some description. Clean-shaven. European-white. I still couldn't place him.

I said, "Who are you?"

"A friend," he said. "I can prove it."

I shook my head. Well, it'd been a shitty day so far and I needed cheering up. "Right, fuck it, come on over then. But my bus will be here in a couple of minutes."

He cut the connection and jaywalked quickly across the street, dodging between a couple of taxis and a cyclist. As he approached I drilled into his face, seeking any familiar shapes. None were discernible. He sat down next to me without preamble, gave a lopsided smile, and tilted his head sideways to look at me.

"You've changed, Kate, but only so much. Different hair, some work maybe, but same attitude."

"Again with the 'Kate'?" I said.

He pulled a face. "Yes, *Kate*. Look, I don't make friends easily, but I liked you and I thought we got on okay. Even when you were seeing that arrogant shit, Jackson."

"I don't know any Jackson."

"You did. Richard Jackson. A buffed-up Army major from Creech. You guys were going at it for a few months. It was the talk of the hospital."

I gave him a death stare. "No, I don't think so, *Pete*. The only Jackson I can vaguely remember is an acquaintance from college. He was a roommate of one of my friends, but I don't think I've seen him for, maybe fifteen years. He was the least 'buffed' person you could meet, as well." I looked him in the eye. "I really think you've got the wrong person, *Pete*."

"Wait," he said, and he pulled out his cellphone. He opened it up and started scrolling through his photo stream. He went back month-by-month until he stopped at a date the previous June. He opened an image, enlarged it with a flick of his fingers and held the phone up in front of my eyes.

"That's you. And by the way, that handsome dude standing next to you? That would be me."

A chill went down my spine. I reached into my jacket pocket, shakily brought out my spectacles, and pushed them up my nose. The picture came into hard focus. It was a photograph of a woman, in a bar, lifting a drink toward the camera. This guy Navarro was next to her, looking awkward but also holding a beer in a salute. The woman was smiling and looked happy to be there. Standing behind the bar was someone I assumed was the barman, making the two-finger bunny ears gesture behind the woman's head. Her hair was a bit blonder, and a lot longer, and her nose was maybe flatter, the cheekbones a little higher. But otherwise it was me. Or my clone.

I looked at Navarro. "Are there more?"

"Another one from that same night." He reached over and flicked the screen sideways a couple of times, scanning through photographs until he came upon the right one. In this, the woman was in profile; arms draped around a tall muscular man wearing a white T-shirt and desert army BDU pants. She was planting a kiss on his cheek as he looked toward the camera winking.

"Richard Jackson," said Navarro.

As I stared at the picture it felt as if my world was tumbling around my ears. This time I was more certain that the person in the photograph was me, but I had no recollection of the scene, or the occasion. And I had no idea who Richard Jackson was.

"I don't understand," I said. "Where was this taken? And when?"

"In a bar called Joey Malone's – one of your frequent haunts back at Indian Springs. It is you, but not Sara Clarke. In those days you were Kate Morgan."

I came to a decision. "The Hyatt: it's three blocks away. Let's go and get a drink."

Navarro nodded and smiled. "Good choice. I'm staying there."

I shot him a look. "I'm warning you, though – you better have answers for me."

The Hyatt lobby bar was dark-lit and modern, tables and booths geometrically arranged around a rectangular space enclosed by tall cubes of wooden strips and hanging lights of various styles and aesthetics. Frank Sinatra was warbling quietly from above, entreating everyone to 'take it nice and easy', and there was a quiet burble of conversation from a smattering of office workers wearing crumpled suits and sipping the first of many post-conference drinks. A not unpleasant mixed aroma of scented candles and freshly brewed coffee tickled my nose.

Navarro led the way over to the bar itself, a long structure at the rear of the room backlit orange and yellow with a huge cabinet of hard liquor glittering invitingly. There were about a dozen barstools, and a couple at the end were unoccupied, so we slid in. I draped my coat over the back of my chair and sat down, popping my handbag on the bar.

Navarro was trying to catch the eye of the barman. I still couldn't place him. This close up, there was still nothing recognizable about him. I scrabbled around in my handbag for my cigarettes, then remembered I wasn't allowed to smoke inside. Getting irritated with Navarro's inability to get service, I stood up and leaned forward on the bar and waved down the full length to a bartender who was cleaning glasses while in deep conversation with a shapely blonde in a cocktail dress.

"Hey, some service here, please?"

The barman heard me and nodded, making his excuses to the woman. Navarro gave me a look. I shrugged. "Use what you got, isn't that right?"

The barman, a good-looking Italian type with bright even teeth and gelled black hair, sauntered over and leaned in toward me. He gave me a mega-watt smile and ignored Navarro. His name badge read *Paulo*. "Hi there, what can I get you?"

I sat back down and inclined my head at Navarro, who looked flustered and irritated at the same time. He pointed at the rack of whiskies. "Suntory please, on the rocks."

Paulo turned to me, but before I could reply Navarro said, "She'll be having, if I remember, a Kraken and coke, with lime."

10

My chest tightened and my mouth dried up at this throwaway line. How did he know?

He shrugged out of his tweed jacket and wrapped it around the small backrest on the barstool. He put his room key on the counter and Paulo took it and walked away to get our drinks.

I snapped my fingers. "Let me see those photos again?"

He nodded and passed his phone over. I opened the first one and stared at the face looking back at me, the one with Navarro by my side.

"How do I know that's not photoshopped?"

"You don't," he replied. "But it isn't. Why would I?"

"Then why don't I know you?"

Paulo returned with our drinks and a couple of ramekins filled with bar snacks. There was an awkward silence while he arranged everything on coasters and added little plastic accoutrements before slipping the tab in front of Navarro, with his key. When he'd finally sloped back to renew his conversation with the blonde in the dress, Navarro took a sip of his whisky and looked me in the eye.

"What's the last thing you remember about Indian Springs?"

"I've no memories at all, seeing's I've never been there," I said with a flash of annoyance.

He slid around a little so he was facing me. He had twitchy eyes, flicking left and right to check out the room and its occupants. He'd arranged his drinks and the ramekins in neat parallel lines, which caused me to raise my eyebrows. He rolled the ice around in his glass and took a long drink, crunching the cubes in a very irritating way.

"Alright," he said, with a smirk. "How long have you been working here in Motor City?"

"Eighteen months."

He shook his head and gave a lopsided smile. "Not possible. Six months ago you were working with me at Indian Springs. You left, very abruptly. Soon afterwards Clem left too."

"Clem?"

"Clem Reynolds. You and he were the only two medical officers at the hospital. He was the town general practitioner as well. Everything was left in a bit of a state when you both upped sticks, but the Army drafted in two military MOs to fill the positions."

I sat back and took a deep breath. "Okay, I'll go along with this for a while. Tell me more."

"You'd been there for approximately six months," he said, "working in the ER. I remember thinking we were lucky to get someone like you, with all your previous ER experience."

"This is bullshit." I raised my glass to my lips and took a big drink. "I've never done an ER rotation."

Navarro put his glass down and crossed his arms. "Do you want to hear this?"

I pulled a face. Shrugged.

"You left the day after that strange guy was brought into the ER. Remember him?"

"Of course not."

Now he gave me a withering look. "A truck going full on hit some guy walking down I-95 in the middle of the night. When he got to the ER he was comatose, you called me in and we did scans. And this is why I remember it so vividly. The scans were absolutely anatomically perfect. There were no injuries, no defects of any kind. It was like looking at a textbook representation of a human body."

"That makes no sense."

"Ah, but there were witnesses. Two guys from out of town. The front of their truck was all bashed in."

"So what did I do with him?"

"You wanted to take him to theatre; Reynolds disagreed. Then the guy woke up. The next day he'd left the hospital and all his records had gone missing. I went looking for you, but you'd not clocked in that morning, which was weird in itself. You were rostered on. I went back to review his scans, but they'd been deleted from the system. Luckily I'd sent a copy to someone I know in Vegas for a second opinion. You see, there was something wrong with the scans themselves. There was a kind of interference pattern, an abnormality I'd never seen before."

"Did you hear back from your buddy in Vegas?"

Navarro looked furtively around the bar, and leaned in confidentially. His voice lowered a touch, and I had to lean in as well to hear what he was saying. "No, he never replied."

"Oooh, sounds awfully like a conspiracy theory hatching here," I said mischievously.

Navarro didn't take the bait, but stared into his drink. "I went looking for you, you know, so that we could, like, chew it over. But I found out you'd left the hospital. Clem as well. *Poof*, just like that." He snapped his fingers.

"So what happened to you then?" I said.

He laughed humorlessly. "A couple of days later I heard that due to 'national security concerns' the US Army was taking over the running of the hospital, and everyone was to be relieved of their positions. I was clearly getting sacked, but they were coy about using that phrase. I've been looking for work ever since – no one from the hospital will give me a reference."

A headache was starting. "Is that what this is about? A scam to get a job? You wanting a reference from me? Are you going to offer me money next? Is a big brown envelope going to appear in a second?"

His eyes blazed. "Kate, you were my friend. I came here for an interview and then I saw you in the cafeteria. Dr. Kate Morgan. Clear as day. I called the Emergency Room and they'd never heard of you."

"Of course they'd never heard of me. My name's Sara Clarke. And this is nonsense. I think we're just about done here."

Navarro looked angrily at me. "Please, Kate, what's this all about? A new identity? Are you in some kind of witness protection program?"

"Pete, I'm not this person you think I am."

He put down his glass and leaned back in the chair. "Tell me about your family."

I glared at him. "You're kidding."

"No, indulge me. This is for real."

"I'm an only child," I said, sighing. "My parents live in Miami. Not much to tell."

He shook his head and made a kind of 'tch-tch' sound. "Not so. Not according to you. You told me your father died of cancer and that you were completely estranged from him. Oh, and that your five-year-old daughter died in the ER when you were on duty at the Memorial in Chicago."

"Really? Now I'm also a grieving mother?"

He nodded slowly. "You told me many times that the reason you moved to Indian Springs was that you needed to get away from Chicago. Too many memories there."

I shook my head. "These aren't my memories, Pete. I've never been to Chicago. And a dead daughter? That's some fucked-up biography you've concocted for me."

He put his drink on the table and pointed at me, an angry look on his face. "No, Kate. This is your real life. And there's more. The other reason you went to Indian Springs was that your father used to be a test pilot at Creech Air Force Base in the 70s. You were proud of that. Showed me loads of photos of him and you. Sitting in those old jets."

"This is bullshit," I whispered.

He smiled. "You were a cute toddler, Kate."

I tried to get a read on him. Tried to figure out what angle he was playing. Or whether he was, indeed, deranged, and I was right about the meds.

"Kate, look closely at the photos," he insisted, gesturing with his phone. "That's you there. I've got no reason to make this up. What's going on with you?"

I downed the last of the Kraken, grabbed my coat and struggled into the sleeves. Navarro jumped to his feet and tried to put a hand on my arm but I shrugged him off and put my sunglasses back on so I didn't have to look at him.

"You showed me a picture of your daughter once," he said. "She looked like a mini-version of you. Her name was Kelly."

There was a sinking feeling, as if perhaps a rabbit hole was going to open up beneath my feet if I let this go any further. His words were buzzing around my head like a fly you can never swat. I pulled the collar up around my neck and turned sharply on my heel without another word.

Navarro's raised voice stopped me in my tracks.

"Kelly died, Kate. She died in your arms. Why are you denying all this?"

I furiously span back to face him. "Fuck right off now, Pete, if that's really your name. Don't you dare follow me."

"The photos, Kate," he said. "That's you."

"Fakes," I said. "Go find some other poor sucker."

I hurried through the bar to the door that exited directly onto the street. Stopping, I took a deep breath and closed my eyes. I was annoyed with myself, frustrated that I'd been taken in by a nutjob. Clearly the guy had issues.

But what about the photographs? They must have been doctored. I turned and looked through the glass of the door to see Navarro now in animated conversation with the blonde in the cocktail dress.

Cursing under my breath, I strode away.

TWO

The Moynahan was an upscale block in Corktown, Wayne County, a 1920s building renovated in pale pink and red rising ten stories from the entrance hallway and coffee shop up to the leisure center on the top floor overlooking the Detroit River. I took the elevator to the sixth level and walked the short distance along the deep-pile carpets to my apartment. A solid red door with an old-fashioned knocker and an ultramodern entry system faced me, and I swiped my key. The latch unlocked with a satisfyingly secure-sounding clunk. I entered; the lights automatically flicked on and I threw my jacket into the built-in closet and leaned against the wall to unzip my boots, which I also threw into the closet. I walked past the den and straight into the kitchen where I grabbed a large heavy-bottomed glass from a shelf. There was a half-empty bottle of Kraken on the table, so I popped some ice from the machine and poured myself a few fingers. I wandered over to my small balcony, where there was a single-seat lounger, table and a dainty stainless steel BBQ set. A couple of tired, plastic-looking plants were my only concession to decoration out there.

I took a long drink, letting the spicy rum linger at the back of my throat. My head was buzzing, and the start of a migraine seemed to be feeling its way around the edges.

This all had to be wrong.

Someone was playing a game.

Or maybe this was a dream, and I was about to wake up.

Kate Fucking Morgan.

Across the street a couple of floors lower was the top of a neighboring apartment building with a swimming pool lit up electric blue and a few hardy souls doing some end-of-the-day laps. Street noise was muted at this height, but there were distant sirens, and the hum of rubber on asphalt. The sun was setting, the skyline a picture-perfect magenta fading into the approaching blackness. Overhead, the first evening stars were starting to twinkle, and the lights of a wide-body jet coming into Metro Airport could be seen traversing the moon.

I pulled out my phone and checked for messages. None. I was about to put it away when it started vibrating and to my irritation I recognized the number as Navarro's. I closed my eyes and took a deep breath before accepting the call.

"Sara?" came a breathy woman's voice before I had a chance to say anything.

"Who's this?" I said.

There was a pause at the other end, and then, "I need to speak with you. Can you let me in?"

"Who the hell are you? Another one of that Navarro guy's lunatic friends?"

The voice on the other end was patient, calm. "No, but you need to hear me out. Please, can you let me in? I'm standing outside your crib. Apartment 605, right?

I hung up on her, strode through to the door and looked through the peephole. The top of a blonde woman's head was visible and there appeared to be no one else with her anywhere in the hall — the fish-eye perspective covered most of the space. I fixed the security chain in place and unlatched the door, pulling it open a few inches. The woman on the other side looked up and smiled before turning her head to anxiously look behind her. "Can I come in, then?" she said.

"Who are you?" I answered. "Someone else from my past or maybe an alternate universe?"

The woman seemed not to find this funny, and her eyes bored into mine. "I've got answers for you, if that's what you mean," she said. "About what's going on. You and Navarro."

I gave her a fierce look, which she returned coolly. After a few seconds of this I opened the door and let it swing.

"You better have some answers then," I said, turning away and walking into the kitchen without looking back.

She followed me in and closed the door behind her, shrugged out of her long coat and draped it over an arm. She was squeezed into a yellow dress with gold piping, which ended well above her knees.

Right, of course. I should've known. "Followed me from the bar, did you?" I glowered.

"Didn't need to. Got your address from the hospital. And your phone number from your friend Pete's phone, which I relieved him of." She lifted it up and shook it for me to see.

"He's not my friend," I said.

She laid her coat on the counter and walked through the living area toward the balcony. As her high heels click-clacked over the parquet flooring, I checked her out. She had shoulder-length ash-blonde hair, olive-brown skin and a perfectly proportioned face with a straight nose and high cheekbones. Her eyes were dark and framed with long black lashes. She must have been early thirties, perhaps younger. She stopped and turned, taking in the decor, one hand on her hip, the other idly caressing a pendant that dangled in her cleavage. My living room was an open-plan arrangement with two settees and a single chair arranged around a glass coffee table and facing a fireplace with a large LCD TV screen above it. Nothing special.

"Nice place," she said. "How can you afford this on your junior doctors' salary?"

I scowled. "What business is that of yours?"

"Well, I reckon you're looking at three, maybe four thousand dollars a month here, plus all the bills. And these furnishings don't come cheap. Or maybe it's a furnished rental?"

"Who are you?" I said, getting angry. "Are you going to tell me that we were best buddies in another life too?"

She walked up to me and looked me in the eye. She was about six inches taller, mostly due to the heels. In one smooth movement she reached behind her head and removed her blonde wig, shaking her head out to reveal a brunette bob.

I took a step back. "What is this?"

"You don't recognize me, do you, Sara? He really did a job on you."

"Who? What're you talking about?"

"The cover he gave you was flawless, or at least it was until Navarro pitched up. Couldn't have predicted that. Good job I was looking for you as well. Talk about getting a break."

"Who *are* you?"

"My name's Colleen Stillman," she said, still infuriatingly composed. "I work for the FBI. Or at least I did, because after today that may be in question."

"Can I see a badge?" I said, arms folded.

"Hmmm, this is strictly 'off the books'. But I've got something better." She reached into a hip pocket on the dress and pulled out a USB stick. "Do you have a computer? I need to show you this."

I stared at the USB as if it were radioactive. "What the hell is all this about?"

Her lip twitched. "A big, big secret with you front and center. Now, do you have a computer or not?"

I nodded dumbly and led the way to the den. There was a small desk with a MacBook connected to a router and printer in front of the window. A couple of office chairs were scattered around and there was a bookcase, empty of anything apart from a photograph in a picture frame. I turned on the Mac and sat in front of it as it booted up. Stillman leaned over me and picked up the photograph. In it was a handsome couple, mid- to late-fifties, both with dark hair and healthy white smiles.

"These your parents?" Stillman asked without inflexion.

"That's right," I snapped defensively. "You know differently, I suppose?"

She gave a half smile but said nothing, putting the photograph back on the shelf. She passed over the USB that I plugged in. I double-clicked on the drive where a new icon had appeared. A separate window opened, containing six document files and a video file. I went to open one of the documents but she placed her hand over mine, stilling my finger on the mouse.

"Before we do this, I want you to know that I'm breaking a significant number of federal laws here. Even being in possession of this is a felony. However, I don't really have a choice. I need your help."

I threw my hands up in exasperation. "I don't know you, and I certainly don't have any interest in national secrets or federal laws. I'm just a doctor."

She took a deep breath. "I need you to watch this. I don't know if it'll bring your memories back, but there's more to your amnesia. You're part of something huge."

"Right," I said, unconvinced. I looked at the screen, my finger hovering over the mouse. "Which one?"

She pointed to a file named *VHAB_INT.mov*. "Open that one, and turn up the volume."

I double-clicked the file and after a couple of seconds a screen opened with *FBI TOP-SECRET EYES ONLY* flashing in black and white with a *go* arrow at the bottom left.

"No secret password?" I said, mischievously.

She pulled a face. "Hit the button."

The screen cut to a picture of what looked like a police interview room as seen from behind a one-way mirror. The colors were bleached out but the details were sharp. On the screen, frozen in time, staring into the camera across a wide desk covered in papers and photographs was a man dressed in a black suit and tie. He looked like a GQ model, mid-thirties, short black hair, and high cheekbones. Even on a grainy still there were no lines on his face or asymmetry to his nose or eyes. Sitting with their backs to the camera were two guys I assumed were police officers. On the right a grey-haired white man, on the left an African American, both wearing shoulder holsters. Against the far wall were three uniformed police officers, all wearing SWAT body armor and carrying machine pistols.

Stillman reached out and clicked on the pause icon. She turned to me and pointed at the screen.

"Do you recognize that man?"

I shook my head slowly. "No. Who is he?"

Stillman gave me a thoughtful look. "You really don't know, do you?"

"Read my lips – I don't know him."

Stillman leaned forward, focusing on the screen. "Play it."

The grey-haired man leaned over and flicked a switch on some sort of recording device on the edge of the table. Red numbers started to tick over on the bottom right of the picture, counting time forward in seconds and minutes. The images were crystal clear, but there was no sound. I lowered the lights in the den and turned up the volume, pulling the chair close to the desk. Stillman remained standing behind me.

The playback started.

"The time is 1245 hours on Monday, November twenty-third. Conducting this interview are myself, FBI Deputy Director William Hubert, and FBI Special Agent Lawrence Mackie."

No reaction could be seen from the man facing the camera, who seemed to be staring directly into the lens. Then a smile seemed to pull at the corner of his lip, followed by a solitary eyebrow raise.

"This is very formal. Am I to consider myself under arrest?" His voice was mellifluous and velvety, with a trace of amusement.

The man with the grey hair – Hubert – continued. "No, of course not. It's ... procedural. Just for the record. Can you tell us your name?"

The man's head swiveled slowly to face him.

"We are Vu-Hak."

The other guy, Mackie, cleared his throat. "All of you? Or is there an individual here?"

The man folded his arms and looked bored. "One is here."

Hubert looked sideways at Mackie, who sat back in his chair, folding his arms. "Do you have a name?"

The man brought both his hands onto the table and placed them side-by-side before looking back up at the camera. "We have no individual identities. But as I am here alone, I understand your need to address me as an individual. Therefore you can call me ... Cain." He gave a smirk and looked at both men. "Appropriate name, is it not?"

Hubert coughed into his hand and brought up a handkerchief to wipe his mouth. "As in Cain, son of Adam?"

"Do you know your bible, Director Hubert?"

Hubert leaned forward. "Cain was the firstborn son of Adam and murdered his brother Abel. God punished Cain to a life of wandering the Earth and set a mark on him so that no man would kill him."

The man calling himself Cain nodded, smiling like a schoolteacher complimenting a child in class. "Genesis, chapter 4, verses 1 to 18. Although I like to think it should have read 'so that no man *could* kill him'."

I pressed the pause button. "What the fuck is this? They catch some religious whack-job? How is this relevant to me?"

Stillman held up a finger. "Just … keep watching."

I took a breath and let it out, shrugged, and pressed play. Hubert was speaking again.

"So, what happened to Adam?"

"In your bible?"

"No. Adam Benedict. Our Adam."

Cain brought up a finger and wagged it slowly. "Not so fast. I have a condition that you first need to agree to. Under no circumstances are you to seek out and contact Dr. Kate Morgan. She is to play no part in any further proceedings."

I reflexively clicked the mouse over the pause button and stared wide-eyed at Stillman, my heart suddenly trying to jump out of my chest. Cain was again staring straight at the camera, his face unreadable.

"There's that name again," I said. "I think I'm going to need another drink."

"Get me one too," replied Stillman, her face impassive.

Two minutes later, I returned with two glasses full of ice and Kraken.

"Alright then, on with the show …"

Cain's soft voice came out of the speakers again. "… in addition, it is important that my presence is not made public until I deem it necessary. Will you agree to this as well, Director Hubert?"

Mackie could be seen to look anxiously at Hubert, who was shaking his head. "I'm not sure I have the authority to make that call. That would need to come from the president. Your presence here is, to say the least, the most important event in the history of humankind."

Agent Mackie ran his fingers through thinning hair. "Cain, you must realize there are geo-political ramifications of what occurred. Not only that, but the discovery of an alien race brings with it certain religious implications as well. I mean, you clearly realize this, with your choice of name."

Cain's head swiveled towards him. "Do you think religion will survive the discovery of the Vu-Hak, Agent Mackie?"

"That depends on how the information is presented. We need to have careful control over this knowledge –"

"You are getting ahead of yourselves," interrupted Cain.

Hubert brought his hands up in a placatory gesture. He glanced sternly at Mackie before speaking. Hubert shuffled some of his papers around, nervously it seemed. Mackie leaned forward with an elbow on the table.

"Yes, of course. Can we talk about what happened back in Nevada? For instance, where is Adam Benedict?"

Cain sat back in the chair and again folded his arms. "Adam is dead."

He stared into the camera lens, and I felt the blue eyes boring into mine. I froze the image. There was something about him. Something I couldn't quite put my finger on. Just under the surface. Tantalizingly close yet separated by a seemingly impenetrable barrier. Stillman's hand touched my shoulder and I reached for my glass. The ice tinkled as the rum swirled.

"This Cain. Do I know him?"

Stillman was leaning on the wall, staring at the screen. She snapped out of her reverie and shook her head. "Not Cain. But you do know Adam Benedict."

"I don't get it. None of this," I flicked my chin at the screen, "makes sense. I've never heard of an Adam Benedict. Again, what has this got to do with me?"

Cain was still looking out from the screen at us both, like a portrait whose gaze follows you around the room. Stillman pulled the other chair close and grasped my forearm tightly, which made me want to pull away. "This has everything to do with you. You're not who you think you are, and I don't know why. But he," she glanced back at the monitor, "he does."

I shook my arm free and pushed away from the desk. "I think I'm going to ask you to leave."

Stillman sat back and placed her palms on her knees. She closed her eyes for a second, and then looked back at me. "There are five minutes left on this recording. You need to see it through."

We locked eyes for what seemed to me like a minute or more before I reluctantly nodded.

Hubert was speaking again. "How did Adam die?"

Cain smirked. "Saving humanity, obviously."

Hubert and Mackie looked at each other, quite nervously. Hubert cocked his head to one side and rubbed a finger absently against his lip. "And yet, here you are. Why don't we feel 'saved'? The wormhole closed – we thought permanently – and yet you're here."

There was a flicker of some unrecognizable emotion on Cain's face. "It was a simple matter to recreate the conditions leading to the opening of the wormhole, once we knew the requisite elements. Opening and closing the portal is now at our discretion."

Mackie was shaking his head, looking at Hubert. "How can you control a wormhole? We thought the initial conditions which created the Trinity Deus project were unique."

"They are not. We can control gravity."

"But, according to our experts, a gravitational field strong enough to create a tunnel in deformed space would also destroy this space in a fraction of a second."

"Correct. Unless there is an opposing force."

"A force strong enough to control such energies?"

"Yes, what you call 'dark matter'."

The screen froze. Cain's face was impassive, and his arms were folded. Stillman shrugged. "There's a gap in the recording here of about three minutes. I don't know if it's been deliberately deleted or cut. Or by whom."

"What's dark matter?"

She nodded. "I had a conversation once with Mike Holland about this stuff. He said that without it – whatever it is – the galaxy would fall apart. Somehow this stuff is keeping it glued together."

I was none the wiser. "Mike Holland?"

She looked at me strangely, eyebrows pulled down. "Used to work with me at the FBI. Scientific Director. Very smart guy."

"Where is he now?" I said.

"Dead."

"Not so smart then," I wisecracked.

Stillman ignored me and restarted the video. Hubert scratched his head. Mackie was speaking.

"Help me out here then. Adam said you were coming to destroy our world. You say he 'saved' humanity, and yet you're here. What's changed?"

Cain sniffed, a very human-like gesture. "A great many things."

Hubert and Mackie said nothing. The silence lasted a minute before Cain smiled and sat back in his chair. He looked around the cell, taking in the soldiers behind him and the green/grey concrete walls. He folded his arms and addressed the camera.

"Adam Benedict died trying to close the portal. He nearly succeeded. During the process we accessed his thoughts and neurological processes. What we discovered was ... interesting. He had managed to resist us, resist assimilation and subjugation by the Vu-Hak that traveled with him. We also discovered that the Vu-Hak that co-inhabited his host machine had been irreparably damaged."

Mackie carefully laid his pen down on the table, and frittered around with it, squaring everything off, papers and notebooks. Hubert could be seen to lean backward and put his hands on the armrests of his chair. His knuckles appeared white.

"Cain... are you here, alone?"

Cain shook his head slowly. "More Vu-Hak are here."

Mackie sat up sharply. "How many?"

"Many. In various locations around the planet. We are undetectable. But it is critical that humanity is kept in the dark, and that you do not spread panic throughout the world. That would have unfortunate consequences."

"But," said Hubert, "won't they all look like you? I mean, the machine host's appearance was based on Adam Benedict."

Cain blinked again, slowly. "How little you know of our capabilities, Director Hubert."

With that his face suddenly blurred, as if depixelated on a computer. Like a melting candle, his features twisted and sagged and then took on a new shape. Blonde hair sprouted from the skull and the features started to soften, chiseled cheekbones becoming rounder, the nose becoming smaller and flatter. The lips fattened and shortened. The skin darkened and the figure sitting in the chair seemed to shrink and morph into a smaller female humanoid figure. Then the screen froze, with the female staring up into the camera with green phosphorescent eyes.

I sat back in the chair, heart pounding in my chest, leaping up into my throat and threatening to choke me. Stillman's hand was on my shoulder, and I could just barely hear her saying, "It's alright," but the pulse in my ears was a jungle drumbeat and I could only focus on the person looking at me out of the screen.

Myself.

THREE

I took a long swallow of the Kraken with trembling hands and let the ice fragments rattle around inside my mouth for a few seconds before they slid down my tongue and back out into the empty glass. I couldn't take my eyes off the screen, where my doppelganger stared back at me. The likeness was uncanny, almost perfect, although there were no age lines or wrinkles to be seen, giving it a showroom dummy-like effect. Absently, I ran my finger down my own face, tracing the shallow groove I knew was present from the edge of my nose to the side of my mouth. I ran my tongue around my teeth, upper and lower, taking in the crevasses and sharp edges, the warmth of the gums. I swallowed again, just to feel it happen and nothing to do with the saliva that was building up and pooling in my pharynx.

"It has to be a fake, right?" I said. "I mean, images can be manipulated easily these days …"

Stillman shook her head. "I wish it was, believe me."

"But how do you know?" I insisted, hearing the tremble in my voice. "The photos Navarro showed me, this recording … how do you know it's all true?"

"Because I was there, Kate. When all this shit first hit the fan."

I took a deep breath. "Is there more?"

"That's all we have," said Stillman, regarding me silently, concern showing in her gaze. "There were no recordings on the hard drives at the station house where this interview happened because Cain destroyed them. However, I'd already streamed them into the cloud, which he didn't know about. Lucky for us."

"What happened next?" I asked. "After he … became me."

Stillman shook her head. "I truly don't know. Hubert and Mackie were found unconscious, their memories wiped. The soldiers and other FBI agents were incapacitated. There was no sign of Cain."

"So he could be out there, pretending to be me?" I was horrified. Then realization dawned abruptly, like a slap in the face. "Wait the hell up … am I, me?"

Stillman reached out and touched my arm, gently this time. "You're not Cain. But then, you're not Sara Clarke either."

My guts were contracting, my skin was clammy and I was starting to hyperventilate. I leaned on the desk, looking at Stillman, searching her eyes. There was sympathy there, and she gave a lipless smile and a slow nod.

"Your name is Dr. Kate Morgan. And you're probably the most important person on the planet right now."

"But why? What's going on?"

A smile pulled at the corner of Stillman's mouth. She stood up and stretched, her tight yellow dress pulling high up on her thighs. She cricked her neck sideways and walked out of the den, flicking a look back over her shoulder at me. "We need to make plans."

My eyebrows furrowed and I stood to follow her. "Plans?"

There were rattles and squeaks as she searched noisily through my fridge and cutlery drawer in the kitchen. She pulled out a hunk of foil-wrapped cheese and a half-bottle of Chardonnay. She looked up before emptying a pile of crackers and potato chips onto the kitchen table. "Sorry … famished. Hope you don't mind."

"What sort of plans? What are we going to do?"

She cut a triangle of cheese and sandwiched it between two crackers. "Got any quince? I'm a sucker for that."

I rubbed my knuckles into my eye sockets as Stillman uncorked the wine and poured a couple of large measures.

"Getting me shitfaced may not help your planning," I said.

Stillman merely waggled the glass at me, and with only a slight reluctance, I took it and gestured over to the couch. I moved the throw cushions around so we could sit facing each other and Stillman sat sideways on, pulling the dress down as she did so and tucking her knees in. She grimaced at the maneuver, shuffling to get comfortable. "Got anything less ridiculous I can wear? This really ain't my style."

I gave her a watery smile. "You sure? I can see you rocking that look in the Hoover building."

She gave a little snigger and raised her glass to me. I reluctantly clinked it and we drank in silence for a while. I looked around the room, taking in the furnishings, wallpaper, widescreen TV. Was this me? Nothing now seemed right. It seemed sterile, bereft of personality, no longer belonging to me, but to some stranger.

"I have amnesia, and a new identity," I said, trying the sentence out to see how it felt. "Did he – Cain – do this to me?"

Stillman pursed her lips. "Pretty sure, yes."

"Do you have any theories as to why?"

"Kinda. But first, I'm pretty sure all that," she gestured back to the den where the laptop was, "was smoke and mirrors."

"What do you mean?"

"Didn't you notice that Cain gave almost no details about what the Vu-Hak are actually doing here on Earth? That worries the fuck out of me. The Vu-Hak aren't like us. We don't know much about them apart from the fact that they have no empathy for humanity … oh, and they're murderous bastards."

"How do you know all this?"

She was looking at a point above my head. "Because Adam Benedict told you – and you told us."

"Us, being …?"

"The FBI of course. Hubert, Holland, me …"

My wine glass found its way to my hand. "So who was Adam Benedict? You said I knew him."

"Yes, from when you worked in Indian Springs."

"Ah, there you go with parts of my biography that I'm still to hear about." I took a sip, and then a larger swallow. The wine was making me feel a little woozy and more confident. "So how did I become so important in all this?"

She hesitated and leaned back among the cushions. "Adam Benedict – the real, human Adam – had been to the Vu-Hak galaxy. By accident. He'd stumbled on an intergalactic portal, a gateway of sorts, in the Nevada desert – a product of the Cold War's atomic bomb tests. Adam – with a friend – found it, and to cut a long story he went through, dying en route. The aliens, these Vu-Hak, found him as soon as the portal dumped him in their galaxy. They downloaded his consciousness into a machine body that looked exactly like him and sent him back. Oh, and they sent one of their own Vu-Hak with him as a companion in the same machine."

"So Adam's the guy in the ER Navarro told me about?"

She nodded. "The police were interested in him by then, but he took you with him on a kind of road trip from Nevada to California."

"But why me?"

"At some point during that trip, he must have 'bonded' with you – is that the right word? You made a connection?" Stillman was smiling tightly and raised her eyebrows. "Anyhow, to cut a long story short you and he shared some common ground. That much was evident."

"I'm just not feeling anything," I said, trying out a little sarcasm.

Colleen was looking at me strangely. "You should. Adam Benedict died not only saving the world from the Vu-Hak, but saving you, specifically."

The wine now tasted a bit flat and I wondered how long it had been in the fridge.

"Maybe he was in love with you?" she said, a twinkle in her eyes.

This made me look up. "Did he tell you that?"

"Of course not," she replied. "But it made sense, at the time."

"No, none of this makes any sense. If Adam is dead, then why did Cain wipe my mind? What am I to the Vu-Hak? I'm nothing. Just another human, a bipedal carbon-based life-form of which there are seven billion or so on this planet."

Stillman was looking past me, a thousand-yard stare into the darkness beyond my balcony. "You aren't nothing. I wish I could convince you of that. I wish you could remember him. Remember everything." She blinked and looked up at me. "We need to find Cain."

"Do you know where to start?" I said.

"Yes, but if we get close it'll be hard keeping under his radar. Did I mention he can read minds and manipulate electrical fields, gravitational waves and a lot of other such shit?"

I laughed, only slightly hysterically. "Great. So, what could we possibly achieve then? Why can't we go to the authorities? Your old FBI buddies?"

"I told you, all documentation of the Vu-Hak and Adam Benedict has been removed. Erased. I was lucky to get away with that file. No one knows. We're in this on our own."

"I'm going to be no use to you. I can't remember anything."

Stillman put her drink down and took my hand in hers.

"I've an idea. Lie down on that couch."

FOUR

Stillman's voice echoed around my head, slurring and languorous. My breathing slowed as she counted somnolently backward from ten. Her almond eyes sucked me in like a black hole, spinning and distorting my perception of time. Everything became unfocused, floating in a space filled with thick gelatinous foam. My heartbeat, a slow sonorous thudding, was pulsing in my ears as the feeling in my body drained away and my vision narrowed to a pinpoint.

Vestiges of a dream teased me, shimmering in the blackness, images nonsensical and random, like flicking through channels on a foreign language TV.

A light chilly breeze coated the back of my neck and my nose twitched as the smell of freshly mown wet grass drafted past it. I heard birdsong, the Doppler effect of passing insects, the distant hum of traffic from a freeway and the low rumble of an aircraft.

I blinked and opened my eyes.

I was sitting on a cold and hard park bench, wrapped in a thick black coat and wearing gloves. The sky was overcast, the trees sparse as leaves danced from branch to earth, gold and red, covering the grass with an autumnal quilt before the winter snows hid them forever.

A grey single-track road, cement cracked but serviceable, empty of cars or walkers, wound into the distance over a hill. White tombstones lined its grassy verges, each one a couple of feet high and one foot across, spreading six deep and as far as the eye could see.

Arlington National Cemetery.

"It's a beautiful world, don't you agree?"

There was a man sitting next to me on the bench. Jet-black hair, cut short. An aquiline nose, cheekbones high and prominent. Pale white skin, almost waxy. He looked at me with irises of cobalt and bottomless black pupils. His eyebrows were perfectly symmetrical, sloping downward to give him a serious visage. He was wearing a dark suit and dark tie, clumsily, like he'd just learned how to knot it.

He gave a half-smile. "Or perhaps you and your kind just take it for granted?"

I felt myself frowning. "My kind?"

There was a tickle inside my head, like hundreds of spiders crawling around the lining of my brain. His eyes flashed with the sparkle of hidden emeralds lying deep within.

Humans

His lips didn't move, but the words came, nevertheless. Anxiety grabbed my tongue and dried my mouth. The fear in my chest tightened and pressed harder, starting to suffocate me.

"Who are you?" I said.

His mouth twitched and he blinked slowly.

I'm not who you think I am

A shiver started in the back of my neck and dribbled down my spine. "Adam?"

He turned away and looked along the road. There was a red structure in the distance, a series of arches and buttresses which marked the old ceremonial entrance to the cemetery, the McClellan gate. The top of the Pentagon was just visible over the trees.

I swallowed hard. "I heard you'd died. Saving us. Saving me."

He shook his head and looked up at the sky, at the storm clouds expanding from the west.

No one has been saved

The temperature continued to fall, and the wind was picking up. I pulled my collar around my neck and lowered my chin into the fabric.

"I don't understand," I said. "The portal opened. They should be here. We should all be dead."

A few raindrops splattered on my coat, and then a few more sprinkled onto my skin, cold and wet. A man walking some kind of bulldog passed us, pulling his coat tighter around himself. The dog looked at us in passing, sniffing the air before being pulled back to heel. The insectoid buzz of couple of helicopters on station somewhere out of sight could be heard.

I felt a hand closing around mine.

You're afraid but you don't need to fear me

I managed a nervous smile. "I don't fear you, Adam. Why should I?"

He removed his hand and turned away to gaze over the field of tombstones. The wind was picking up and with it the noise of the leaves rustling in the trees. The sky was darkening, and with it my mood. Dread was creeping in slowly, numbing my brain.

I am not Adam. You may call me Cain.

His mind was closed tight, giving nothing. No emotions, no humanity or alien-ness. Zip. He was a blank page.

"You are Vu-Hak though?" I said.

He looked away again and the silence was deafening. My stomach heaved with sudden nausea and bile climbed up my gullet. Tears pricked my eyes, and the wind blew them across my cheek. I let them flow.

It had all been for nothing.

"So that's it? It's over?" I said.

It is not over

He put a hand on my cheek. His touch was cold, like he was pressing ice cubes into my flesh. A wave of electricity cascaded through my mind, and a mosaic of images flashed in front of my eyes, too fast to process. In an instant they were gone.

"What have you done?" I said, swallowing hard.

He stood up and extended his hand, palm upward. I took it and he pulled me to my feet. He was very tall and I had to crick my neck to look into his face. The green phosphorescence was gone from his eyes, leaving only the glorious blue-black orbs.

I have given you what you need – you will know when to use it

"What've you done to me?" I said, my voice rising.

He let go of my hand and stepped back to look at me. He seemed to be re-appraising me, sizing me up, deciding what to do. His eyes narrowed.

You must be hidden from yourself

"Hidden from myself? Why?"

There was a twitch at the side of his mouth, and I thought one of his eyebrows lifted a notch.

For your protection, and so you will not be tempted to use this information until the time is right

"How will I know when that time comes?"

You will know

He turned on his heel and walked away toward the McClellan gate, his voice still echoing around my head.

Enjoy your new job – Sara

FIVE

I woke up suddenly, as if a hypo of adrenaline had been emptied into my jugular. My heart was pounding and I took a deep breath to slow the rate. Every thought was in 3-D and high definition, every forgotten memory now bursting through open doors.

I jerked upright and felt a hand on my shoulder. "Whoa, girl," came Stillman's voice from behind me.

She was holding a glass of water and, with a raise of her eyebrows, offered it to me. I gratefully took it and quenched my thirst, only now realizing how dry and parched my mouth was. The room was in darkness, the only light coming from the deck where my nightlight was shimmering orange.

"Colleen, I …" I began.

She shook her head and wrapped an arm around my shoulders and pulled me close, gently rubbing my arm. I sank into the warmth of her side, appreciative of the simple gesture. Then I pulled her closer, wrapping my arms around her as the world around me melted away as I squeezed back. In her embrace, the world stopped on its axis.

"Welcome back, Kate," she said, giving the top of my head a gentle kiss.

I took a long, shuddery breath.

"How long was I under?"

Stillman shrugged. "Maybe an hour."

I blinked in surprise. "Did I say anything?"

"Lots, at first."

"And then …?"

"Then you slept. I've finished your wine, by the way."

I leaned forward, head in hands, and ran my fingers through my hair. The dream was still crystal clear, but its meaning eluded me. My previous life, however, did not.

"Are you okay?" Stillman's voice was full of concern.

"No."

Kelly's face was burned into my retina. My daughter. My dead daughter. Dead now for over a year. Her pretty blue eyes, the curly blonde hair, her playfulness, her kindness. But where was the grief? I felt empty and there was heaviness, a weight on my shoulders that seemed to be crushing me. Was it because I had been forced to forget her existence? Tears started to well up but remained in check as the nothingness took hold of my soul and threatened to suffocate me.

I sat back and took another drink. Stillman was studiously watching me, so I tried a smile. "I know who I am now. I remember my real life. But I don't even remember starting at the hospital here in Detroit. It was as if I'd always worked there."

"It was deep cover, to say the least."

"Cain must have been able to manipulate all the admission paperwork, applications, everything." I said, shaking my head. "My apartment, clothes … what the fuck? How is that even possible without me knowing anything?"

Stillman just shrugged. "Think how powerful Adam was. The ability to get inside other people's minds. Infiltrate electronic systems. Probably wouldn't have been too difficult for Cain."

"But what I don't know is why Cain blanked my mind and gave me another identity."

Stillman shrugged. "According to the tape we watched, he clearly didn't want the authorities – me included – to find you. He specifically told Hubert to leave you alone."

"Yes, but why?" I said. "If Adam is dead, what do I have to do with anything anymore?"

Stillman gave a forced smile. "Clearly you still have a part to play in future events."

We looked at each other in silence. Then Stillman twitched upright.

"Oh, now then. I've something for you."

She reached for her purse and snapped open the clasp. A second or two later and she was handing me a small see-through jiffy bag with a lock of blonde hair in it. I stared at it like it was kryptonite, my heart lurching in my chest.

"What's this?" I said, but knowing the answer.

Stillman's smile was kind. "We found this at your old place in Indian Springs. You kept it by your bed."

I slowly took it from her outstretched hand. The hair was ash blonde and plaited, with a couple of loops of elastic keeping it together. The tears came and I did nothing to quell them. The loss was instantly more than my heart could take, heavy dark clouds swamping and crushing my soul.

"Thank you," I managed.

The knock came quietly at first, and then more insistently, louder and faster. Then there was silence. I stared at the door, unmoving. Stillman got up, taking the glass from my hand.

"You expecting visitors?"

I shook my head.

She moved to the side of the door, and I followed, staying behind her. She gestured to the peephole for me to take a look.

"Stand directly in front of it. That way whoever's there won't see the light as you uncover it."

I nodded and noticed that she'd produced a gun from somewhere. She held it in a two-handed grip pointed at the floor and flattened herself against the wall. For a fleeting moment I considered asking why I was the one front and center, but she gestured with her head to the door and so I carefully flipped the peephole up.

"It's Navarro," I whispered.

Stillman's brows furrowed. "How the hell did he find you? There's no way he followed me."

"Well he's here," I said tightly. "What are we going to do?"

"How well do you know him?"

I thought about that. Navarro had always been a bit standoffish at Indian Springs, and had a bit of a reputation as a loner. An ex-Marine, he'd gone into medicine late and gravitated towards radiology, a specialty where he didn't need to interact with patients very often. Despite this, I'd gotten along fairly well with him, and I felt bad because I'd so emphatically denied knowing him a few hours earlier.

"He's okay," I said. "Harmless. He may be able to help us. He was there when Adam Benedict was brought in to the ER."

Stillman chewed on her lip, then came to a decision. "Alright, let's see what he wants."

I made sure the chain was secure and opened the door about three inches. Light from the hallway poured in through the gap. Navarro was standing there, hands in pockets, looking back at me. There was a thin film of sweat on his face, as if he had just been for a run. Or climbed a bunch of stairs. Well, this was the sixth floor.

"Pete, what're you doing here?" I said.

He blinked a few times and his neck gave a little sideways twitch, as if he'd had a little electrical shock. He looked up and down the corridor before leaning in toward me and putting a hand on the doorjamb.

"Let me in," he said.

Goosebumps exploded on my skin and a cold chill brushed down my neck and spine. I said, "Sorry, Pete, hold on for one moment, will you?" and shut the door gently.

"Something's not right," I whispered to Stillman. "Can you feel it?"

She shook her head but raised the gun a couple of inches, whispering back, "What do you mean?"

I wasn't sure, but a general sense of foreboding was suffocating me. The kind of dread animals might experience while being herded on the road train for the slaughterhouse.

"Let me in," came Navarro's voice again, now husky. I looked in the peephole again. His eyes were wide, the irises all black, like pools of oil.

Stillman grabbed my sleeve and pulled me toward her. "We should talk with him. We need all the help we can get."

My hands were shaking and I felt giddy and nauseated.

"Are you okay? What's wrong?"

"Can't you feel it?" I said again. "It's ... I know it's a cliché but ... as if something just walked over my grave."

"I can't feel anything," she said, staring at me.

"It's like ..." I looked up, my eyes widening as realization hit me. "It felt like this whenever the Vu-Hak got inside my head."

Stillman glanced at the door. She inched forward, gun held up at the side of her head. There was a scratching sound, like fingernails clawing on wood. Deep breathing, slow and wheezy.

"Please Kate, let me in," came the voice.

Stillman looked at me but I shook my head, my eyes shooting her a warning. "No way."

"You said he might be able to help," she whispered.

"What if it's not him?" I said, starting to hyperventilate.

"He's not a machine," she said.

I closed my eyes and tried to picture the machine Adam. The perfect but plasticky skin, the lack of ageing lines or crow's feet or any disfigurements. A human copy, convincing, unless seen up close. I sneaked a peak through the hole again at Navarro and saw the staring eyes, bloodshot and watering. A furrowed brow. Sweaty and pale. Buzz cut hair, blotchy scalp.

Not a copy. Not a machine.

Definitely Navarro.

I reached up to unhook the chain and open the door again, and then everything seemed to happen in slow motion.

Navarro kicked the door in.

There was an explosion of broken wood and plaster as the lock and chain guard burst free. The door blew off the hinge and hammered into my shoulder. I tumbled backward, losing my feet and falling heavily over a chair. Somehow I rolled without hitting my head on the floor but crashed into the wall opposite. Navarro took a step through the entryway and Stillman raised the gun two-handed and pointed it at his head. Before she could fire Navarro launched himself at her, arms flailing and knocking the gun flying out of her hands. He grabbed her around the neck and pushed her up against the wall, and then she was lifted off the ground, pinned, trying to loosen his grip while kicking her legs against him.

I looked around for the gun but couldn't see it, so I picked the chair up and swung it into his back as hard as I could. He staggered against Stillman, losing his grip, and she took the opportunity to punch him in the face, again and again, straight-arm punches, vicious and accurate. Blood started to seep from his nose, which had flattened against his face and looked broken.

I picked up the chair again and swung it, aiming for the back of his head. It connected and there was a sickening thud as his head jerked to the side with the force of the blow.

But he didn't fall.

He raised an arm to block Stillman's punches and swung a fist at her at blinding speed. She just managed to see it coming and ducked, letting it crash into the plasterwork. The wall indented and cracked and when he pulled his fist out of the hole, there was blood on the paintwork and over his knuckles. Stillman ducked under his arm again and jabbed him in the kidneys, which caused him to fold over and let out a hiss like a deflated balloon. As she moved in for another punch he threw an elbow into her face, which she deflected onto her shoulder. The force must have been significant, because she spun sideways and her feet gave way.

Navarro moved toward me and I held the chair out in front like a lion-tamer. His face was expressionless, his eyes soulless, black and empty.

"Pete, what the fuck are you doing?" I managed in between breaths.

In response his lips curled back in a feral grin, and there was that familiar tickling sensation behind my eyes. Fear and anxiety were being kicked around my brain, hyper-activating my adrenal glands. Sweat started to drench my skin, my heart thumped in my ears, my breathing accelerated even faster. Paralysis took hold as the fear spread throughout my body, shutting down my muscles and my nerves. I couldn't move.

Then the voice of the Vu-Hak was in my head.

We have found you Kate Morgan

Navarro lunged forward and grabbed hold of the chair, pulling it out of my hands and flicking it away in one movement. I stared into his eyes, frozen, waiting for the green phosphorescence to flash as the Vu-Hak moved in for the kill.

Then Stillman jumped back in and got Navarro in a headlock, jerking him aggressively to the ground so he was bent in two. His reached up to scrabble for her hands but she viciously twisted, using her weight and momentum like an MMA fighter.

The spell was broken and the paralyzing fear left me all at once. I grabbed his legs and pinned them down as he kicked and twitched, attempting to get out of Stillman's grip. His fingers went up to her face and she buried her head in his neck as he tried to gouge her eyes out. She was panting hard, veins standing out like hosepipes on her forehead and temples.

"Get ... my ... gun!" she ground out. "There!"

Her head flicked to the doorway where the Glock was lying against the frame. It was about six feet away, which might have been six miles given that Navarro was likely to break free any second.

"I've got him. Quickly, Kate! He's strong!"

I took a deep breath and crawled over his legs as fast as I could, keeping my body weight on his until the last possible moment. I pulled myself toward the door, heading for the Glock, stretching out my hand, fingers grasping. As my finger brushed the metal of the barrel, there was a sharp tug and my hair was pulled backward and my head slammed into the floor. My vision blurred as the pain lanced through my skull. I twisted and he lost his grip and I awkwardly rolled, bumping up against the wall. Stillman had her legs wrapped around his neck in some sort of judo hold, and she was batting away his hands as they now tried to grab her thighs. His face was bright red and his eyes were bulging, but still he kept swinging away, the odd fist connecting with Stillman's chest and body. She was tiring, and I could see he was not going to tap out anytime soon, if at all.

I scrambled to pick up the gun. I had no idea if the safety was on or off but I assumed she would have had it ready to go. I held it with both hands and pointed it at Navarro. "Pete," I screamed. "Give it up now!"

There was no response, and he kept struggling and punching, the impacts getting bigger and more frequent.

Stillman grunted, head down, "The legs, Kate! Shoot him in the legs!"

I took a deep breath. The pain in my head had somehow dulled the Vu-Hak presence and lessened the fear. I took aim at Navarro's left shin, closed my eyes, and pulled the trigger.

The report was loud in the confined space of the corridor, and the recoil hurt my wrist, but my shot was accurate. A hole blew out of his pants, followed by a squib of blood. At this close range the bullet passed through his leg and carved out a divot on my floor. To my astonishment, there was no let up in Navarro's attempts to get out of Stillman's grip. Both arms and legs continued to thrash, like he was being Tasered.

"Again!" Stillman shouted.

I targeted his other leg, higher up above the kneecap, and pulled the trigger twice. Two big holes ripped through the trousers and a geyser of blood shot out vertically. An artery. Crimson sprayed the wall like a Jackson Pollock painting. Within a few seconds I guessed about a liter was pooling under his leg. The human body has about five liters in total and with one fifth already gone he was looking at hypovolemic shock.

Stillman released him and pushed herself away like a crab, taking huge deep breaths and scrabbling toward the far wall. Navarro lurched to the side, collapsed, and then, using one arm, started to push himself to his feet. His leg bent out from under him and with a crack his shinbones snapped, horrifically ripping through his trouser leg. Despite all this he started to crawl toward me, mouth opening and closing soundlessly. Blood continued to pour out of his leg and he slipped on the mess but continued his advance, looking like a nightmare vision from a Dante painting.

Then Stillman was by my side and yanked the gun out of my hand. She pushed me out of the way and fired twice into his face. The back of his head exploded as the 9mm rounds blew out, taking blood and brain and skull to complete the wall decoration.

His head dropped, and he fell in a pile onto the bloody carpet.

SIX

I leaned against the wall, my heart going like a trip hammer and adrenaline coursing through my body. Navarro lay face down in the doorway, the back of his head a dark bloody mess. Behind him, blood spattered the corridor leading to my elderly neighbor's door. Hopefully she was out of town.

Stillman edged toward Navarro and stepped gingerly over his body to close the front door. She kicked his leg out of the way as it jammed in the gap.

"Help me move him into there," she said, pointing at my coat closet.

I was frozen to the spot; I started to shake as the adrenaline left me. What had we – had I – done? Navarro wasn't a Vu-Hak: he was a human being. And now he was dead in my house. While I didn't fire the killing shots, that didn't make me feel any better. I had helped kill someone … someone I knew as a colleague, and maybe a friend. Did he have family, a wife maybe, and children? I didn't think so, but I hoped not.

"Kate," Stillman hissed. "Snap out of it. We don't have much time. How long do you think it'll be before the police get here?"

I nodded. "Not long."

Every resident on this floor would be on their phones right about now, dialing 911, reporting gunshots in the Moynahan. People would be panicking, the building going into lockdown.

I still didn't move and was fixated on Navarro's mutilated leg, and the expanding pool of blood oozing towards the door. Stillman grabbed me by the shoulder and shook me. I managed to tear my gaze away from Navarro and was struck by how calm she looked.

"It's alright, Kate. We had no choice."

"Okay, but what are we going to do?" I said.

"Get the hell out of Dodge, obviously."

"What, and just leave him in my cupboard?"

She briefly averted her eyes and then took a deep breath. "We need to lie low for a while. Re-boot. Figure out what the hell happened here."

"We just killed someone. That's what happened." I was starting to panic again.

"Yes and no," she said. "This was something different."

She wasn't wrong there. Navarro wasn't one of the Vu-Hak machines, that much was clear. But he wasn't himself. "I sensed the Vu-Hak. It spoke to me," I whispered, my voice shaking. "It said that they'd found me. It was controlling Navarro."

Stillman gave me a sharp look. "Controlling him? From where?"

I pointed to the body on the floor. "From there. Inside him."

"Like he was possessed?"

I screwed up my eyes and tried to think, tried to make sense of what had happened. "Yes, it was Navarro's body but his mind was all Vu-Hak. I think he was in there, but he wasn't in charge of his actions. I also got … impressions. Like, a sadistic pleasure in getting another autonomous being to behave under your control."

Stillman's brow furrowed. "I don't understand. They're controlling people now? Why?"

I had no answer for that. If the Vu-Hak had been in one of their machine bodies, then nothing could have stopped it from killing us.

"Maybe there aren't any more machines," she said, slowly.

That pulled me up short. Adam had said that the Vu-Hak were a race of untethered consciousness. That they had forsaken physical bodies thousands of years ago. At some point before that however, they'd transferred their minds into machine constructs in order to travel unhindered through interstellar space.

"Adam told us that organic matter – and that includes those alien free-floating minds – wouldn't survive passage through the wormhole. The machines protected them. The fact that the Vu-Hak are here means the machines are too."

Stillman looked thoughtful. "Okay, they can't be here without the machines."

I nodded. "And Cain is definitely a machine."

"Yes he is."

"So where're the other machines?"

"We need to find Cain and ask him."

Together we awkwardly shoved Navarro into the cubby, and I pushed the door closed. There was a long smear of blood and brain leading from the front door to where we had deposited Navarro.

"Should we clean that up?" I said.

Stillman was already gathering her things together and pulling her coat on. "No time. We need to get out of here before the cops arrive."

"Maybe we should wait for them?"

"You've got to be kidding. We can't trust anyone now." She walked up to me and was in my face, her almond eyes now red-rimmed. "You hear me?"

I nodded silently and grabbed my jacket and beanie from the sofa. The unreality of what had just happened was sinking in. But, considering the experience of having my memories reloaded, nothing was going to seem impossible. My house, the decorations, the keepsakes, the personal touches. None mattered now. None of them were truly mine.

"The police are going to be looking for Sara Clarke," I said. "And unfortunately she looks just like me."

Stillman just shrugged. "It's a big country. I think I know just where to go to be anonymous. And to get help."

We left the Moynahan by the fire exit and joined the pedestrian traffic heading downtown toward the city. It was dark and chilly, and there was a light drizzly rain coming off the lake. An increasing squeal of sirens could be heard as the police answered the multiple 911 calls from our building.

Stillman hailed a cab and we dived into the back seat. The leather squeaked and smelled vaguely of smoke and piss. I caught a glimpse of myself in the driver's mirror, bags under red-rimmed eyes, blonde hair curling messily from under the beanie.

The driver, a very fat Middle Eastern man, looked back and asked where we were going.

"Greyburn Cemetery," said Stillman.

He flicked the meter on and took a wide U-turn on the street, heading south.

"Why the cemetery?" I said.

Stillman leaned close and whispered into my ear, "Fifteen minutes' walk to the Greyhound station."

The rain was bouncing off the sidewalks, huge globs pooling into rivers along the road.

"Why not just drop us off at the bus station?"

She gave me a withering look. "Because when the taxi driver is interviewed he won't be able to say that he dropped two women off at the bus station, will he?"

So there we were. Fugitives, and on the run. I had to revise my thinking.

Traffic was fairly heavy, and ten minutes later we were dropped off at the entrance to the cemetery. Stillman paid the cabbie and added an average tip. Too big a tip, or no tip at all, and he might remember us, I thought. Now I was thinking like a fugitive too.

We waited until the taxi was out of sight and then headed off westwards at a fast pace. Stillman had not had time to change and was still wearing her long dark coat over the yellow cocktail dress and high heels, which were clickety-clacking along the sidewalk. She stepped on an uneven pavement edge and twisted her ankle.

"Fuck," she said, stopping and hopping as she took the stilettos off. "I need to get out of these clothes."

I nodded silently and looked up and down the street. Lights were flickering on sporadically, and the traffic was pretty steady. However, no malls or shopping areas looked open and we were in the wrong part of town for a high fashion raid.

"Over there, looks like no one home." Stillman said, pointing to a couple of apartment buildings. The lower windows on the ground level were dark with half open curtains and certainly looked unoccupied.

"We adding burglary to our crimes now?" I said, only half-joking.

She gave me flat eyes and hustled us across the road toward the apartments, which up close were all grey old stone with solid-looking window frames. We turned into the nearest building and made our way up the stairs to the front door. Stillman leaned on the bell and waited as I anxiously checked passersby and traffic. After a half-minute or so, she rang it again. No answer.

"We're in luck," she said with a twinkle in her eye. "Let's get inside."

She rummaged around her handbag and pulled out a shiny silver tool, which looked like a bottle opener with multiple wires and hooks. It took her four seconds to pick the lock, and we slipped into the house. There was a musty smell of old curtains, and a not unpleasant smell of bolognese sauce. My stomach rumbled and I put a hand on my abdomen and gave it a rub. The hallway was pitch dark and so Stillman flicked the lights on. A series of low-wattage bulbs encased in old-world lampshades flickered, casting orange shadows along the corridor, which was about thirty feet long. At the end was a half-open door leading to what looked like a kitchenette. On the right were doors leading to two other rooms. The left-hand wall was just picture frames, bookcases and plants.

Stillman shrugged out of her coat and popped it onto the hat stand next to the front door alongside a couple of fleeces and an assortment of winter coats.

"Stay here and keep a look out. I'll see what I can find."

She headed up the corridor and ducked into the first room on the right.

The hat stand lived up to its name, with flat caps and woolen hats, a couple of straw boaters and a fedora that wouldn't have looked out of place on Indiana Jones. A very large black beanie with *JETS* on it looked more promising and so I pulled it on, tucking as much of my hair in as I could. I leaned against the front door and squinted outside. There was one dim streetlight and a few late-model sedans parked and an elderly couple walking a dog. I reflexively jerked my head back as they looked my way but when I poked my head out again they were gone.

There was a creak on the floorboards behind me and Stillman returned, wearing trainers, jeans and a sweater, which all seemed to fit her. I guess we caught a break.

"Like my disguise?" I quipped.

"You're obviously a fan of beanies," she said, giving me a crooked smile.

She grabbed one of the fleeces and put it on, throwing her handbag over her shoulder. There was a mirror across from the door and she stood in front of it, checking herself out.

"We good?" I said, anxiously looking toward the front door.

She pursed her lips and frowned into the mirror. "Throw me that baseball cap?"

There were a few to choose from and she settled on a blue NYPD cap. I wondered if the owner was actually a cop, or just a supporter. Either way, I was getting twitchy and thought it was time to go.

Stillman saw me looking and nodded. "Let's get out of here."

I started toward the door but as I reached for the handle a shadow passed by the side window and footsteps could be heard. We pressed ourselves back into the side of the hallway behind the hat stand and waited.

"Wait, the lights are still on …" hissed Stillman.

"Too late," I said.

The sound of a key being inserted in the lock echoed down the corridor, and the door was slowly pushed open.

SEVEN

"Honey, did you leave the lights on?"

The voice was male and croaky, with a southern drawl. Stillman propelled me into the first room off the hallway before the door had fully opened and crowded in behind me. The smell of old clothes and fabrics reminded me of my grannie's bedroom. The blinds were half-drawn, and everything was in monochrome, silhouettes of bric-a-brac and furniture could just be seen on the walls and in the corners. I could just make out a double bed, a couple of wardrobes and a vanity desk. There was another door leading, I presumed, to an en suite. The ticking of a clock synched with my heartbeat.

"The window, quickly," whispered Stillman.

"Can't we just wait until they head into the kitchen, and make a run for the front door?"

She shook her head and pushed me toward the window. It was one of those sash types locked down by a screw. I gave it a few turns and it shuddered open but then stopped with an opening of about twelve inches.

"That's a squeeze, to say the least," I said, pulling a face.

A cool, crisp breeze fluttered through the gap, blowing a few dust motes in my face and making me clamp my fingers over my nose to prevent a sneeze. Creaky footsteps could be heard outside and coming closer, and there was some scuffling on the doorframe and knob. I wondered if it was worth a dive behind the bed, but Stillman was already climbing out the window headfirst, like an escapologist wriggling out of a straitjacket. The bedroom door started to open and a sliver of light made its way through. A hand snaked in, found the switch, and flicked it on. The room exploded with the luminescence of an atomic bomb. I had nowhere to go so I backed up against the window frame as Stillman dropped heavily onto the sidewalk six feet or so below.

A woman entered the room.

She looked to be in her seventies but was sprightly and thin.

She had a beaky nose and moved almost bird-like with a strange bobbing of her head and neck. Her hair was frilly white, like she had a lace doily flapping around her face. She was wearing a green two-piece leisure suit, which looked to be made out of some form of velour material, and a scarf was jauntily knotted around her neck.

She saw me and froze.

We looked at each other, neither saying anything.

I put my finger to my lips and shook my head, eyes wide and pleading. She nodded slowly, her gaze never leaving mine. I beckoned her to come in and she did so, closing the door behind. She gave little sign of being frightened at the sight of an intruder in her house, but clutched her handbag close to her chest with both hands. We stared at each other silently, waiting for the other to make the first move.

"We have money," she said in a low tremulous voice. "I'll give you whatever you need."

She held her head high and I felt sorry for her and impressed at the same time. I abstractly wondered if she had been a schoolteacher or a governess of some sort. She looked the type.

There was a hissing-whistle sound from outside where Stillman was gesturing frantically at me to climb out. It would take me time and effort to squeeze through the window and the woman would have plenty of time to try and stop me or run to get her husband. I shook my head at Stillman and turned back to face the woman who hadn't moved any further into the room.

"I don't want your money," I said. "I'm so sorry for the intrusion. We just needed some clothes."

As I said this I realized how stupid it must have sounded.

I was standing there dressed in expensive jeans and a leather three-quarters jacket, certainly not the picture of a homeless bum. And all I had stolen was one of her beanies.

"Let me leave right now," I said, "and we'll be out of your hair. It'll be as if this never happened."

Then the front bell sounded and the woman's head jerked toward the door, her eyes widening. I gestured furiously at her, swiping my hand under my chin.

"I'll get it," came the same croaky voice from down the hallway, footsteps heading toward the front door. "Who'd be calling at this hour? It better not be that Aaron from next door. If he's lost his key again I'm of a mind to tell him we've mislaid the spare …"

The woman and I continued to look at each other, and my heart was pounding away, all the different scenarios whizzing though my mind. All bad outcomes.

The front door unlatched noisily and creaked open. There was no further sound and no further talking. I'd just counted to ten in my head when the bedroom door opened and the man, who I assumed was the husband, entered with his hands above his head. He was stooped and had a heavily lined face, a small amount of white hair poking out from under a peaked flat cap. He looked angry and, like his wife, not in the least bit scared.

Then Stillman appeared behind him, her gun in his back, pushing him firmly but gently. She looked at me, resignation on her face, and shook her head. "What else could I do?" she said.

"Shit, we're taking hostages now?" I hissed.

Stillman just grimaced and pushed the man further into the room. "Let's find somewhere we can lock them in and get out of here."

I frowned. "They've seen us together. They can identify us."

"Doesn't matter. We just need a head start."

The woman was still clutching her bag tightly and had not taken her eyes off me. She had a quiet defiance that was endearing.

"What's your name?" I said softly.

"Margaret," she said. "Margaret Bolton. This is Gerry, my husband."

"I'm sorry about this. It's not what it seems. We're not going to hurt you."

Gerry snorted, tipping his head toward Stillman. "Well, she's got a gun."

Yeah, there was that, I supposed. I looked at Stillman and raised my eyebrows. She made a resigned kind of sound and lowered her Glock.

"We're not criminals, just desperate," I said to the Boltons. "I'm sorry about this but we need to secure you for a time. We can't have you raising the alarm, at least not yet."

"We won't call anyone, so you can just leave," Gerry said, unconvincingly.

Stillman gave him a look. "That's not going to cut it."

I pushed open the door to the en suite and took a quick peek. A fairly large freestanding bathtub occupied the middle of the room, with ornate taps and accessories scattered around it. A toilet and matching bidet were surrounded by shelves and assorted toiletries. There was a single elevated window with a cross frame, which was clearly too small to squeeze a person through.

"This'll work," I said, beckoning Stillman over.

She gave it a quick once over and nodded. She motioned to the Boltons with her firearm. "In you come. This won't be for long. I'll make a call when we're clear and the police'll come and get you."

The Boltons considered this by staring at each other, and then Gerry shrugged. Grudgingly, but without any further delay, they shuffled into the bathroom. Stillman frisked them quickly and found a cellphone, which she confiscated. We heaved the bed and a wardrobe to jam the door closed. It looked secure enough.

"Let's go back out through the front door," said Stillman, putting her gun away. We exited and walked quickly down the stairs to the sidewalk.

"Which way?" I said, looking up and down the street. A couple walking a dog were approaching from the left, and another guy in running kit was making his way towards us from the right.

Stillman pointed toward the jogger. "West Morgan Street is that way, I think."

At that moment the en suite window above us opened with a loud bang and Margaret's head appeared. She stared at us for a second and then shouted at the top of her voice, "Help! Help us!"

The dog walkers, with what looked like a fairly large German Shepherd, stopped in their tracks, now only ten yards from us. The jogger had also pulled up and was looking at us. He had a cellphone in his hand and brought it to his mouth. His face became illuminated as he was connected.

"Help! We've been robbed!" Margaret screamed again.

Stillman looked at me and rolled her eyes.

"Fuck it. Run."

EIGHT

S tillman took off across the street, dodging a slow-moving truck and skipping around a newspaper dispenser on the corner before stopping to check on my progress. I hadn't moved. The jogger was now a couple of yards from me, a tall well-built athletic-looking man with the huge shoulders and upper arms of a guy who spends too much time in the gym. Despite the cool of the night he was wearing one of those sweat tops with the sleeves ripped off. He continued to talk on the phone, giving my description to someone I guessed was the 911 operator. He saw me backing away, put the phone in his pocket and got in my face, blocking the way to Stillman, who was now watching anxiously from the other side of the road. She was clearly hesitating; not wanting to pull the gun in the street with god knew how many people watching.

"You and me are just going to wait here now until the cops arrive," the jogger said, planting his feet in a wide stance. He smiled, secure in his size advantage and masculinity. He had that look about him, the way he held himself, oozing an unassailable confidence.

"It's not what you think," I said defiantly, trying to inject an assurance into my voice that I didn't feel.

He gave a derisory kind of snort, and just folded his arms. They looked like a couple of gas pipes intertwined. He shook his head slowly, as if daring me to make a move.

I took another step back but was grabbed from behind, my arms twisted painfully upward. The German Shepherd was suddenly in my face, barking loudly and salivating. Margaret Bolton continued to scream from the window. Stillman was shouting now, waving her arms and looking up and down the street for a gap in the traffic to come back over.

"Take it easy," hissed a voice in my ear, presumably one of the dog's owners. "We saw you come out the house. Cops are on the way."

He brought more pressure to bear and lifted my arms further upward and backward, which pushed me to my knees. Spots started to appear before my eyes and I became dizzy and lightheaded. I was starting to get angry and distressed in equal measure.

Then Cain's voice boomed in my head.

I have given you what you need. You will know when to use it.

"What the …?" I grunted.

"Stop struggling," the voice from behind me came again.

I have given you what you need

And just like that, everything changed.

The world was suddenly moving in slow motion, so accelerated were my thoughts. I could triangulate the exact location of the people around me with my eyes closed. The dog was subtracted to a ghost-like image consisting of pixels and blurred lines. The woman holding the leash was holding him back, but was happy to let him strain and pull in my face to scare me. I could read the thoughts of the jogger, already seeing his name in tomorrow's local paper having assisted in the arrest of a hardened criminal such as me. The man holding my arms was excited and sure of himself, telling himself he was just wanting to do the right thing, to be a local hero. I sensed the Boltons behind their window, now quiet and watching the events unfolding with some satisfaction. And Stillman, concerned for me and scared about what she would have to do in order to extricate me, and herself, from this situation.

All this went through my mind in a microsecond.

My awareness was hyper-acute, my brain working like a supercomputer, analyzing every scenario and probable consequence in real time. My muscles twitched as the neurological signals driving them were accelerated. Everything was in overdrive, supercharged. My reflexes, strength, speed; all were somehow optimized to maximum performance. It was like being a passenger in a supercar, with someone else driving and in control.

What was going on?

Without really thinking about it I span around and launched

myself off my knees, the force of my turn easily dislodging the guy's grip on my arms. I grabbed the front of his shirt and yanked sideways. He flew through the air, landing a good ten feet away, bouncing and tumbling into the gutter. His dog reflexively jerked backward a couple of feet and stopped barking, as surprised as his owner at what had just happened. I shot out a hand and cuffed the dog around the mouth. Its head jerked sideways and it let out a whine before scampering backwards, tail between its legs. I pulled the lead out of the woman's hand and the animal dashed into the road, dodging between the cars, and vanished out of sight.

The meathead jogger hadn't backed off and started to move in toward me, arms out like a wrestler, going for a hold. I took a big step in, invaded his space and thrust my open hand into his face. His nose flattened, and there was a squelchy sound and a snap. He staggered back but didn't fall, even as the blood sprayed from the nostril that wasn't closed off by the new deformity. He gave a snarl and dropped into a crouch and bunched his fists before swinging a haymaker into my face. I easily ducked under it and without conscious control my arms became a blur, fists finding his face easily. One, two, three punches, *rat-tat-tat*. He rocked back on his heels but kept his feet. Shaking his head, he swung again, a large roundhouse punch that if it hit me could have knocked my head off. However, there was no chance of that happening. The punch landed on my forearm, the impact an abstract sensation, and again I threw a dozen or so blisteringly fast punches into his gut, head, ribs. He winced with each impact and twisted trying to avoid being hit, but it must have been like trying to avoid a swarm of flies.

His size had so far enabled him to stay on his feet but the overwhelming number of blows finally took its toll and he swayed to the side and dropped to his knees, hands over his bloody and battered face. Before he could recover I leaned back and kicked him in the face, using all my weight and speed. The kinetic energy of the blow propelled him backward into the road where he tumbled and rolled uncontrollably while cars screeched and horns blew as the traffic came to a standstill.

My eyes scanned the street, overhead, everywhere, seemingly in tetrachromatic vision, searching for other threats. But there were none. The dog owner was crouched over her partner, cradling his head in her hands. He looked okay, but dazed. The dog was long gone. The Boltons were still at the window, dumbstruck at what they'd witnessed. They stared at me, their mouths wide open, their brains not quite registering the events of the last minute and a half.

With the traffic halted, Stillman ran across the road dodging the stationary vehicles with their gawking drivers. She must have seen something in my eyes because she held up both her hands and pulled up a couple of feet away.

"Whoa there, it's me. What the fuck happened? How did you do that?"

The scene was certainly chaotic. Drivers were getting out of their vehicles, many holding their cellphones up taking photos and video, lights flashing. People were starting to overcome their initial fear and hesitation and were beginning to wander over toward us.

I grabbed Stillman by the arm. "There's no time. We've got to go. Now!"

We took off and jinked down the first side street we could find. The lighting was thankfully dim, and traffic was sparse. I was still seeing things faster and clearer than normal, but the effects were starting to wear off. I picked the first house on the right and pulled Stillman into an alleyway running down its side. As we ran, my vision and senses continued to take in all the surrounding areas, full alert and geo-mapping in real time. My brain was still on overdrive, and it seemed as if I could remember every detail of the streets and houses we passed. Every image was saved and locked in, every bit of my brain, every terabyte of storage, was able to be accessed and processed and made available.

We came to the end of the alleyway and turned into another yard, keeping to the side of the fencing. I set a grueling pace which Stillman followed without complaint, only occasionally grabbing my hand when I periodically pulled up short to sneak a peek around a corner before setting off again. My hair was sticking to my forehead, slick with perspiration, sweat rolling down my back in thick salty drops. My heart was racing but my breathing was easy, and it felt like I could run forever. My feet pounded the tarmac, eating up the yards, as my head swung from side to side taking in the surrounding streets, roads, houses and pedestrians and logging them as potential threats or mere obstructions. Stillman's rasping breathing was sounding more strained as we bolted down a garden path, the sound of our feet slip-slapping and echoing around the walls of two adjacent townhouses.

"Where you taking us?" she managed in between wheezes.

"A shortcut," I said, glancing backward. "We've got a bus to catch, remember?"

NINE

I was exhausted.
As drained as if I'd just completed a marathon. The energy was leaking from my body, like a battery with power dropping by a bar a second, like a deflating bicycle tire. The analogies came thick and fast.

We were slumped in the back seats of the Greyhound bus. It was about half full, but the nearest passengers were three rows ahead. It'd pulled out of the station only a few minutes after we got on board, the driver announcing that the time to New York was approximately eleven hours including a couple of stops and we should make ourselves comfortable. Stillman had bought a couple of Cokes from a machine, and I'd drunk them almost in one gulp. I was on my second Snickers bar, stomach growling noisily like a bear in springtime waking up from hibernation. I wolfed down the rest of the chocolate, wiping my mouth on the sleeve of my jacket.

"Refueling?"

She was watching me carefully, a concerned look on her face. I needed to sleep and felt like a zombie, kinda alive but also dead. My knuckles were red and swollen and starting to hurt. Making fists just intensified the soreness and made me grimace in pain. Stillman reached over and gently ran her hands over them, massaging the joints and tendons. I smiled gratefully and gave her hand a reassuring, if painful, squeeze.

"I'm okay really." I said. There was another pain higher up on my forearm where I'd blocked meathead's roundhouse punch. Suddenly the reality of what had just happened kicked in and I was aching all over, like I had the flu.

Stillman took a deep breath. "Want to tell me what happened back there?"

"I'm still trying to figure it out myself."

"I've never seen anything like that," she said. "You were like a blur. Fast. Like something out of *The Matrix* …"

I looked out of the window at the lights of Detroit. High rises and office buildings winked at me, black boxy structures glittering and shining. I caught my reflection, hair plastered to my forehead, dirty sweat dripping down my nose. I rubbed my eyes and brushed my hair back, tucking some loose strands behind my ears.

"He did something to me," I said.

"Cain?"

I rested my head back and closed my eyes. "It was like a 'fight or flight' reflex but scaled up to the nth degree. Everything was enhanced and speeded up. I felt superhuman. Like I could do anything. See anything. It was … incredible."

"But look at you now," she said. "It's as if you've completely run out of gas."

I nodded slowly. "Like a supercharger on a car. Press the 'nitro' button and 'boom' off you go at light speed."

"And run out of fuel quicker."

"'The flame that burns twice as bright, burns half as long'," I said, quoting Lao Tzu. Where had that come from?

She gave a little laugh in acknowledgement, and then paused a beat. "Why do you think Cain give you this ability? Just so you could kick ass?"

I closed my eyes again, thinking back to the park bench at Arlington. The images that flashed through my mind when Cain touched my face, when he said *I have given you what you need. You will know when to use it.*

"I'm not sure. But I think there's more. Something's been implanted in my head. Something … important."

"Okay. So how do we get it out?"

I gave a weary shrug. "That's a good question. The human brain is like a supercomputer – a hundred billion cells with around a thousand links to other neurones – so a total storage capacity of two and a half million gigabytes. Which means in theory we should remember anything and everything. But we lack the capability to recall everything that's stored there. It's like it's locked behind a door. Corralled off from the rest of us, inaccessible without the right key."

Stillman pursed her lips. "Alright, so we need to find the key. Hey, I could always hypnotize you again?"

I almost smiled. "Tempting. It did seem to work last time."

"Almost too well. Which puzzles me. Memories hidden behind an embedded mental wall often take multiple sessions to recall. If they ever are. But with you, everything came back straight away. As if it was supposed to."

I nodded and we sat in silence for a while. My eyes started to close as the exhaustion took over and the adrenaline drained from my system. Just as I was about to give in to it and go to sleep Stillman put a hand on my arm.

"Do you think the Vu-Hak was controlling Navarro when you first met him on the street? And in the Hyatt bar? You know, before he went all crazy on us."

I thought back to the bar, and then later when Navarro came to the Moynahan. In the bar he was annoying, but nothing struck me as being abnormal, at least not that abnormal.

"I don't think so. But he must have been, right?"

Stillman shrugged. "I hit on him to try and get your phone. He acted like a dick, but nothing else."

"Then how did they find us?" I said.

Stillman closed her eyes, thinking back.

"There was a guy entering the bar just as you left. You squeezed past him, remember? Tall, wrapped in a long coat and wearing a baseball hat with sunglasses?"

"Nah, I was too angry. I just wanted to get out."

"He sat on the barstool next to Navarro. Took off his coat and settled in. I didn't see him drink but by then I was in Navarro's face." She looked at me and smirked. "You know he thought I was a hooker?"

I looked at her, picturing her sauntering up to him in that tight yellow dress, him with his buzz cut and tweed jacket. "I can imagine."

"Hey ..." She playfully punched my arm and gave a lopsided grin. "I'm a Special Agent, remember? Life-long training in interrogation and information gathering. I was just playing a role ..."

I gave a sisterly laugh and nodded. She'd put a couple of sodas in the seat pocket so I grabbed them, pulled the tabs and offered one to her. We clinked tins and took a couple of swigs.

"So what happened next?" I said. "I mean, after you went into the bathroom."

Stillman took another swig. "There was a back door which I'd scoped earlier. I hung around a back alleyway for ten minutes or so then sneaked back into the bar. Navarro had gone. I grabbed Paulo and bent his ear. I'd already given him a hundred bucks and a couple of promises I'd no intention of keeping."

She slumped back in the seat and relayed what had happened next. Navarro had gotten another drink and then looked in his jacket pocket for his phone. It wasn't there. He'd stood up and searched all his pockets and started to panic. His wallet was present and correct, but everywhere he patted down, there was no phone. He looked around his barstool, on the floor, on the bar, but there was no sign of it. Paulo asked him if everything was okay and whether he had lost something, to which Navarro replied that he'd lost his phone and thought he might have dropped it outside. The bartender asked if he maybe should give it a call and see if anyone picks up. Navarro gave him the number and Paulo dialed it from the phone next to the cash register. It went straight to voicemail. Navarro then said that he'd quickly pop outside to see if it was lying on the sidewalk somewhere, and asked Paulo to tell Rachael where he'd gone. Paulo asked who Rachael was, and Navarro had flicked a thumb toward the restrooms. The bartender told him that, as far as he knew, her name was Colleen.

"You gave him your real name?" I said.

Stillman shrugged. "Meh. Paulo wasn't the sharpest tool in the shed. I doubted there'd be any blowback."

I smiled. "Then what happened?"

"This is the funny bit. Navarro said to him: 'Wait … what? She said it was Rachael. That she comes here all the time.' To which Paulo replied – and I liked this bit – 'Sorry, but I've never seen her before. And believe me, I would have noticed someone that hot …'"

I stifled a giggle and Stillman gave another shrug as if to say 'Well, it's true.' "Navarro made his way to the restrooms at the back of the bar, but by then of course I'd long skedaddled."

I thought back to when I left the bar through the front exit onto the street. "The guy I passed at the door. I think you're right – that was the Vu-Hak."

Stillman looked spooked. "If it was, it ignored you and me and went straight to Navarro. Why?"

"I've no idea. Also, it was in human form. Again, why wasn't it a machine, like Adam? Or Cain?"

"If it was a machine I'm pretty sure we'd all be dead," Stillman said softly.

"I reckon the Vu-Hak found Navarro in the bar after he'd spoken to me and you. It must have been following Navarro, not us."

"And Navarro led it to us," she replied, nodding slowly. "So, what, are they everywhere? Floating and watching?"

I suppressed a shiver. The thought hadn't occurred to me. If Navarro wasn't infected when we first met – if 'infected' was the right word – then maybe the alien was waiting for the opportunity to get someone close to me. Someone they knew had contact with me previously. I glanced up the aisle at the other passengers, all of whom were now either sleeping or had their heads buried in books or magazines. Were any of them …? No – I couldn't let my mind go there. Could I? I screwed up my eyes and tried to think.

"Remember when he – the Vu-Hak – Navarro – whatever, spoke to me in the apartment, and said 'We've found you'? Maybe it just got lucky."

Stillman looked thoughtful. "We need to know why they're looking for you. I mean, you're right – if Adam's dead why do they care?"

Of all the questions, that was the million-dollar one. What was I to them? I closed my eyes again. So many questions, so many unknowns.

Stillman suddenly jolted out of her seat and grabbed my arm again. "Do we even know if the Vu-Hak died when I killed

Navarro? I mean, what if it just 'jumped' out of his body and is watching us now?"

I thought about it but then shook my head. "But then how'd we manage to escape? It could've just jumped into your body, or mine for that matter?"

"If that's how it works," said Stillman.

"No, it can't work like that," I said slowly. "I think that when we killed the 'host' body – I mean, poor Pete – then we somehow killed the Vu-Hak."

"But you don't know for sure," Stillman objected.

"No. There's very little we know for sure," I said.

She turned away and was quiet again, and fatigue washed over me like a tsunami. Every muscle appeared to be atrophying and giving in to gravity. I needed a warm bed and a dreamless sleep.

"Eleven hours to NYC. Remind me why we're going?"

Stillman had closed her eyes. A smile twitched at the corner of her mouth. "Bill Hubert's holed up there. He may be able to help us."

"Hubert? I thought you said his memory was wiped?"

The smile widened. "Well we now know how to fix that, don't we?"

TEN

I must have slept most of the way because it seemed like we pulled into the bus station in downtown NYC only moments later, Stillman gently shaking me awake. After a quick bathroom stop we hustled onto the platform and through the morning commuters up the escalators to 7th Avenue and the entrance by Madison Square Garden. Sunshine reflected from the windows of a tall office building across the street and the noise of the city hit me as taxis and limos honked and wheezed and bumped along at snail's pace in the rush hour of a weekday morning in the Big Apple. The streets were covered with old snow, dark grey from the pollution of the passing trucks and cars. There was the smell of coffee coming from a street vendor who was also sizzling up what looked like some kind of pastry frisbee. Diesel fumes from a passing truck lingered in the still air. People walked fast, heads down looking at their smartphones or plugged into their favorite music. Impatient commuters dressed in ski or puff jackets frowned at slower walkers navigating the crowd, coffee cups in hand, lost in their own worlds. Tourists, mainly Asians from what I could see, drifted in groups or collectives, peering at maps and guides as they shuffled around in search for their first point of interest of the day.

I stopped on the sidewalk behind the silver traffic protectors and stared at the dozens of yellow cabs lined up nose to tail. My breath rose before me, and my heart fluttered like a butterfly as another wave of anxiety washed over.

"Ever been to New York?" shouted Stillman into my ear.

"Nope."

"The Empire State is just a block or two away. Straight down East 34th. Want to go?"

I turned and shook my head, lips tightly compressed.

"We should go," she continued airily. "It's only a couple of hundred yards from where we're going to be anyway."

"Colleen, I don't feel safe here," I said, watching the crowds and looking for any giveaway signs of alien possession, whatever they might be. Horns, fangs, whatever.

She gave a weary sigh. "The population of Manhattan Island is nearly two million. New York City is eight and a half. I think we'll blend in okay."

I thought about the Vu-Hak, and what, if anything, they thought of cities like this. Did they once live like us, in concrete towers, where the trees are potted and slotted into specific spaces, where people eat and sleep and work and play according to the ticking clock? I recalled how I felt during my interactions with the Vu-Hak that shared Adam's machine body. I recalled the coldness, the sheer alienness of the mind that had filled me with dread and terror.

"Let's get off the streets," I said.

Stillman gave me a look then nodded. "Alright, let's go." She gestured across to the other sidewalk. "That's the way: we're going to the Langham, on 5th. It'll take us five minutes, tops, if we walk fast."

We set off at a quick pace, dodging around the tourists like people on a mission, which I guessed we were. I popped my sunglasses on in a vague attempt at disguise, to which Stillman gave a smirk before putting some of her own on. I wondered if we looked like those women on *Sex and the City*.

As we rounded a corner on 5th avenue past a Pret a Manger, the pink and grey concrete facade of the Langham came into view. A concierge dressed in a dark grey suit was flagging down a cab for some departing guests who were checking their phones, oblivious to the chaos walking past them. The Empire State Building rose majestically above the hubbub further down 5th, towering above the other high-rises. Images of King Kong crawling up its side popped into my head.

"What's Hubert doing staying here?" I said to Stillman as we hopped across the street just as the lights changed, braving a taxi whose driver didn't give a shit about red lights or pedestrians actually crossing on green. Perhaps the pedestrian lights were just guidelines, not rules.

"Would you believe he's on vacation?"

"What, on his own?"

Stillman shrugged as we squeezed through the rotating door of the main entrance. "He's career FBI. Two failed marriages and four kids who don't speak to him much. Real shame. He's one of the good guys."

I remembered she had a soft spot for him, and I'd wondered whether there was more to it than that. There was a significant age difference, but hey, no judgment from me.

We crossed the foyer and stopped at the reception desk, a single long rectangular block of granite staffed by a half-dozen black-shirted attendants. A bellboy looked over at us but soon lost interest when it was clear we'd no luggage to give him and therefore no tip.

I pulled Stillman back as she was about to grab one of the check-in staff. "Do you really think this is a good idea? If Hubert's memory was truly wiped by Cain, we might not have much chance of getting anything useful. Also, what if he's ... you know ... one of them?"

She folded her hands and looked at me sternly. "Kate, I think we've got to give it a go. Bill Hubert's got no memory of the interview with Cain but actually, no one officially knows what happened in there, as I told you. I'm the only one who knows shit because I managed to get hold of the video feed."

"Okay, so ...?"

"So ... Bill is 'certain' of two things. One, that Adam is dead and two, the invasion was prevented. As far as he's concerned, the whole Vu-Hak thing has been put to bed and hidden from the public – because officially it 'didn't happen'. You know, like Roswell, all over again."

I frowned. "Roswell was bullshit. Nothing happened there."

Stillman shot me a sideways look and cracked a half smile. "Are you sure?"

I snorted, wondering if she was kidding. "Does he remember me?" I asked.

She nodded. "Of course. He remembers everything up to and including Cain's appearance. You need to understand – you disappeared off the map after that. No one had a clue where you went or even why you vanished. Now we know what happened, of course."

"So, after I went missing, did anyone look for me?"

She gave me a look. "To be honest, there wasn't much enthusiasm to find you."

I wasn't sure how to take that, so I said, "Do you think just seeing me will jog his memory?"

She shook her head. "I think it's unlikely. I mean look how you managed to go all Jason Bourne on us. It took hypnosis to unlock what happened to you and I'm still not sure why or how that worked as well as it did."

"Maybe there was some sort of implanted trigger in my head?" I suggested. "We know Cain definitely put some stuff in there."

Stillman shrugged. "Wouldn't put it past him, that's true. But anyway, regarding Hubert – even if you tell him what happened to you, that's not why we're here. There's more to that Cain interview, remember. We need to know what else happened before Hubert and the others were knocked out and their memories wiped. That information could be vital. It's those gaps in the tape that have to be relevant."

"Let's hope so," I said.

Stillman turned away and waved to catch the eye of a check-in attendant. I wandered over to the dispenser and poured myself a cup of water flavored with some kind of minty leaf. I leaned back against the wall and checked out my surroundings. A family of four was squeezing through the revolving doors, two little girls laughing playfully as they jammed in together to the amusement and vague annoyance of their parents. Another bellboy followed through a side door with a mountain of their luggage balanced on a golden trolley. The concierge nodded at me and smiled, before picking up his own telephone and dialing a number.

My paranoia started up again, but then Stillman tapped me on the shoulder.

"Fourteenth floor. He's in."

The elevator interior was all mahogany, dark mood lighting and floor-to-ceiling mirrors. There was no Muzak. A small TV screen embedded into one of the mirrors advertised the evening menu for the hotel's restaurant and cycled into an advertisement for some kind of financial broker service. Well, I supposed this was the Langham, after all.

Stillman jabbed a finger on the *14* button and we smoothly started our ascent. I noticed she was tapping her foot nervously. She noticed me noticing and gave a smile.

"I'm fine. Been a hell of a twenty-four hours."

No argument from me. I tried to smile back but couldn't. It was likely we'd only just gotten past the first curve of this particular rollercoaster.

The elevator doors swooshed open and we stepped out onto the fourteenth floor and followed the arrows down a long corridor, passing a couple of maids cleaning one of the rooms. There were tray tables on the floor covered with the detritus of last night's room service, and newspapers hung from door handles in posh brown tote bags. We stopped outside 1425. The Do Not Disturb light was on the door control panel, and a similar instruction was hanging from the handle.

Stillman knocked on the door, two loud impacts reverberating down the corridor. She put her hand into her handbag, and left it there, where I assumed she'd put her Glock. My heart started to hammer away and I felt nauseated again. There was no answer and I nervously looked at Stillman, who set her face and knocked again, harder.

A few seconds later the door opened and William Hubert stood there, resplendent in his hotel robe and slippers. His grey hair was askew, and he looked unshaven and as if he'd not been sleeping. His eyes flicked from Stillman to me and back to Stillman.

"Jesus. Talk about a bad dream," he rasped.

"Can we come in?" said Stillman.

His rheumy eyes fixed on me and a smile cracked his face. "Hello Kate. I thought we'd lost you."

I nodded, my breathing coming easier. "You've no idea."

"Well, yes, come in ... Excuse the mess, I wasn't expecting visitors you know."

He opened the door fully and stood back, waving his arm expansively into the room while pulling the robe tightly around his waist. Stillman went first, and I tentatively followed, checking over my shoulder. One of the maids in the corridor had stopped working and was watching us go in. As she saw me looking she quickly looked away and went back to her trolley.

Anxiety joined Paranoia as my trusty sidekicks.

The room was generously sized. There was a desk set with a couple of chairs on one side where Hubert had plugged in his laptop. A comfy-looking couch with a coffee table faced the TV, the table buried under a silver tray and the remnants of Hubert's breakfast. The bed was unmade and the TV was showing muted CNN. There was a smell of coffee from the Nespresso machine on a shelf by the window. Bright sunshine poured in, and the view was tremendous, looking uptown along 5th.

I sank into the couch and Stillman hovered for a few seconds before joining me.

Hubert wandered over to the Nespresso machine and glanced over at us, saying, "Can I fix you a cup? Got a few choices here ... lots of pods left over."

I nodded, almost without thinking. "That would be great, thanks. Anything caffeinated will do."

"Espresso? Colleen, you too?" He looked over at Stillman who shook her head, staring at the TV screen.

"Anyone like something to eat? I can order room service ..."

My stomach rumbled at the thought of food, but I really hadn't liked the look the cleaners had given us. Was I being overly suspicious?

"Anyway then, Kate," he began, pressing a couple of buttons and putting a purple pod into the hatch on the front, "I can't wait to hear your news. Did you go on a 'finding yourself' kind of road trip after, well, you-know-what ...?" He winked at me.

I glanced across at Stillman, who raised her eyebrows, and actually was looking quite pissed off.

"Finding herself?" she said. "You mean after the little matter of you dropping nuclear weapons on your own troops in order to kill the first alien encountered by humanity?"

Hubert stopped what he was doing and froze. His head dropped and he slowly shook it before turning back to face us. "Colleen, I thought we'd been through that."

Stillman's voice was like ice. "We talked about it, yes, and then you got me transferred out of your division. Remember?"

"That wasn't my doing. After my little problem it was thought that the division needed a shakeup as well. I was reassigned too."

"Wait," I said. "What problem?" Stillman nudged me in the ribs, and I turned to her. "What? What am I missing?"

Hubert walked over to the couch and perched on the side closest to Stillman, and focused on me.

"Kate, I had a sort of stroke. A mini-cerebrovascular accident, they called it. I was found in one of the interview rooms, unconscious. I had a couple of scans, which were okay, and I recovered fully, but at my age it was thought I should take some personal time. After a suitable period of 'time out' I came back to find my position taken over by another senior agent." He looked at Colleen. "And most of my team had been assigned other positions too."

Stillman stood up, walked over to the TV and turned to face us, arms folded. "Bill, there was no stroke. It was a set up. It was the Vu-Hak."

Hubert's face had gone white. "What do you mean?"

"They're back. They never went away. We're in big fucking trouble."

Hubert frowned and started to shake his head like a dog drying off after a swim. "No, no, no … that's not true. Adam stopped them. There've been no sightings for six months. I would have known."

I walked over to the window and stared up 5th avenue, at the tourists and citizens going about their lives, oblivious to what was coming. The veritable calm before the storm.

"Mr. Hubert, your mind was wiped. Mine too. It's happening and we're out of our depth. Can you remember anything at all?"

"Nothing." His voice was a pained whisper.

Stillman had gotten up and was pacing the room. She stopped and looked fixedly at Hubert. "Hypnosis brought Kate's memories back. Maybe we should try you."

Hubert shook his head. "Won't work, I'm afraid. I'm not susceptible to hypnotic suggestion. It's one of the FBI requirements, as well you know."

"We've a copy of a recording," I said. "It might jog your memory."

"A recording of what?"

"A formal interview between you and a Vu-Hak called Cain. Mackie was there too."

Hubert looked aghast. "Mackie? But he's dead. Heart attack on his farm."

Stillman stopped pacing and hugged herself. "No, I don't think so. Your memories of the incident were selectively wiped by Cain. A heart attack is too convenient to be how Mackie really died."

Hubert was frowning. "I don't understand. Why?"

"That's one of the things we need to find out," I said.

We pulled the curtains and Stillman plugged the USB into Hubert's computer. She selected the file and the image of Cain came up, facing the camera looking over the heads of Hubert and Mackie. Stillman pressed the green arrow and the onscreen Hubert, his back to the camera, leaned over and flicked a switch on the recording device. Red numbers started to tick over on the bottom right of the image, counting time forward in seconds and minutes. The playback started.

"The time is 1245 hours on Monday, November twenty-third. Conducting this interview are myself, FBI Deputy Director William Hubert, and FBI Special Agent Lawrence Mackie."

Hubert leaned over and stopped the playback. He shook his head, as if clearing his vision. "I have absolutely no memory of this ... and yet ... it seems familiar."

"Keep watching," I said.

He clicked the mouse again, and the recording resumed. I watched Hubert closely as the onscreen conversation between the alien and the two FBI men proceeded. Hubert twitched by my side occasionally, but made no comments, even as he and Cain clashed over Adam's death and the supposed closure of the wormhole, which obviously had not happened. Then the tape abruptly stopped as they were discussing 'dark matter'.

"There's a gap of three minutes here," I said, reaching over to grab the mouse. "Let me just fast-forward ..."

"Wait," said Hubert, placing his hand over mine. "Just wait."

"Are you okay?" Stillman said, concern in her voice.

Hubert was frowning, his eyes blinking as if to clear his head. "Yes, I believe so." He took the mouse and right-clicked over Cain's face.

A dialog box *Password* – - – – - – – - opened.

Stillman sat back. "What the fuck? How did you know to do that?"

Hubert shook his head. "Just came to me. And guess what? I know the password."

He typed *TR1N1TY2*.

There was a burst of static and another screen appeared, replacing the interview. On it, Cain's face in close-up stared into the camera. Just visible behind him were a couple of bodies lying on the floor and what looked like bullet holes in the walls. Grey smoke drifted at low level. Cain started talking, and his eyes glowed phosphorescent green.

"Director Hubert, if you are watching this then Colleen Stillman has obtained the recording of our conversation. I embedded a trigger, which would allow you to access this hidden section. I apologize to Ms. Stillman for using her in this way –"

Stillman's finger stabbed the mouse and the recording paused. "Used me? I found that recording myself ... by good old-fashioned detective work as I was going through some old data files."

Hubert smirked. "Colleen, do you really think that anything that happened was accidental?"

Stillman said nothing, folding her arms and looking pissed.

Hubert pressed play again, and Cain continued in a monotone. "I implanted an organic neural switch in Ms. Stillman's mind, which would have allowed her to find the recording at a time I deemed suitable. That time is now ..."

Stillman paused it again. "That bastard. He's using all of us." Now she *sounded* pissed as well.

I gently took hold of the mouse and looked her in the eye. "Colleen, I think we should just hear him out, don't you?"

For a long second she glared at me before looking away and nodding grudgingly. I pressed play and sat back. Cain's sonorous tones filled the room again.

"The Vu-Hak are on Earth in huge numbers, and they are looking for Kate Morgan. They are looking for her because they want to find me, and they know I have implanted key information into her mind, and given her a new identity, one that she will believe is real. The information she possesses will enable her to find me. It is very important that she remains hidden from the Vu-Hak or everything will be in jeopardy."

With a trembling hand I pressed pause and stood back. Stillman and Hubert looked at me, concern in their gazes. There was so much to process, and a headache was coming on. At least now I had proof and some closure as to what had happened. But the 'why' still eluded me.

Specifically, why me?

And if what Cain was saying was to be believed, he was a traitor to his own race.

Hubert interrupted my train of thought. "I don't understand any of this. We know how powerful they are. If they're here in force, they would just take over, easily. Wouldn't they?"

Stillman threw me a glance before turning to Hubert. "They aren't here in the machines. They seem to be free-floating ... ghosts of a sort I guess. Spirits. Untethered consciousnesses. They're able to take over humans' bodies. We encountered one at Kate's apartment and it tried to kill us. If it'd been a machine, we'd be dead."

Hubert frowned. "But how? Adam said that the machines

were necessary for transport through the wormhole. Didn't he say that the gravitational forces in there would annihilate organic matter?"

I nodded. "He did say that."

Stillman inclined her head to the screen. "Let's hear the rest of the tape."

I pressed play and stood back. Cain was still staring unwaveringly at the screen.

"I'm performing vital work that is necessary for the survival of the human race. If I am prevented from completing this work, the Vu-Hak will win. It should be nearing completion in six months, and therefore the fact that you are watching this means the six months is nearly over. You must therefore find Kate Morgan, keep her safe from the Vu-Hak, and bring her to me. She will know where I am.

And then he dropped the bombshell.

"Tell her Adam is alive, and he sends his regards."

ELEVEN

Adam was alive. That thought ran around my brain like a headless chicken, bouncing off the inside of my skull bones and freaking me out. Hubert had drifted over to the Nespresso machine again and was fiddling with the pods and switches. There was burbling and gurgling as the milk frother did its thing.

He glanced over his shoulder at me and said, "I wonder what vital work he's talking about?"

"At least we know why Cain wanted Kate," piped up Stillman with a forced smile. "Adam's got a soft spot for you. I mean, what's the human race to Cain?"

I couldn't focus on any other aspect of the recording; just Cain's throwaway line at the end telling me that Adam had survived. Adam must have done something to delay the invasion and certain annihilation of the human race, and not only that: he survived. But what were the consequences for him – and us – given that the Vu-Hak were here anyway?

"So are the rest of us just on borrowed time?" Stillman said to no one in particular.

She'd gone to the window so I joined her there and looked out over the metropolis, at the Empire State building, and at the people below, oblivious to the forces conspiring against them.

"This can't just be about me," I said, suddenly feeling very weary.

"No, we have to assume there's a bigger picture," said Hubert, handing me an espresso and Stillman a latte. "The key section of the recording is when Cain said that you know where he is. Do you have any knowledge of that?"

I shook my head and sipped my espresso.

He tapped my skull with a gentle forefinger. "Cain planted stuff in there. Maybe you should try hypnosis again?"

"I can't believe this is just a repressed memory," said Stillman. "Cain implied that you'd know where to go to find him, so perhaps you should just pick a destination, see what happens?"

"Really?" I snapped. "You want me to pull a place out of my head? And what, we'll head straight there?"

Stillman's lips tightened. "Maybe. Look, Cain said two things of importance. That you need to remain hidden from the Vu-Hak, and that we should bring you to him. We need some sort of plan, some direction. We can't just sit here."

"We could do exactly that. This room may be the safest place of all. They don't know we're here."

Hubert looked up. "I think it's safe to assume they're targeting acquaintances of yours, Kate. Like me, for instance."

A chill tickled the back of my head, like an icy finger. "Are there lots of people who know you're in this hotel?"

He kept a poker face, but his apprehension was palpable. "I don't think this is a good place to stay at all," he said ominously.

"Right," I said.

I sat down at the computer. Maybe inspiration would strike, after all. The video was paused on the image of Cain staring out of the screen. I leaned forward and peered more closely. My hand moved to the mouse, and I clickety-clicked here and there before raising an eyebrow and sitting upright. I'd enlarged the image of Cain from the beginning of the interview and blown up his face so that his eyes were all that we could see. Despite the video feed quality, speckles of green phosphorescence shone eerily in the black of his pupils.

"How about I go to Google Earth and stick a pin on the monitor?" Stillman said, in an attempt to lighten the mood.

"I've thought of something," I said.

Hubert came to stand over my shoulder and I pointed at the image of Cain's eyes.

"He was talking about the name he gave himself," I said, "and then he made you think of bible class, remember? The bit about how God made Cain 'wander the earth, and having a mark on him', and all that?"

Hubert leaned in as well, staring intently at the screen. "You think he was trying to tell me something?"

"Well, the 'mark' comment is interesting. Survey markers or marks are objects placed to mark key points on the Earth's surface."

He pursed his lips and looked unconvinced. "That's a stretch, but even so how does that help us? He hasn't exactly told us where he is."

"Maybe he's not telling. Maybe he's showing. Showing me."

I pressed play but ran the file in slow motion. At first nothing happened, the green fluorescence subtle and twinkling, like sea creatures at the bottom of the ocean. Then suddenly there was a red flash, first in the left eye and then in the right. A fast irregular sequence that went on for a few seconds before the familiar emerald glow returned.

Hubert beamed. "Genius, Kate. Well done."

"What?" said Stillman, hands raised.

"He's just given us a sequence of letters and numbers in Morse code."

"Can you read it back?" I said.

"I'm a tad rusty. Give me a minute with this recording and I'll see what I can do. If I can just get it to run at half that speed again, I should be able to make it out."

He bent down and started to work with the laptop. Stillman looked at me and gave a big shit-eating grin, which I returned. We gave him some space to work, and as Stillman went to the bathroom I prepared myself another espresso. My hands weren't shaking yet so my caffeine levels were still sub-optimal.

Hubert stopped scratching with the pencil, and put it down, beaming.

"Yep, they're co-ordinates. Latitude and longitude to be exact." He pushed the paper over to me:

Latitude 75 02' 35" S

Longitude 47 15' 28" W

Stillman returned from the john, pushed Hubert out of the chair and pulled up Google Earth. The familiar spinning globe appeared.

"Okay then: let's find out where he's hanging."

She tapped in the co-ordinates and the globe started to turn.

The southern hemisphere expanded as we tracked south into the Polar Regions.

"Antarctica?" I said.

Hubert leaned over my shoulder. "The Weddell Sea. Covered by a permanent massive ice shelf."

Stillman was looking puzzled. "What's he doing there? Is he underwater?"

I had my iPhone open at Wikipedia. "Well if he is, he could be easy to spot. Apparently it's got the clearest water on the planet. 'A clarity corresponding to distilled water' it says here."

"So how do we get there?" said Stillman, looking at Hubert. "We'll need an icebreaker or a fucking submarine!"

"I know a guy," Hubert said quietly.

I'd boarded the airplane alone, tickets paid with cash from a wad Stillman produced from her bag.

I didn't ask.

The desk staff must have thought they were helping some kind of drug dealer or whack-job as I handed over thousands of dollars in one-hundred-dollar bills. Stillman and I'd fought over whether we'd attract more attention paying in cash, or whether a credit card booking would just flag us up to any watching Vu-Hak. Were they watching? We had no clue, but ultimately we agreed it'd be safer with non-traceable cash. Unfortunately I didn't have time to grab a false passport, this being real life and not one of the Bourne movies. However, my passport was Sara Clarke's and therefore officially *was* a false document, and it raised no flags at all. Maybe the Vu-Hak hadn't yet deduced my cover name, despite one of their number dying in my apartment.

Maybe we'd be in luck.

The first leg from New York to LA passed quickly. I was shoehorned in the middle row at the back of the plane, and, despite the noise of the kitchenette and the toilets, I managed a couple of hours of dreamless sleep. The woman in the window seat must have had a bladder the size of a peanut given the number of times she squeezed past me to go to the toilet, and she didn't stop drinking coffee all the way. I felt like she was a kindred spirit. Luckily she hadn't been hungry so I'd put aside my prepared uncommunicativeness to beg for what remained of her meals as well as my own. I told her I'd missed breakfast, but as she handed them over she looked at me like I had worms.

At LAX I ran like Usain Bolt across to the Tom Bradley Terminal and made my connection to Brisbane with five minutes to spare before the gate closed. The flight was thankfully quiet, and I was soon getting organized at a window seat in business class on Qantas's newest acquisition, a 787 Dreamliner. I downed the arrival champagne almost in one go, and sank into the seat, my body feeling battered and bruised and crying out for more sleep. I ordered an ice-cold New Zealand Sauvignon Blanc, grabbed six packets of peanuts from the trolley, and stared blankly at the personal TV screen showing a map of the route. It was twelve hours until we landed at Brisbane, a big modern city on the southeast corner of Queensland. The plan was to get a connection from Brisbane to Tasmania, where we would all regroup. Stillman and I had decided to meet up separately in Australia, for safety. Certainly neither of us wanted to travel with Hubert, who would be making his own way to Tasmania in order to arrange for a US Navy submarine to pick us up. It was all on the 'down low' as he called it.

The guy in the seat opposite and facing me was young, trim, mid-thirties, and Australian, dressed in an expensive business suit and sporting combed-back reddish hair. In another life I might have started a conversation straight away, but when he caught my eye and crinkled a (not unattractive) smile at me I looked away awkwardly and started fiddling with the screen, pretending to search for a movie. I put the headphones on so he got the message I was not in conversation mode. I found a noise-cancelling switch on the headphones, and the cabin sounds muted away.

We took off smoothly, the big engines whining and then doing that scary drop in power thing as we banked north before rising gracefully over the ocean and settling into our course across the equator and down into the southern hemisphere. I closed my eyes. The low thrum of the engines was soporific and the alcohol was kicking in. I could feel myself starting to drift off, so I put the seat into a semi-recline position and took a couple of deep breaths. I'd always been able to get off to sleep fairly quickly, even after answering my pager and calls in the middle of the night. I'd learned of a technique called "4,7,8" – basically you breathed in for four seconds, held your breath for seven and breathed out slowly for eight. Your heart rate and respiratory rate slowed down and you magically fell asleep. Just like that.

Well, that plus a gallon of wine.

There was a bit of turbulence, a subliminal rumble that made my stomach drop a little and my anxiety levels rise, but we soon smoothed out again and I resumed my count. Sleep came over me like a blanket, but not a blanket of warmth – a blanket of cold and frigidity. My eyes got heavier and heavier and within a minute sleep took over.

TWELVE

The dream started immediately.

It was as if someone had adjusted the colors of the universe, as easy as twisting one of those plastic dials on an old TV set. The sky was brighter than it should be: iridescent hues of turquoise and cobalt. The trees were phosphorescent green and burned onto my retinas, leaving wiggly after-images. Buildings and bridges glowed with an amber hue. Grey roads and highways appeared as sleek rivers of jet-black tarmac painted with perfect electric white lines. Streetlamps and windows glowed blue. Really blue. Electric blue. Front yards of run-down houses that had been disheveled with the decrepitude of late winter were a riot of colorful blooms.

Everything was so right it was wrong – really wrong.

The picture abruptly changed as a grey house shimmered into view. I recognized it as my house in Indian Springs. A house, but not a home.

I'd moved there from Chicago after Kelly's death, and it never felt like a home, just a place to throw my weary bones after a twenty-four-hour shift.

The picture changed again to my POV and I was walking up the driveway to the door. The curtain in the front room twitched. Someone was in there. The door was locked and I slapped the wood, the effect sounding like a bell tolling.

A face appeared at the window.

Kelly.

My daughter.

She gave a huge welcoming smile and I could feel my head melting and caving in. She had a little smudge of something on her forehead, a fleck of blood I remembered from when I identified her at the morgue. She held up her hand and pressed it against the glass and my own hand reached out and matched her gesture like one of those soppy chick flicks. We touched fingertips, only a couple of millimeters of glass separating us. I imagined my molecules diffusing through the solid glass, mixing with hers, connecting.

"Can I come in?" I heard myself saying in a shaky voice, my breath coming in ragged gulps.

She continued smiling and nodded slowly, moving her hand down to the doorknob on the side. The door opened in slow motion and she was there facing me. Her skin was blue-grey, a pallor I associated with death, but her eyes glowed with a green shining light that fitted the palette of the world we were in. She moved out of the way and I walked past her into my house, through the kitchen and into the living room. The sofas and coffee table were exactly as I'd left them. My bag was on the chair, upturned, its contents spilled over onto the floor. Lipstick, compact, pens, hankies, scraps of paper ... and a photograph of Kelly.

She appeared soundlessly by my side and picked up the photo, turning it in her little hands so I could see it as well. I remembered the photo. It had been her birthday, a couple of weeks before she died. She was wearing pajamas because we'd just had a sleepover with four of her friends and she was still high with the excitement and joy of just being a little girl on her special day surrounded by love ...

Grief bit me with such ferocity I thought it was going to suck every emotion out of me and leave me an empty shell. But then Kelly took hold of my hand. She spoke to me, but her voice was adult, measured, unrecognizable.

"Emotions. The very feature that make you human. Happiness, pride, excitement, satisfaction, contentment. Every emotion that you consider good. But what would you be if you didn't also feel hurt or pain or despair? You can't have good without bad. There is no light without darkness. Does that sound right?"

This wasn't my daughter. I let go of her hand and took a step back. "You're one of them, aren't you?"

She smiled again and jumped up on the sofa to sit facing me. She swung her feet back and forward and interlaced her fingers on her lap.

"Them?" she said, innocently.

"Aliens. *Vu-Hak*." I ground out the word.

Her lip twitched and her eyes glowed a little greener. The effect was to make her skin greyer in such a way that it looked thicker, more leathery, as if all the blood had leached into her core or drained into her feet. Her blonde hair hung on her face like pastry draped over cut apple. Dirty, straggly and corn-like.

It was as if she was decaying in front of me.

Another chill came over me but I willed my subconscious to fall in line. I wasn't going to retreat or act scared. I wasn't going to give them a show of weakness. I would show defiance and surety, even in my dream.

"Where's Adam?" I said.

The alien imitating my dead daughter shrugged, looking blankly at me. I folded my arms and returned her stare, daring her to look away first. She did, but not before breaking into another chilling smile.

"That's the question, isn't it?" she said. "I think you know where he is. You will tell me."

I desperately tried to hide how fearful I was. I knew now they were inside my mind, though they weren't yet controlling me. Was this something Cain had given me as well? The ability to erect some sort of barrier to their psychic infiltration?

"Humanity's time is up," the simulacrum intoned. "You are already well along the path of self-destruction. You play with technologies you do not understand and cannot control. Your distrust of your own species and access to world-destroying technology leads to only one conclusion. The end of humanity. Our presence has just brought the deadline forward."

The alien jumped off the sofa and wandered over to the front window, pulling itself up on tippy toes to look out. This action was so incongruous that I stifled a laugh. It heard me and turned sharply.

"Where is Adam?" she insisted.

"He's dead, didn't you know?" The lie slipped out, smooth and easy, like grease running down a pole.

Anger flashed in her eyes and I tried to remain composed.

"Tell me about Cain," I said.

"Who?" she replied, innocently. Or was it *truthfully?*

The conversation was over and the alien looked into my eyes. There was a pressure in my head that hadn't been there before. Icy fingers were infiltrating my mind. My thoughts were slowing down, my neural pathways and connections becoming clogged and blocked.

This had all been smoke and mirrors.

A distraction.

She was trying to take over my mind.

If she did, it was all over.

I screamed as loud as I could, the sort of scream that would curdle your blood. It flowed through my brain and kickstarted some primeval pathway. Adrenaline ripped through my body.

I woke up.

THIRTEEN

I opened my eyes to find the world had gone to shit. Vibrating. Blurring at the edges. Shaking and rattling like a subway line.

Oxygen masks bouncing everywhere.

People screaming.

The atmosphere felt stretched and gossamer thin. My stomach lurched and acid burned the back of my tongue. I swallowed it, grimacing, feeling the heat behind my sternum. Magazines and glasses and plates were flying around as the airplane lurched violently up and down. One of the stewardesses who had served me earlier was hanging on to the armrest of a seat; a passenger had his arms around her waist as she was thrown every which way. Her head was bleeding, a crimson river running down the side of her face. She caught my eye and her mouth opened soundlessly as we lurched again and she was thrown up in the air, slamming her head into the overhead bin.

The locked steel door to the flight deck was about ten yards away, a few rows forward. I waited for the aircraft to stabilize for a second and snapped my seatbelt off and threw myself forward out of the seat. I noticed that the Australian was missing but didn't have time to process this as I pulled myself around his seat and out into the aisle. The aircraft dropped again like a stone, bouncing me about as gravity came and went. I held tightly to the seat and my feet planted once again on the deck as the plane pulled up. I caught a glimpse of the sea out of the window as we banked over at a severe angle.

We looked to be pretty low.

I pulled myself along toward the flight deck, past the toilets and kitchenette, which was littered with cutlery, metal pots and pans, and swimming with liquid and food debris. After what seemed like a lifetime of reaching and pulling I finally got there. It was a solid grey metal barrier, cross-hatched with rivets like an industrial plate. The handle was locked solid. I banged on the door but couldn't hear the noise of the impacts, such was the screaming of the engines and the rattling as every loose object in the cabin ricocheted off every surface. Back down the aisle, past the forest of masks, no one was coming to help me.

Cain's voice blew through my mind like a hurricane, sweeping everything aside. *I have given you what you need. You will know when to use it.*

Well, I thought, now's the fucking time.

I grabbed the flight deck door's handle and pulled.

Nothing happened.

I put both hands together and pulled it towards me, waiting for the surge of superhero strength to pull the door off its hinges.

Still nothing happened.

My fingers were red with welts and wet with perspiration. I gave them a death stare, willing them to transform into hands of steel. Anything to get the door open.

Then, a presence at my shoulder.

The Australian.

His hair was disheveled, his tie was askew, and his jacket was missing. His shirt was soaking and there was blood coming from his left ear and a swelling under his eye the size of a golf ball. He reached out a hand just as the aircraft lurched forward again and I flinched, batting it away. He careened into me, our bodies becoming tangled and crushed into the corner of the doorframe. I panicked and went to push him away again, but he grabbed hold of my wrists.

"It's okay," he shouted in my ear. "Let me help you."

I wasn't convinced.

"Where were you?" I shouted back.

He glanced over his shoulder and nodded down the cabin. "In the john. Didn't want that on my obituary! *Matt Hamilton: Died taking a shit.*"

The airplane banked again, this time steeply to the right. I wondered how much longer we had before we hit the ocean.

"Let's get this door open," he yelled.

We grabbed the handle, his hands on top of mine, and pulled

with all our might. It was bending but it wasn't going to be enough. It was futile. Matt's veins were bulging in his temples as he continued to strain, but I'd already relaxed my grip and slid my hands away.

"Come on! We can do it!" he said.

We were moments away from death, and there was nothing we could do.

I have given you what you need. You will know when to use it.

I shook my head and clenched my fists, knuckles whitening and nails digging into my already red raw palms. I hunched down, curling my head into my chest, my face reddening as frustration swept off me like waves of molten lava.

Then it happened.

I knew what to do.

I pushed Matt to the side and identified a panel on the wall, hidden behind a notice with various instructions and warnings for the cabin crew to give during announcements. It was flush to the wall but there was a recessed button, not clearly marked. I stabbed it and the panel sprung open. Inside was a simple red handle, a door release.

I closed my eyes and pulled the handle. There was a click and the door popped opened an inch and then blew open as if a bomb had gone off in the cockpit. Matt and I pressed ourselves against the side as the door slammed into the wall. A glance into the cockpit showed that the window in front of the pilot was smashed, every warning light seemed to be on red and sirens were howling. The sea was visible, sun glistening on white-topped waves, maybe a few thousand feet below.

I forced my way into the cockpit, the gale force winds making me lean forward at an acute angle. The pilot turned and his eyes were blank and emotionless. He pushed the yoke left and the plane surged and tipped and Matt and I were thrown sideways. I crashed into one of the empty jump seats and Matt vanished out of sight, tumbling into the space behind the door. The other pilot, belted into the left-hand seat, flopped side to side like he was boneless, unconscious, or dead – I couldn't tell. His head impacted the window, leaving a smear of blood on the glass.

I knew I had to get to the controls, but I had no idea how to fly an airplane. The flight deck was all multifunction lights and electronic switches and there were two head-up displays, like in fighter jets.

Then, as if I'd requested it online, the information was there in my head. The controls of the 787 were tagged and familiar to me, as if I'd flown it all my life. I knew where everything was. I understood aviation lingo. The autopilot controls, primary flight display, navigation display, engine identification, crew alerting system and flight management system control unit.

I just had to get the no-longer-human pilot out of the way.

As I weighed up my options, Matt pushed past me and launched himself at the pilot, fists swinging and pummeling. The pilot started to fight back, his face still unnervingly devoid of emotion. I ducked under the swinging arms and leaned over the co-pilot to release his seat belt. I grabbed him under the arms, heaved him out of his seat and pulled him over the long central pillar onto the floor. I was about to jump into his seat when Matt was thrown onto me as the airplane jerked to starboard and the nose pulled up. We both tumbled and crashed into the wall, the back of my head hitting a bank of switches. Matt's face was even more battered and bloody and he now had long scratches down his cheek. He wiped his face with his sleeve and attempted to get up but the pilot was already starting to push the yoke forward: the computer was screaming "PULL UP, PULL UP."

Matt stared at me with eyes like saucers, and I could sense the terror radiating from him.

"I'm sorry," he said, tears welling up.

However, I felt weirdly calm and composed. The same surge traveled through my body as when I'd faced the strangers outside the Bolton's house. I'd been plugged in again, supercharged. I put a hand on Matt's chest.

"Trust me," I said.

Then I leaped onto the pilot.

The wind continued to howl through the open window hurricane-like, but it felt as if I was wearing magnetic boots or my feet were part of the airplane's structure.

The pilot's arms came up and he started flailing at me but I ignored the wild swings and grabbed his seatbelt. I ripped it off the arm of his chair, tearing the fabric like paper, and grabbed him by the front of his shirt. In a single movement I lifted him up and over the yoke and threw him at the open front windshield. He careered through the HUD display and his leg got caught on the way and wrapped around the top of the screen, snapping at a wicked angle, blood spraying into the cockpit with the wind.

Then he was gone.

FOURTEEN

I sat in the pilot's chair and squinted at the controls, the fierce buffeting air making it almost impossible to look forward. Matt climbed into the seat on the left and strapped himself in. The attitude indicator was blue at the top and brown underneath in equal amounts, indicating that the aircraft was level for the moment at least. Our airspeed was 255 knots, altitude was 3650 feet but slowly ticking downward.

I took hold of the yoke and pulled on it gingerly to bring the nose up.

"Do you know how to fly?" shouted Matt. "Cause I sure as hell don't."

"How hard can it be?" I yelled back.

I did seem to understand what all the controls were for, but that was like knowing all the ingredients that made up a curry and having no idea how to put them all together in the right order. Despite the convincing scenarios shown in movies and television shows, no untrained passengers have ever had to fly and land a large aircraft like this in the real world.

I closed my eyes, mainly to stop myself being overwhelmed with the sensory overload and the seriousness of the situation. Breathing deeply helped me focus, and I told my body that I was in control, and to calm the fuck down.

My hands hovered over the autopilot control as I wondered what would happen if I engaged it and we were too low. I guessed that if everything went tits-up I could just turn it off again. Fuck it. I pressed the AFS button and took my hands off the yoke. The aircraft continued to fly at the same altitude, and at the same speed.

"Yay," I said.

Matt seemed too terrified to take his eyes off the sea.

The co-pilot's headset was lying on the center console wrapped around the throttle, so I ducked under the hurricane and put it on. There was a PTT button on the yoke, which I activated and pulled the microphone close to my lips. I found the transponder LCD and flicked it to 7700, the emergency code.

"Mayday, Mayday. This is Qantas five-six repeat this is Qantas five-six. We have an emergency. We are ..." I checked my watch "... about two hours out from Brisbane. We've lost both pilots and need assistance. Over?"

I had shouted as loud as I could, but the noise in the cockpit was still deafening and I wasn't sure whether anyone would be able to hear me. I turned to Matt.

"So you're definitely not a trained pilot then?" I yelled.

He shook his head and sat back in the chair looking pale and clammy.

Right.

I squeezed out of the chair and leaned close, my lips touching his ear. "We should be okay for now." I pointed at the airspeed indicator. "Keep an eye on the speed. We need to stay at this velocity. Big jets like this can't stay in the air at less than 150 knots or so. We go too slow, we stall and crash."

He nodded, looking like a deer caught in headlights.

My hand moved over the LCD dials and switches, moving instinctively flicking a switch here and there.

I wondered if I *could* fly this thing.

"Just make sure this needle stays in the green zone," I continued. "The autopilot should keep us going at this level. If the airspeed starts increasing we're probably going down, so disengage the autopilot and pull gently back on the yoke."

He reached out and grabbed my wrist. "Why ... where are you going?"

I flicked my head to the rear. "I'm going to see if the co-pilot is dead or just knocked out."

"Wait up," he said, eyes boring into mine, fear written all over his face. "Who are you? How did you do that?"

"Do what?" I said.

"The pilot," he shouted. "You threw him out of the window like he weighed nothing."

I wondered what I could tell him that would help our

situation. There was movement behind and I saw the co-pilot trying to ease himself up from the floor. His eyes were flicking left and right, beats of nystagmus hinting at a concussion. A spot of blood bubbled from his right nostril.

"Hey, it's okay. How you feeling?" I said.

"I'm …" he started, and then twisted over and vomited.

I kneeled by him as his abdominal muscles stopped contracting and the heaving ceased. I offered him a cloth, which was lying on the floor, to wipe his mouth. He gratefully accepted it and sat back against the bulkhead, breathing deeply. He looked a shade of green I'd not seen outside of a Grinch movie.

"Where's Tom?" he said, looking at Matt in the pilot's chair. Then he seemed to register the gaping hole in the window and the gale force wind blowing through the cabin. "What happened?"

Matt turned and gave a manic laugh. "She threw him out of the window, mate."

I gave him a 'shut the fuck up' kind of look and put a hand on the co-pilot's arm. "Listen …"

"Peter," he said.

"Listen, Peter. The pilot's dead. Gone. We're two hours from Brisbane. I've got us flying level on autopilot. Do you think you can take over? Get us home?"

He winced but nodded, so I helped him to his feet. He swayed a bit but seemed fairly steady after a second or two. He put his hand on the back of the co-pilot's chair and shakily slid into the seat and buckled up. Matt looked over and reached out for a shake, ducking under the wind.

"Hi, I'm Matt. No clue what I'm doing here, but happy to help."

Peter nodded again and settled his hands over the controls. He wiggled his fingers like a concert pianist and closed his eyes. Almost like he was looking for inspiration. I tapped him on the shoulder to break his concentration.

"You sure you're okay?" I said.

"Yes, yes. Really."

"You've landed this before, haven't you?"

He swallowed. Looked me in the eye. The twitching of his eyeballs had decreased in amplitude.

"Over a hundred landings. All simulated." He smiled apologetically. "We generally land on autopilot."

"Can you do that from this altitude?" I asked.

He gave a dismissive shake of his head. "We're much too low. We have to climb up and make a proper approach."

I stared at him unblinking, as Cain's words echoed again.

I have given you what you need. You will know when to use it.

I put my hand out and touched his temple. A jolt of electricity like a build-up of static charge traveled between us. He gave a little jerk and sat upright, his face taking on a serene, composed look.

"You can do this," I said.

"I can do this," he repeated.

"Okay then, get us down."

Matt was looking at me strangely. "What did you just do to him?"

I ignored the question again and looked away. "You'll need to help. You good with that?"

His brows furrowed. "I guess, but what're you going to do?"

"I'm going to check on the passengers. Make sure everyone's okay. Let them know what's happening."

He put out a hand to stop me. "What the hell just happened?"

I wasn't sure what to tell him that wouldn't make him think I was insane. But then, after what he'd just witnessed, the truth might appear less crazy than my wildest fabrication.

"Later," I said. "Once we're on the ground."

FIFTEEN

We descended into Brisbane just as the sun was coming up, brilliant gold and orange hues exploding like a furnace in the east as the first slither of sun peeked over the skyline and the river glowed liquid gold and silver. We'd come in over a huge metropolitan area, larger than Los Angeles, sprawling in all directions along the floodplain of the river valley toward the Great Dividing Range in the west. I was surprised when Matt told me the population was only 2.5 million. LA would have crammed ten times that number of souls into the same area.

A huge and not unexpected cheer erupted from all cabins as the wheels touched the tarmac, like a charter aircraft taking novice flyers and the elderly on their first trip abroad. As we taxied in, dozens of fire trucks and police vehicles accompanied (forcibly escorted, probably a better description) us to our temporary stand four hundred yards from the main terminal. I squeezed Peter's shoulder in a gesture of 'well done', and he slumped forward in his seat after shutting down the engines. He fumbled with the mic and announced to the passengers that everyone was to stay sitting until the police had been through the aircraft, and the accident investigators and fire chief had given the all clear to disembark.

Matt had gotten up from his seat and was stretching, looking out of the broken cockpit window at the terminal building and the rising sun behind it. Hundreds of faces could be seen behind glass viewing areas watching with excitement the full emergency services on standby and gawking at the damage to our aircraft. I hoped there were no remnants of the pilot smeared along the paintwork from the window.

The guilt sat not on my chest but inside my brain. What I'd done I couldn't undo. I'd killed another man. Alright, a man possessed by an alien who was trying to kill me, and everyone on the airplane, but an innocent human being all the same. Could I have saved the pilot and killed the Vu-Hak, or was the human mind in there already dead? I thought about Navarro and tried to remember whether I could sense him as he tried to kill Stillman and me. I didn't think so, but I didn't know for sure.

There was a knock on the cockpit door and it opened to reveal Stillman herself, and a couple of severe-looking police officers. She looked at the devastation and shook her head slowly before giving me a smile and opening her arms, leaning in for a hug. The hug was very welcome; I felt tears welling up as I buried my head into her shoulder and her hair.

"It's okay," she whispered, "you're here now. I heard all about it. You had no choice."

I pulled out of her embrace, irritably wiping my eyes, keeping my voice low too. "It's not okay though, is it? How can we be safe? They seem to be able to easily find us."

She frowned. "I know. I wonder if that's just a function of their numbers. Plus bad luck on our part."

I looked around the cockpit, only now taking in the mess, broken dials, torn leather and bits of plastic and glass strewn around. Smears of blood were coating the windows.

Stillman saw me looking and put a finger up to my face. "Hey. We need to focus. Hubert'll be waiting for us. I'm getting you out of here A-SAP."

"How're we going to explain this away?"

"A 'birdstrike'," she whispered. "You flew through a flock of seabirds. The local authorities will take it from here. They've been briefed. The Australian Federal Police are on board. No one'll know the truth and that's how it'll stay."

"This guy, Matt. He was there. He saw what happened."

Matt had been watching our exchange with interest. His hair was still disheveled and a bruise was spreading over his scratched cheek. This actually made him more attractive, but I suppressed the thought. He gave a shrug and an almost apologetic smile.

"Sorry," he said.

Stillman let go of me and walked over to him. They stared at each other for a second and then she burst into a big grin.

"You idiot. I said look after her, but really – landing a 787?"

He smirked and flicked his head at Peter who was still slumped in his chair, eyes red and baggy. "Nah, it was all this guy. I just did what he told me to do." He then looked at me and his face went all serious. "Actually, it was Kate who saved us all. Oh, and I still haven't figured out how you did what you did, by the way."

I turned to Stillman, eyes wide. "You know this guy?"

She gave a half smile and a semi-apologetic shrug. "I guess introductions are in order. Kate, this is Matthew Hamilton. Matt works for the FBI. I asked him to babysit you, incognito."

I felt my face reddening. "Babysit me?"

At that moment, thankfully, a couple of armed police officers entered the flight deck. Stillman conferred with them for a minute before turning back to me.

"We gotta go, hon," she said and held out a hand.

I reluctantly took it and let her pull me out of the seat. The police officers led the way and we threaded down the aisle past the devastated cabin and onto a disembarkation ladder. As we exited the airplane a fierce heat reflected off the tarmac into my face. The air was humid and heavy and smelled of aviation fuel and I was sweating even before I'd reached the bottom of the steps. It was hard to breathe; Brisbane was a sub-tropical city, and it was early summer.

We were bustled into a white airport van and driven at speed around the taxiways to the airport's administration block. We pulled up outside a set of sliding doors and another van swung in behind us, disgorging half a dozen heavily armed police officers. Stillman led the way into an office painted grey with one floor-to-ceiling window facing a bland corridor, which led to the lost-goods store. A wall-mounted A/C unit was blasting frigid air at maximum into the small space, and I shuffled underneath it, feeling instantly better.

The office had a single desk in the corner holding a computer, an open notebook and a stack of papers under a rock-shaped paperweight. There were a dozen or so swivel chairs surrounding an oval table and a bookshelf laden with papers and files was in the other corner. A plasma TV on a wall was tuned to a local news channel. Above the sliding doors a camera swiveled on an insectoid stalk, red light blinking.

Stillman gestured to the chairs and so we all took seats around the table with Hamilton and Stillman sitting either side, almost like they were protecting me. Maybe they were. Two of the police officers sat opposite me, both fit and tanned and far too young.

One of them brought out his walkie-talkie, keyed a channel and said, *sotto voce*, "They're here."

Stillman gave me a poker face.

The door opened again and a man walked in, three-day stubble clashing with his neatly pressed suit, the kind you only see on high-priced lawyers. Or gangsters. He had grey hair pulled back in a tight ponytail and his clear blue eyes took in the room with a single sweep. He pulled up a chair and fished in his pocket to extract a big mobile phone which he placed face up on the table between us.

"Just so you know, I'm recording this," he drawled.

"Who are you?" I said, irked.

He gave me a weird smile and played with the buttons on his phone. Stillman leaned sideways and placed a hand on my arm.

"Kate, this is Cole Harvey. He's with the American consulate here in Brisbane. He can help us."

Harvey finally stopped dicking around with his phone and looked at me, his eyes as immobile as the rest of his face. "I've been in touch with Director Hubert while you've been in the air. I've organized your transport to Hobart. The RAAF are going to take you there. Amberley Air Force Base is about forty klicks south west of here. We've got an Airbus KC-30A coming in tonight and it'll fly you down there in the morning."

"No more commercial flights," said Stillman. "We're going under the radar. Off the grid."

I tried to match Harvey's stare, waiting for him to blink. Waiting for some sign of subterfuge or betrayal. He obviously knew enough about what was going on, and who we were, and that didn't make me feel any safer.

"I was under the impression that the fewer people knew, the better?" I hissed to Stillman, an edge to my voice.

She sighed and sat back in her chair. "Kate, while you've been in the air, there've been developments."

"Such as?"

Harvey took this as his cue and stood up. He walked across to the wall TV and picked up the controller from a little nook on its flank. He flicked through the channels to find a saved FOXTEL newscast. "Yes, developments. Things are spiraling out of control. Things that aren't going to be easy to contain for much longer."

He pointed the controller at the screen and clicked play. The program was CNN's *The Situation Room*, and its lead anchor, Wolf Blitzer, was speaking while green-screened behind him was a large office building's main entrance. There, dozens of uniformed soldiers were running across the lawns toward a pillared door where two bodies were lying on the grass next to the public benches along the concrete pathway. The soldiers were approaching the bodies cautiously, guns pointing, circling and giving hand signals to each other.

Blitzer was saying "… the suspects were killed as they exited the building, having ignored calls to drop their weapons and surrender. We have obtained video from inside the building, taken on a phone and uploaded to YouTube a few minutes ago. Please be aware that some viewers might find this footage – which is unedited – disturbing."

The picture transitioned to a shaky video taken from behind a table where the phone's owner was huddled. There was a blazing fire coming from a corridor to the left, dark black clouds billowing horizontally as if blown by a fan. Crashes could be heard in the distance. Gunfire. Screams. Cries.

Two men in dark suits emerged through the smoke. Both were wearing lanyards and were clean cut, Special Agent-types. They were carrying guns in both hands and firing indiscriminately. People could be seen cowering against walls, behind upturned chairs and tables, hugging each other and screaming hysterically. A soldier appeared from off camera and started firing at the men. The impacts of the bullets caused them to jerk backwards and clouds of crimson puffed horribly into the air. I expected them to go down but they didn't fall, and to my horror directed their fire at the soldier who twitched and danced before collapsing in a crumpled heap.

One of the shooters noticed that he was being filmed and walked toward the camera. The person behind the phone was pleading, begging, but still continued to film. The shooter was seen in close-up, his face showing no emotion, no rage, fear – nothing. His skin was greyed, his mouth open with lips slightly parted and his eyes as wide as they could stretch. Some emotion, some feeling seemed to change his expression, but it disappeared before I could identify it. It was like reaching desperately for an escaped balloon, the string dangling so tantalizingly close but the wind pushes it away and it's lost forever.

Then he brought the weapon up and fired. The picture jumped and went dark.

Harvey paused the video, and I closed my eyes, aware that I'd been holding my breath.

"Oh my god," I said.

"Those shooters were on the president's security detail," said Harvey. "Impeccable backgrounds, young families, no red flags." He paused. "They killed thirty-four people before the army took them down."

"Vu-Hak," I said. "In human bodies."

He nodded soberly. "There was no warning. Apparently they were doing their job right up until they 'turned'."

Hamilton spoke up, his voice tight. "Why this particular building? What were they doing there?"

Cole shrugged. "It's one of the FBI's administrative offices. There's many scattered around the country."

The screen had frozen on the face of the shooter. Eyes now burning with anger in a face that a moment ago had been as blank as a canvas waiting for a painter's inspiration.

"They're looking for information," I said. "Specifically, the whereabouts of Adam Benedict."

"And your whereabouts," said Stillman.

"This has been happening around the country," said Harvey, his voice a little shaky. "Break-ins at the White House, FBI offices in New York, CIA at Langley. Multiple perps, indiscriminate deaths, every one unconnected, and yet connected."

"They're not hiding anymore," said Stillman.

SIXTEEN

Stillman and I had booked under false names in to Brisbane's W Hotel, a trendy modern high-rise with a glass facade overlooking the river in the CBD. I sat on the couch and peered through the curved windows out onto the city's south bank, where there was one of those sightseeing carousel wheels (or 'Eyes') that every city now seems to have. A few passenger ferries buzzed up and down the river at speeds far greater than they should have been able to. These were the CityCats, jet-powered passenger boats that actually looked like a lot of fun from where I was sitting. However, I doubted if I would get to do any touristy stuff.

I'd spent the day in a fabulously comfortable bed with a selection of pillows that seemed to be designed specifically for me. I awoke after nine hours of dreamless sleep to a sky the sun had dyed pomegranate pink. The beauty of the sunset only intensified my pain. People were dying, and it might be because of me. I glared at the mocking swirls of color, the whites of my eyes looking pinker in the sunset's reflection through the glass.

There was a quiet buzz from the door. Then two, followed by three more. Stillman's code.

I pulled the robe tightly around me and went over, standing by the door's side and not looking through the peephole.

"Hello?" I said softly and with a fair amount of trepidation.

"*Remember tonight ...*" came a voice.

I smiled. The quote was Dante, and what we had agreed.

"*For it is the beginning of always*," I replied.

"Great, so open the fucking door."

I undid the latch, pulled the chain through the sneck and furtively opened it. Stillman was standing there, also in her robe, hair wet from the shower. She looked up and down the corridor before entering.

"Sleep okay?" she said.

"Actually not bad," I replied. "Considering."

She nodded and wandered over to the chaise longue by the window. She picked up one of the magazines and flicked through a couple of pages. Adverts for perfume, impossibly skinny models in clothes no one would ever be seen wearing in the real world, a picture of Roger Federer with a humungous watch on his wrist. The sort of crap I've seen in every hotel room I've ever been in.

I folded my arms and waited.

"We've got a couple of hours," she said eventually. "I think we need to change your appearance."

I grunted. "I like a dress-up. Do I get a wig, like yours?"

"Ha, no. Remember, the Vu-Hak are predominantly looking for you. Looking, being the operative word. They aren't in your head, and you seem to have a way of preventing them getting access. So I think we should at least narrow the odds of you being recognized on the street."

"What d'you have in mind?" I said.

Her eyes crinkled and she reached into the pocket of her robe and brought out a pair of scissors and a bottle of brunette hair dye.

I groaned.

I barely recognized the face in the mirror. We'd found an electric razor in the drawer and Stillman had licked her lips and gone to work. She'd shaved the back of my head and cut the top and sides into a severe bob like something Lisbeth Salander would rock. Then she'd dyed my blonde locks a deep brunette, and she was now sitting in front of me putting the finishing touches to the edges.

"Maybe a dragon tattoo on my neck, just here?" I said, tracing an outline from my shoulder blade to my jaw.

"It's not bad, you know," she said, pouting.

I raised my eyebrows.

"No, really, I've missed my calling. I used to do all my brothers' hair when they were kids. Got so good their friends started paying me to do theirs."

I nodded grudgingly as a mischievous thought popped into my head. "Did you do Matt's as well?"

Stillman stopped, scissors in mid-air. "Remember I'm armed with a deadly weapon before you go further down this road."

I broke into a grin and waited.

She groaned. "Yes, look okay we dated for a while. A couple of years ago. But we both soon realized it was a mistake. He's actually a really good guy. More like a brother, now, actually."

"Is he coming with us to Antarctica?" I asked.

Stillman continued to work on my hair, snip-snipping and occasionally stopping to lean back and admire her work. "Yes. And that Harvey guy too."

"Why?"

She put down the scissors. "Come on, Kate, think about it. They both know too much. We can't leave them behind in case the Vu-Hak acquire them and find out where we're going."

"Acquire? Is that what we're calling it now?"

"What would you suggest?"

"'Possession'? 'Infection'? 'Violation'?" Any of these would fit, I thought.

Stillman started cutting again and murmured. "Perhaps it's time to once again ask ourselves what we really know about this fucked-up shit we're in the middle of?"

I raised a hand to stop her messing with my hair. "We know enough. We know they're looking for Adam, and therefore they're looking for me in order to get to him. And there're thousands of them …"

"Yes, but let's unpack it," she said, pushing my arm down and getting to work on my fringe. "The Vu-Hak are here on Earth, but in the form of … what? Ghosts, of a sort? In essence I suppose like how they'd existed in their own galaxy at their last evolutionary step."

I nodded. "'Untethered consciousnesses' was I think how Adam referred to it."

Stillman stopped cutting. "So how does that work, exactly? Are there some laws of physics that they're breaking?"

I'd given this some thought already. "I'm pretty sure a mind can't exist, can't think, without the physical structure – neurones and so on – to map on to. Think of the grey and white matter in our brains as the hardware. The consciousness is the software that runs on it."

"So, when your brain dies, so does your mind."

"Yes, absolutely. We know this for a fact. Think about what happens when someone is lobotomized or suffers a stroke. The hardware is damaged and as a consequence there's nothing to support the operation of the software. So, at the extreme, when the brain dies it's like there's nothing capable of generating thoughts anymore. No consciousness. End of everything."

"Alright then: how do the Vu-Hak exist as ghosts?"

"You're thinking of ghosts the Hollywood way. The Vu-Hak must still exist in some physical sense. Maybe they're a bunch of molecules floating around but non-randomly. They're interacting through chemical or electronic bonds we don't understand in order to remain associated and banded together as an individual entity."

Stillman took a minute to process this. "Well here's the deal breaker. Does the Vu-Hak consciousness 'die' when the human it's infected ceases to exist? Or do they just leave the body and go back to floating again?"

That was a really good question. I pictured the scans of the Adam-machine and the structure in his head, which might have contained the hardware analogous to the human brain. Perhaps the consciousness – human or Vu-Hak – was dependent on some structure there in order to exist in a physical setting.

"Supposing then, as the Vu-Hak mind maps onto the existing neurones in the brain of a human, it forms a kind of electric-organic bond with the human host. When the human is killed suddenly, maybe the complexity is such that there isn't time to disentangle and leave – which dovetails with the fact that we haven't yet seen one jump during a host's sudden death?"

Stillman nodded slowly. "That's as good a theory as any." She then looked at me, eyes narrowing. "They don't seem to be able to get into your head. How is that?"

"Whatever Cain put in here is acting like a sentry." I tapped my temple with a finger. "The Vu-Hak on the airplane tried to get in and take over but I was able to stop it – at least temporarily. I'm not at all convinced that it's a foolproof barrier, though."

"I hope you're wrong about that," she said.

We were both quiet for a minute. Stillman sat back in the chair and looked at me in the mirror, admiring her handiwork. "Do you think Adam's destroyed all the machines?"

"They're pretty indestructible. A nuclear bomb just peeled the outside layer off him." I picked up a brush off the dresser and started to tug it through my hair. "What if he's hiding them at the South Pole and we're just leading the Vu-Hak right to him?"

Stillman looked worried but gave a quick shake of her head. "The embedded message from Cain was pretty damn clear – *Find me. Come to me.*"

"Yes, but the message was from Cain! A Vu-Hak! Who definitely *was* in possession of one of those machine suits."

Stillman pulled a face. "Do you really believe Adam convinced a Vu-Hak to help him?"

"Maybe Cain is the Vu-Hak that was with him all the time?" I said. "You know, the one he said had died."

Stillman looked at me as if I was an idiot. "The homicidal, evil one? That one?"

I racked my brain to try and come up with something that would explain everything, make logic of what was going on. A theory of everything. Something that would package all the chaos into a nice little box of order.

"Cain didn't *act* evil in the slightest. He's implanted information I can apparently access as and when I need it, not when I want it …"

Stillman picked up the thread. "When the portal opened, Adam went through and then nothing happened. The invasion didn't occur and the wormhole stopped opening."

I paused for thought, and then continued. "A week later, Cain appeared to me at Arlington Cemetery and gave me amnesia, while leaving cryptic clues with Hubert and you about 'end times' and such stuff." I continued combing my hair, pulling the teeth through my wet bangs, trying to get used to the new look. "That was six months ago."

Stillman nodded. "Cain told us that Adam was 'almost ready' and that the survival of the human race was at stake."

"What's Adam been doing for six months?"

"We'll find out soon enough."

She got up and walked to the mini-bar area, squatted down and peered in the fridge, rattled around for a few seconds and came up with two cans of beer. "Peroni Nastro Azzuro in cans. Never seen these before."

She brought them back over and we pulled the tabs together and clicked the cans in a *salut*. I took a big mouthful and sat back. Stillman took a drink herself before leaning in, our noses almost touching, fighting a smile.

"Here's to nice things in tin cans."

SEVENTEEN

The USS *Jimmy Carter* (SSN-23), a US Navy nuclear fast attack submarine, Seawolf class, cruised at a leisurely twelve knots on the surface of the western Weddell Sea, approximately twenty nautical miles east of the Antarctic Peninsula. Ploughing a white-capped furrow through the emerald waters, its smooth streamlined hull produced a silent, tidy wake in its passing. I was up on the external bridge at the front of the conning tower and the icy wind blasted my eyes, pinpricking my cornea with sharp particles the size of pinheads. My nasal hairs had already frozen over so I'd pulled up my turtleneck for warmth.

The morning sky overhead was powder blue but there were grey clouds bubbling up and a watery sun was just visible on the horizon. Hundreds of icebergs littered the surface of the sea, creviced walls patterned with geometric shadows and the kind of whiteness that could blind you if you weren't careful. They appeared static but were gracefully moving with the tide and ocean currents. Beautiful, but treacherous if taken lightly.

In the middle distance was a snow-capped landmass with craggy rock formations sculpted over tens of millennia by the movement of glaciers, crashing ocean waves and howling winter winds. I peered through my binoculars and saw that the snow and ice stopped directly at the water's edge. The shore consisted of a grey rocky beach covered in snow for a few hundred yards where it gave way to a vertical granite cliff. It looked like an inhospitable place, made even less attractive by a blanket of cloud pouring off the distant mountains like dry ice at a rock concert.

"First time in southern waters?" said Captain Benjamin Powell, who was standing next to me, scanning the cliffs with his own binoculars.

I nodded. "Pretty much. I was expecting the sea to be more you know, frozen. There's just little icebergs bobbing around."

Powell grunted and continued his lookout. His face had an angular structure, with high cheekbones, deep brown eyes and a tanned skin that betrayed his mixed heritage. I'd heard he was a serious man – 'taciturn' was the crew's kindest description of him – with a ten-year history of commanding Seawolf-class nuclear submarines.

"They used to call this 'Iceberg Alley' a decade or so ago," he said after a comfortable silence. "There were tens of thousands of the buggers in those days. Polar scientists gave many of them actual names. After their kids, comic-book heroes, sports stars. Global warming's melted most of them of course."

I gave a short, ironic laugh. "Well, we could start naming these new ones. You go first."

He laughed as well, a deep throaty noise, which had a surprising amount of warmth in it. He pointed at the nearest iceberg, a bluish-white snow-topped oval mass floating a few hundred yards off our starboard side.

"I'm gonna call that one Caesar," he said. "Take a note please, and prepare a report for your boss."

"Right." I chuckled. My boss. Hubert. Who also happened to be Powell's brother-in-law and the reason we were 'passengers' on a US Navy submarine in the Antarctic Circle.

"I had a dog called Caesar," he murmured, almost to himself. "Beautiful nature. Golden Labrador. Died a few months ago."

"I'm sorry to hear that. Was he old?"

He shook his sadly. "No. Six. Hit by a truck."

"That sucks," I said.

It did. I remembered that I had a dog as well. A dog that was left behind when the shit hit the fan in Indian Springs and I was given a false identity and disappeared for six months. I wondered what happened to her. I hoped my neighbor, who'd been looking after her, had just adopted her after I 'went missing'. I doubted whether I'd ever be able to call and check.

"Your turn," said Powell, interrupting my reverie.

I spotted a smallish iceberg, resembling a glacier mint. Strangely squared off and symmetrical, bluish snow sticking to its sides, the sun glinting off bits of exposed ice.

"Alright, see that one over there? I hereby name it 'Luna'." I glanced up at Powell who was looking puzzled. I shrugged. "I had a dog as well. She was a cross between a spaniel and a poodle. Lovely girl. She … went missing."

Close enough.

There was a clanking sound from behind us, and Matt Hamilton emerged from the conning tower hatch. Stillman had said he was one of the FBI's rising stars, a high achiever who graduated first in his class and was on a fast track all the way to the top. He'd been on Hubert's personal staff for a month before the Vu-Hak arrived and everything went pear-shaped. His history with Stillman, a brief romantic fling before settling into an easy, platonic relationship, needed further exploration.

Maybe later.

I noticed that he was wearing a Navy woolen hat and a big white rope cardigan. He'd clearly sneaked off to do a bit of shopping before we boarded the sub in Hobart.

"Been to knot-tying classes as well, sailor?" I sniggered.

He shot me a lopsided smile along with a single raised middle finger as he maneuvered into the space between Powell and me. He brought a steaming flask to his lips and took a sip.

"Whatcha doing out here?"

Powell ignored him, resuming his survey of the icebergs.

Taciturn.

I pointed to the distant, barren shoreline. A less hospitable coast could not have been imagined. "We're pretty much there. We're not far from those co-ordinates he gave us."

Hamilton shrugged. "Okay. So now what?"

Powell looked over at me as well and I felt a little annoyed. I was the civilian here, and yet it was as if this whole escapade was being directed by me, and that I knew what lay ahead.

"I don't fucking know," I bit out. "It's not like I planned any of this."

Hamilton laid his hand lightly on my shoulder and squeezed. "I know, Kate. I'm sorry. It's just, well, you do seem to be in the middle of it all."

I gave my shoulder an irritated twitch, but before I could say anything I might have regretted there was a crackle from the comm.

Powell reached over and flicked a switch, bringing the microphone to his mouth. "Powell."

Hamilton pulled his headphones on and listened in, and I grabbed the third pair from the console.

"Skipper, ET-Comm. We're getting something. Onshore. Fourteen point six miles SSE."

I brought my binoculars up and twiddled the focus wheel. Onshore breezes were fluffing up an icy mist from the snow but there was nothing of note on the beach apart from rocks and the glacier rising into the distance.

"That's over those mountains," said Hamilton. "We'll need to disembark and go take a look."

A few small icebergs bobbed in the water between the *Jimmy Carter* and land, but nothing insurmountable.

Powell grunted into the microphone. "OK, I'm coming down. Get the director out of his bunk and tell him we'll be meeting in Operations in five. Slow us to 3 knots."

"Aye aye, skipper. Slow to 3 knots."

Hamilton took another slurp of his coffee. "I'll grab Colleen and Harvey. Suit up."

Matt and I followed Powell down the icy steps, feeling the warmth percolate through from the sub's interior. We made our way past electronics, pipes, conduits and wiring, past seamen who shot us frowns and sharp looks, and entered Operations, a cramped space just off the tower. Down here the rumbling and throbbing of the engines was subdued, like a sleeping giant. There was a nice smell of coffee coming from an industrial-looking machine in the corner, and a pile of pastries sat invitingly next to a selection of mugs and cups. A large wall-mounted monitor fizzed with white noise and wavy lines. Shelves bulging with magazines, manuals and logbooks hemmed in a rectangular table covered with nautical charts. Six chairs and a couch surrounded the table. The whole room was claustrophobic and functional. Like every other space on a submarine, I guessed.

I pulled off my anorak, helped myself to an almond croissant, and shuffled along the couch so I was sitting next to Powell. Hamilton took the opposite side. The sub's communications officer, a tall guy who introduced himself as Eddie Wong, squeezed in next and pulled out a keyboard from under the table. He started twiddling with the dials and controls on the monitor, and the screen morphed into a live image of the *Jimmy Carter* seen from above, maybe twenty or thirty yards in the air.

"A drone?" I inquired.

He gave me a curt nod. "That's right. Long-range military version. Armed as well."

"So, we going to bomb whatever we find?" I asked sourly, remembering how well that had turned out back at the crater in Nevada.

Wong didn't answer but Powell explained in a patient tone. "The armaments are standard issue, a couple of small missiles, defensive really. It's not like those aircraft-sized drones we use over the Middle East. Drones like these aren't used for interdiction, just intelligence gathering."

Wong swiveled away from the monitor and ducked under the edge of the table, which to my astonishment came alive. A built-in LCD screen powered up and projected an electronic map pulsing with latitude and longitude and depth markers and shiny objects labelled with numbers and letters. In the center was a black submarine-shaped icon that I assumed was the *Jimmy Carter*. The coastline was mapped out with slope lines and altitude markers, and the scale seemed to indicate that the table width represented about twenty miles either side of us.

There was a commotion outside and Stillman entered, followed by Hubert and then Cole Harvey. Stillman was wearing a Navy-issue coverall, dark blue with grey splotches. A rectangular Velcro-backed nametag was on the right breast pocket and a US Navy patch on the left. Her hair was wet and combed straight back. She gave me a smile and shuffled in beside Hamilton, who gave her a little fist bump. Hubert was still in his suit, braces and tie, and just nodded as he squeezed in and sat on the other side of Powell. Harvey was wearing a pair of jeans and a T-shirt, his grey hair still ponytailed and his stubble making him look grizzled but actually quite cool because he was surprisingly well built. He had a tattoo on his bicep that looked like an eagle sitting on top of an anchor holding a trident and pistol. He saw me looking and he grinned and flexed his arm. "Know what this is?"

"Frat ink?" I grinned back, winding him up.

He gave me an open-mouthed look. "Dude … this is the Seal Trident."

"You were a Navy Seal?"

"You betcha," he replied. "Feel safer now?"

I stifled a laugh and Stillman raised her eyes to the ceiling.

"Alright, let's get to it," said Hubert, helping himself to a bear claw pastry. "Y'all know each other so I'm going to hand over the briefing to Captain Powell and Mr. Wong here. Ben, can you bring us up to speed with what you've found?"

Powell grunted and leaned over the table. He swiped the desktop like a huge iPad, moving the whole image laterally. He took us over the coastline and the altitude markers started to climb as we approached a dry river valley. A mile or so further inland the picture became pixelated, as if the upload speed had just crashed.

He pointed to the blurred section. "The signal is coming from this area here. We can't get an exact fix on it."

"What sort of signal?" I asked.

"Difficult to be certain. It's radio wave, low frequency and with a very, very long wavelength, right, Eddie?"

Wong shrugged. "It's not typical, but yes it's probably radio. Radio waves are generated artificially by transmitters, of course, but they can also occur naturally."

Powell was nodding his head. "Yes, storm-generated lightning for example, and also astronomical objects."

I frowned. "But you think this is some kind of directed signal? Not a naturally occurring phenomenon?"

He stretched out and pointed to the map again. "This area

corresponded to the exact co-ordinates Bill provided. Something or someone is producing it."

"Why is it so blurred?" Hamilton said. "Did you guys forget to upgrade your wifi?"

Powell didn't find that funny. "This map is generated from military satellite data. It should be crystal clear, like everything else in the area."

I folded my arms. "So we need to go take a look."

"Safety first. Eddie, send in the drone."

Wong turned back to the wall monitor, picked up an intercom and punched a number. He spoke a few words into the microphone and then flicked a glance at us over his shoulder. "Pilot's sending it in now."

Powell nodded. "Onscreen."

Wong flicked a switch on the monitor and we were now looking out of the drone's nose camera as it flew at speed over the coastline toward the snow-covered granite cliffs. It looked as if it was going to crash but then veered left and headed through a gap in the wall into a valley cut deeply in the shoreline. Dark shadows loomed either side and the operator-pilot increased the altitude so we were flying over the edges and tracking the valley's course inland. The camera switched briefly downward and we could see that the riverbed consisted of a thin ribbon of water bordered by smooth rocks of various sizes. There was a haze of light snow and mist, although visibility was remarkably good.

"I thought the weather was pretty shitty over there?" said Hamilton.

Wong glanced up. "These are computer-enhanced optics. True visibility is only five yards or so because of the blizzard."

"Isn't this the wrong season for blizzards?" I asked.

Powell shrugged. "This is the Antarctica. Shit happens here. Although I agree the weather looks a little more wintry than usual."

"Glad I packed my snowboard then," snickered Hamilton, again getting a cold stare from Powell.

The camera changed to the forward POV again. The valley was widening although the cliff edges were still sharp and forbidding. Directly ahead was a misty oval shape, like someone had breathed on a pair of glasses before cleaning them.

"Is that —?" I began.

"Yes," said Powell. "That's it. Whatever it is."

"Slow it down," said Hubert. "Take us higher and over the top."

Wong mumbled something into the intercom and the drone slowed and started to climb. The blur enlarged and soon became separated from the valley below. If the scale was anything to go by, it was about half a mile wide and high. It seemed to continue for miles into the distance, but perspective made it difficult to judge.

"How close are we?" I said.

Wong pointed at the monitor, indicating some numerals and flashing lights down the side of the screen which I hadn't noticed before. "Approaching two hundred yards, give or take," he said.

"Can we stop and hover?"

He looked at Hubert and Powell for confirmation, and the latter nodded wordlessly. Wong gave the command and the drone's forward speed dropped off and the picture stabilized. The blurred object appeared to be teardrop shaped, and we were at the widest point on the front edge. There was a faint image visible underneath, black and featureless but quite opaque.

Hubert leaned back and folded his arms. "Speculation? Why can't we see it?"

Wong pursed his lips. "Maybe a distortion field of sorts. Jamming our signals but also jamming the visible spectrum too."

I squinted at the screen but nothing changed. I concentrated hard, wondering if any of the implanted information from Cain would suddenly appear and all would be revealed.

Nothing happened.

"Should we try and fly the drone through it?" I said to Hubert.

He looked at me for a few seconds, weighing it up.

"I agree with Kate," interjected Stillman. "It's why we're here, isn't it?"

Hubert gave her a sharp look before taking a deep breath. He turned to Powell. "Ben, this is your ship. We're civilians. Your call."

Powell nodded slowly, weighing it up. After a few seconds he said, "Eddie, fly the drone through the field. Slowly, mind."

Everyone turned his or her attention back to the screen, as the drone started moving again. It descended slowly and as it approached, the structure behind the blur started to take shape, remaining black and homogenous but with sharp angles and boxiness replacing what I'd initially thought was more like a smooth black tadpole.

"Seventy yards away ... sixty ... fifty," intoned Wong, reading the data feed coming in down the side of the picture like a waterfall of red dots.

Just then there was a flash of sunlight and the drone picture shook and turned upside down and went black as we lost the signal.

Hubert looked at Wong. "What happened?"

Wong was on the phone to the drone pilot and held up a finger while he received his report. He nodded thanks and hung up. "The drone flew into a solid wall. It broke."

EIGHTEEN

The blizzard had intensified as we'd come ashore, flakes whirling in an angry vortex from a bleak silver sky. I'd expected the coldness and the sting on my face, but not the ferocity of the wind and the blinding whiteness of it all. At one point the snow had become so thick that it resembled confetti flakes, each crystal the size of my thumbnail. I pulled the neoprene facemask around my mouth and nose as the ice particles stabbed my exposed skin what felt like a million times per second. Slush was sliding down my collar into my neck and between my cuffs and gloves. My toes were already starting to tingle and the snowdrifts were up to my knees and making me drag my legs as if I'd had a stroke.

Stillman and Hamilton were walking slowly next to me, hunched over, heads down, not speaking. Harvey and Wong and a couple of marines were drafting behind us, if that were possible at our snail's speed. I flicked a glance over my shoulder and caught Harvey's eye. He gave me a thumbs up. Was he enjoying himself? I shook my head and more icy sludge slithered down my neck.

My earpiece buzzed and I activated the comm with a sideways motion of my head. "Go ahead?"

"Kate," crackled Hubert's voice, just audible above the gale. "We're losing you on infrared and visual. What's the sit-rep? You copy?"

I stopped walking and turned away from the blizzard, snow pelting the back of my coat and hat. "We must be a hundred yards or thereabouts from the anomaly," I shouted into the microphone. "Visibility is virtually zero. Hope we don't just walk into that force-field or whatever it was that brought down the drone."

Stillman appeared next to me and pawed at my sleeve. She pointed ahead, eyes wide through the ice-encrusted mask. The barrier was visible; a mirage in the desert, glassy and shimmering.

"We're there," I said to Hubert, back on the *Jimmy Carter*.

"Activate body cams and do the survey."

"Copy that."

Harvey fanned out to my left, taking one of the marines with him. The other marine stuck with us, as did Wong, who was fumbling to get his body cam to work. It wasn't long before there was a noticeable change in the volume of the wind and the sound of the snow under my feet transitioned from the squeak of fresh snow to the crunch of melting snow. My boots splashed through shallow pools of water in between the drifts.

"Easy does it," said Hamilton, pulling on my sleeve. "We don't know for certain where that barrier begins."

Wong brought out a piece of equipment the size of a briefcase, which he laid on a mound of snow. He opened it to reveal touch-sensitive screens and dials, not dissimilar to a *Star Trek* tricorder. I went over and squatted down to see what he was doing.

"Eddie, what can you tell us?" I shouted into his ear.

"Not much," he answered. "There's definitely a jamming signal interfering with all my instruments. I can't even tell you what the temperature is just now."

"It's cold, Eddie," I said.

I caught movement in my peripheral vision and looked up to see Harvey waving his arms about twenty yards closer to the barrier. The microphone was no longer functioning so Wong and I trudged over to join him. He was standing over the downed drone. It was about six feet long, gunmetal grey, with four upturned wings and rotor blades and a forked tailpiece.

"It looks like it's in one piece," I said.

Harvey nodded. "It's weird. It crashed into the barrier, so why isn't it busted up?"

Wong kneeled down to examine the machine, running his hands over the smooth white side of the main fuselage. He turned one of the rotors, letting it spin for a few rotations before stopping and spinning it the other way.

"Seems okay," he began.

Without warning, the drone powered up, its rotor blades

whipping up a storm and driving the snow in all directions. We scrambled out of the way as it awkwardly lifted off and hovered a few feet in the air, nose swinging left and right.

I turned to Wong. "Eddie, can't you turn it off?"

He opened the tricorder thingy and started scrabbling around the switches and dials with his gloved fingers. Realizing his mistake, he pulled his facemask down and peeled the glove off with his teeth. He jabbed a few buttons, glancing at the drone in between actions. Nothing seemed to be happening.

"Dude," said Harvey. "Why'd we even bring you?"

Wong gave him a death stare and continued to jab away at the screen. I edged closer to Stillman and leaned in to her, covering my mouth with my glove, and shouted directly into her ear over the noise of the drone.

"I've a bad feeling about this. Something's not right."

Stillman's head bobbed up and down, and she pulled off her own gloves, reached into her pocket and brought out her gun. She gestured for Hamilton to do the same. The drone reared up into the air and two small rockets dropped from under a wing and fizzed toward us. We dived to the ground and they shot past, exploding against the barrier.

"Non-homing munitions," yelled Stillman. "That's why we're still alive. Stay down!"

Harvey and the marines brought their guns to bear on the drone. There was a rapid burst of fire and it was peppered with bullets and broke apart, crashing gracelessly into the snow. It fired another rocket as it hit the deck, the missile streaking toward one of the marines. There was a small but substantial explosion as the warhead discharged and the marine jerked backward, shrapnel shredding the front of his anorak. Harvey was also knocked to the ground but jumped up quickly and ran to the downed soldier. I started to run to him to see if I could help but my feet were locked in place like they were glued to the floor. There was a tingling – a kind of static charge around me – and my stomach plummeted like in an elevator. Nausea clawed at my throat, and I swallowed to force down the bile that was ascending my gullet.

I looked to see how the others were doing and saw a balloon-like protuberance oozing from the barrier, rolling like breaking waves over surf. I yelled at Stillman but my voice was muted, deadened by whatever was causing the static. The wave washed over Stillman, then Hamilton and then it was on me. My body shivered as it passed through, one of those uncontrollable shakes you get when you have a fever, then my feet were swept away and I face-planted into the powder. I screamed and tried to grab onto rocks, gravel or anything on the ground, but just left long furrows in the snow as I was pulled in.

The last thing I saw was Harvey running at full pelt toward me and suddenly being repelled as if tied to a rubber band.

Then I was on the other side.

NINETEEN

"How the hell is it so hot this side?"

Matt Hamilton rubbed his face, already dripping with sweat, and blew out his cheeks.

Stillman and Hamilton were sitting next to me on the grass, jackets off and wafting their caps in front of their faces to cool off. The storm was gone and a warm breeze ruffled my hair, bringing with it the suggestion of a balmy day. It was hard to comprehend the hypnagogic quality experiencing this in an Antarctic environment.

On the other side of the barrier, the snowstorm continued, flakes melting on contact. I could just make out Eddie Wong staring in at us, wide-mouthed. Harvey was kneeling over the injured marine, applying a field dressing to the side of his head.

I shrugged out of my anorak and gloves and stood up to stretch. Then, and only then, I turned to face the object. The thing. The … alien structure.

Or whatever I should call it.

Jagged black edges pointed and indented upward, clefts in shadows dark and ominous. I walked the ten yards or so to its nearest edge and absent-mindedly ran a hand over the shiny burnished surface, lustrous as a gemstone. The ambient temperature increased the closer I got, but its surface was cool to the touch, in fact almost icy cold compared to the air. There was a gentle vibration of what I guessed was some kind of machinery: the low amplitude thrum reminded me of the purring of a big cat.

I moved slowly, running my hand along the side. My reflection was visible in its mirror-like surface.

My thoughts were blank: a strange occurrence, as normally they were twisting and turning and generally suffocating me with their whispers.

"What are you?" I said softly.

A voice, feminine and mellifluous, came out of nowhere. "It

is a self-replicating machine that is autonomously capable of reproducing itself using the raw materials found in its local environment."

Walking toward me was a woman of average height, very pale, with a shaved skull, angular features and wearing what resembled a white hospital gown.

"Kate —" shouted Hamilton, leaping to his feet. He'd drawn his gun and was pointing it at the woman in a textbook FBI two-handed stance. Stillman also had her gun out, but was holding it by her side.

"Weapons will not be necessary, Agent Hamilton," she said. "We brought you here to be safe."

"Stay where you are," he warned.

I tried to concentrate, to focus my thoughts, to get some feel for what she was. What *IT* was. But there was nothing. However, I didn't get any bad vibes. No sense of the Vu-Hak. She wasn't trying to infiltrate my head. This was something different.

"It's all good, Matt," I said, waving him off.

The woman approached me but stopped a few yards away. Up close, her features were waxy and baby-like, no lines or blemishes: showroom-dummy perfection.

"Why'd you leave the others outside?" I said.

She folded her arms and her mouth twitched into a half smile. A cold chill blossomed within my chest and the familiar feeling of spiders running around inside my skull appeared. My vision blurred as her voice reverberated in my mind.

It is not safe out there.

I rubbed my eyes and blinked, trying to clear my head. Hamilton and Stillman were frozen in place, like a movie that had been paused. Hamilton was still pointing the gun. Stillman was looking angrily into space, mouth open. The woman walked over and disarmed them both. She flipped the guns around and handed them to me, like she was Wyatt Earp in *Tombstone*.

"We need to talk, you and I," she said, this time aloud.

"Release my friends, then we talk."

"Don't worry about them; it's nothing permanent."

She waved a hand at the object and bubbling appeared on the surface as if something was coming to the boil. A protuberance appeared, rapidly enlarging and taking the shape of a couch, which dropped soundlessly to the grassy floor.

"Are you Vu-Hak?" I said, more calmly than I felt.

She hesitated, and then blinked slowly. "Of course not."

"Then who or what are you?"

She walked over to the couch and sat down. She looked up at me and patted it, encouragingly. I remained standing.

"Are you going to answer my question?" I said.

She smiled and said, "How did you get here?"

"Not until you tell me who you are," I insisted, starting to get angry.

Would you prefer I read your mind to get this information? You will not enjoy the experience.

I laughed. "I've been there before. Do your worst."

She stared at me and her face creased, awkwardly, into what I assumed was an attempt at a smile. It seemed plastic, lines in the wrong place, like a prototype of what a face smiling should look like. She folded her arms in her lap and looked up at me. "Come on, I don't bite."

I moved closer and tested the surface of the seat with my hands. It gave way, reassuringly, and had the texture of an old leather settee.

Without taking my eyes off her, I sat.

"Good," she said. "Now we can talk."

"Not until you release my friends."

For a brief moment her eyes closed and she cocked her head sideways, like a dog hearing something out of the range of human hearing. Then her eyes opened lazily and I caught the last vestiges of a greenish glow.

"Very well," she murmured.

Stillman and Hamilton came to life, as abruptly as if someone had just pressed *play*. Hamilton quizzically looked at his empty hand and then over at Stillman who was already stomping toward us. I guess the sight of me and this strange woman sitting on a couch protruding from the side of a spaceship (which is now what I thought it was) may have appeared jarring, to say the least.

"Who's your new friend?" she growled.

The woman/thing facing me looked up at Stillman. Her eyes were the deepest black, but with speckles of green phosphorescence flickering from right to left, not quite rhythmically, but near enough. Even sitting, she was completely still and calm. There was no extra movement, no twitching or glancing away. A statue.

"You're not human, are you?" Stillman said, slowly.

The woman returned her gaze to me and it was instantly unsettling. She looked at me, through me, past me, like she'd seen something fascinating two inches behind my eyes. I waited for the voice to appear in my head again, but this time she spoke aloud. "No, but I am not your enemy."

"You're a machine," Stillman said tightly.

The woman glanced up at her, a mischievous smile flickering at the side of her mouth. "You mean like a robot?"

"Yes."

"You couldn't be more wrong."

"You're like Adam," I said. "You're one of those Vu-Hak machines."

"Adam who?" she said, her eyes guileless.

I shook my head. "Let's not play that game."

She seemed to find that amusing. "Do you want to know who I am? Or actually – what I am?"

I thought I already knew the answer, but I nodded slowly.

"Close your eyes," she said.

I did, and the darkness was immediately replaced with an explosion of colors and patterns, spinning and coalescing into a small globe of light. It danced for me, spinning like a firefly before spasming and growing into a tumescent ball of silvery liquid. Deep matt blackness appeared at its very center, rapidly expanding until stars and novae flickered into existence. They formed a cartwheeling galaxy, an outer rim of young stars and a bulls-eye core with spiral arms extruding from a massive black hole at its center. My own face appeared in the center of the black hole, unnatural green eyes glowing with unearthly phosphorescence.

"What's this?" I said.

Do you understand your place in the universe?

I shivered and couldn't stop staring at my face. My eyes pulsed emerald as if with each heartbeat. Electricity discharges framed my head, blue-yellow flashes outlining a backdrop of ruined cities and burning skies.

"Are you talking about me," I said, with a shiver, "or humanity?"

She paused.

Both.

The reply was drawn out, as if the word had multiple syllables.

The images vanished and my eyes snapped open.

"A view into your future," she said. "The end is near."

"What do you mean? I thought Adam had saved us. I don't understand."

She looked down at her hands, which were resting on her thighs. She said nothing, but her silence was more unsettling than anything she'd said so far.

"Are you Cain?" I said, although there was nothing familiar about her thought patterns.

She shrugged. "Perhaps we are all Cain?"

What the fuck did she mean by that?

Stillman interrupted, pointing over my shoulder. "Kate, something's wrong."

Harvey was waving from the other side of the barrier. He pointed at the Marine on the ground, who, even from this distance, looked grey and ashen. Wong was still staring in at us, useless as ever.

I turned on the woman. "Let them in, can't you see they need help?"

"It is not safe," she said, calmly.

"Yes, so you said. Why won't you let them in? You brought us here to keep us safe, so do the same for them?"

"This is a mistake," she said.

Maybe it was, but I wasn't going to let someone die if I could help it.

"Let them in or we're leaving," I said, although I wasn't sure how I was going to quite follow through with that particular threat.

We locked eyes for a moment and then she nodded.

There was a rush of wind as the barrier opened and a circular aperture ten yards wide appeared. Snow started to blow through and cold Antarctic air mixed with the subtropical atmosphere around the ship. I ran through the aperture to Harvey, Stillman and Hamilton close behind. Harvey was leaning on the marine's leg, pressing some kind of dark cloth on it, and he'd tied a belt just below the groin.

"He's not doing well," he grimaced. "I think there're penetrating injuries to his abdomen, but more importantly I think some of the shrapnel hit his femoral artery. Look …"

He lifted the cloth up and there was an immediate spurt of blood, arcing into the air. I knew a potentially fatal injury when I saw one. He needed urgent medical intervention. The woman hadn't moved from the makeshift seat and was watching us, expressionless and silent.

"Can you help him?" I shouted, the wind now howling and the blizzard picking up again.

She gave no answer, no sign she'd heard me. Her head was cocked to the side, as if she was listening for something.

I came to a decision. "Let's get him in there. We need to get him out of this cold."

With some co-ordination, we managed to lift him while Harvey applied pressure on the femoral wound. There was a dribble of blood coming from the marine's mouth as well, and his lips were navy blue.

I turned to Eddie Wong, who hadn't moved. "Eddie?" I said. "Some help here, please?"

Then I knew we were in trouble.

TWENTY

I'd missed the signals because of the cold.

I could tell when a Vu-Hak was near because of how they made me feel. The abnormal, irrational fear. The cold chills running up and down my spine. The primeval sense of something bad approaching. The urge to look behind.

I'd missed it all.

A piercing whistling started, rapidly increasing in pitch and loudness. My head felt like it was going to explode and I brought my hands to my ears and screamed, losing hold of the marine. I rolled over on my back and squeezed my eyelids together tightly.

Pain seared through my skull, hotter than a branding iron, my mind conceding to the torment, unable to bring a thought to completion. Without my meaning it to, my body curled into something fetal, and all the while the pain burned and radiated.

I opened my eyes to see Wong standing over me. He was holding the marine's submachine gun. The hole at the end of the barrel looked a foot wide.

He smiled.

You have brought us here.

"Please, no ..." I began.

But in that moment I knew it was narcissism, delusional to think for a second that they would exercise anything like human compassion. They appeared in my mind more like shadows than physical beings, black smoke in a dark void. Each form rippled whenever it moved like disturbed water. They didn't care what or who we were.

"Don't do this," I pleaded.

We have no more need of you.

He pointed the gun at my head and I closed my eyes.

TWENTY-ONE

I could feel soft sheets and warmth on my skin. My eyes were closed but light was squeezing through my lids. They flickered and I tried to open them but the effort was too much: they were so heavy it was as if they were glued together.

To say I felt weird was an understatement.

I had no idea who I was.

Lying there, motionless, I debated whether or not to get up. My muscles felt weak, drained of energy. There was a smell of … flowers, yes that was it. Freshly cut flowers. Pollen. I could hear a faint droning noise, like a vacuum cleaner, and some beeping sounds. Low voices in the distance.

My eyes opened.

I was lying in a bed in a sterile, magnolia-painted room. White unpatterned sheets were pulled up to my chin, and my bare feet were poking out over the footrest. Sunlight was slicing through blinds on a window to my right. There was a door at the bottom of the bed with a window halfway up.

I brought my hand up to my face. I was wearing green pajamas. I wiggled my fingers. So far, so good.

The beeping noises became more insistent. I matched my breaths to them and slid my eyes sideways. There was a monitor with wavy lines and red lights winking on and off on a bedside table. Wires protruded from another box and snaked toward me, disappearing beneath the sheets.

There was a quiet knock on the door. I closed my eyes.

The handle clicked and made an un-oiled squeak as it opened.

"She's still out," came a softly spoken voice. Female.

"We need to talk with her when she wakes." A man's voice. Not trying to be quiet. Authoritarian.

Law enforcement?

Footsteps approached, and fingers took hold of my wrist. Soft, slender cold fingers looking for a pulse.

I kept my eyes closed.

"What do those readings tell you?" I heard the man say.

The woman sighed as she let go of my wrist. There were scratchy noises as if she was writing and then the sound of turning pages.

"Just that she's stable, not in any danger," she said.

Heavy footsteps moved away, and the door opened and closed. After a couple of seconds there was a quieter footstep as the woman moved around the bed to the monitors. I sneaked a quick look, assuming that if she saw my eyes move she would think it was just a reflex. I caught a glimpse of her. Pale, blonde, average-height, early thirties. Nice bone structure. A stethoscope around her neck. A white coat with a name stenciled below the pocket.

Dr Kate Morgan

There was some fumbling with my sleeves as she rolled them up and then tightness as she wrapped a blood pressure cuff around my arm. Next came the wheezy sound of air being pumped in and a slow hiss as it was let out. She fussed around a bit more and then went still. I held my breath and was about to open my eyes to see if she'd left when I got a whiff of her perfume and a pressure on my arm as she leaned forward. Her cool hand pressed on my forehead, as if she was assessing my temperature.

"Come on," she whispered. "Talk to me again."

Had I already spoken with her? Did I know her or did she know me?

I felt her lean back and disengage.

"Okay then, I'll be back in half an hour to check on you. Don't go away."

A mild rebuke in there somewhere.

The door closed and I opened my eyes fully.

In a single motion I sat up in bed. The movement was easy so I flicked the sheets off and swung my legs over and onto the floor. I walked across the room to where there was a small sink with a mirror.

I bent down to see my face and staring back at me was no one I recognized.

Lumpy, half-formed features, like Play-doh or putty.

Empty, black eyes, like those in a doll.

It wasn't my face, though I had to admit to myself I wasn't sure what my face *did* look like.

I took a deep breath and leaned on the sink, shaking my head. "It's a dream," I said to my reflection. "Wake up. Wake up."

Then there was a tickling on my skin, and a feeling of pressure behind my eyes. A strange disquiet came over me, a feeling of restlessness and butterflies in my stomach.

Then the voice came.

It isn't over. It's just starting.

My eyes flashed fluorescent green and I staggered back from the sink until my backside touched the bed. I shakily sat down and brought my hands up to my eyes. There was a blur as my fingers touched and I noticed the absence of fingerprints, and the waxiness of the skin. The monitor had stopped bleeping and all the wavy lines had flattened. I blinked and they all started up again, assuming normal, healthy human values.

"No, no, no, no …" I murmured. "This can't be right."

TWENTY-TWO

Wake up.

The voice boomed around my head, echoing as if bouncing from a distant cave. There was absolute darkness, obsidian and impenetrable. I tried to open my eyes again but nothing happened. I couldn't feel my arms or legs. It felt like I was weightless: insubstantial, drifting, maybe in a flotation tank, maybe in space.

My thoughts accelerated like I was on speed or cocaine, and I tried to slow them so that I could breathe, but they just exploded, a flight of ideas without connection or direction. Breaths came in ragged gasps, and my heart hammered inside my chest such that it felt as if my skin was wafer thin and the organ would burst out. Nausea washed over me.

You are safe now. Try and relax.

A familiar voice. Strangely asexual, like a neutered Siri.

I immediately felt calmer, as if I'd been given an IV shot of anesthetic and was about to drift off into oblivion.

I tried to speak, but no words came.

Unease blossomed within me and the silence was unnerving. There were no traffic noises, no birds singing, nothing.

The atmosphere felt brittle, like it could snap.

This had to be a dream. A dream suffused with sensations so real that they came with physical attributes. Everything would be fine. I willed myself to wake up. True reality beckoned.

Visual sensors are coming online. Diagnostics are running.

The voice in my head was directionless and everywhere, but the darkness remained absolute, an ocean of stygian doubts and apprehension in which my consciousness seemed to be floating.

Your memory will soon return. The patch is offline but the connections are fully formed. Your mind is adjusting to its new environment and settling into its new template.

The darkness abruptly peeled away and I blinked involuntarily. I couldn't move my head, but my eyes roved left and right, hungrily taking in what they could. A small white oval-shaped room. The walls were pristine, clinical, silvery. On the ceiling were a number of slit-like openings ranging from a few inches to a few feet long and a few inches wide. Hanging out of these slits were about half a dozen cables, moving organically, up and down. One was approaching me, its end blinking red and green, and as it got closer a small metallic instrument emerged from the tip. I could feel myself withdrawing as it got closer to my eye, but I still couldn't move my head; nor could I blink. I waited for the pain as it penetrated my eyeball, but none came.

After a few seconds, with a whispering noise like leaves in an autumnal park lane, the instrument withdrew and vanished into one of the slits like a snake retreating into its den.

"How do you feel?"

The voice was now audible and not in my head, coming from my side.

I took a deep breath. "I'm not sure."

My voice sounded strange. There was an abnormal resonance to it, like I was recovering from laryngitis or a hangover.

A face came into view. Pale, shaved skull, angular features. A woman's face. Ageless and yet aged. She smiled awkwardly, and my mind exploded as memory returned.

Eddie Wong.

The gun.

The Vu-Hak.

"Where am I?" I got out, panic rising.

She smiled, a better attempt this time. "You are inside the ship; all is well."

I tried to move my head and get up but again nothing seemed to work. I grimaced and closed my eyes, concentrating hard, willing my limbs to obey me.

"Are my friends all right?"

She paused for a few seconds before replying. "I told you it was a bad idea opening the barrier."

"What do you mean?"

"I could not sense the Vu-Hak in him until Wong approached you. Then it was too late."

"What about my friends?" I repeated, trepidation rising.

"Do not worry, the Vu-Hak has been killed."

"That's not what I asked."

She ignored me and moved out of my line of sight. There was some prodding and little twitches in my arms as if someone were jabbing me with a cattle prod.

"You still have no motor functioning. This has been ... a difficult procedure. We were not ready to attempt this. Or even expecting to attempt it at this time."

She moved back into my line of sight and her expressionless face now seemed to show concern. "We had to leave quickly. The Vu-Hak had already communicated with others on the submarine. They were coming. They could have ... gotten to me. I am sorry ... about your friends."

I closed my eyes as the pain hit me out of nowhere. I hadn't seen it coming. I'd failed them. Colleen, Hubert, all of them. An awful hollowness gnawed at my insides as waves of wretchedness threatened to engulf me, body and soul.

"It wasn't your fault," the woman said gently.

There was an emerald tinge to her eyes, but the whites were visible, making her look human enough. I made to get up, but nothing happened. I moved my eyes, but that was all I could do. I started to panic. "Why can't I move? Am I ... paralyzed?"

I bit out the last word, my heart hammering again, not wanting to hear the reply but desperate to know. The woman was no longer smiling. She looked away for a second and then leaned closer. I felt her hand on my arm.

"You died."

Death.

A shadow that lurked in the dark, watching and waiting, the icy chill of his breath only a heartbeat away.

All my working life I'd taken care of the dead and the dying.

Patients. Family. My daughter, Kelly.

But I'd never been afraid of dying myself. I'd never really dealt with the notion that someday this would happen to me.

Was this the afterlife I'd never believed in?

My eyes opened and the woman was still there, silently watching me, motionless, like a statue.

"Am I still dead?" I asked, aware of the irony.

"Clearly not."

"Thank you," I said.

She nodded. "You are welcome."

"I can't move. There's no feeling."

She blinked slowly as if deciding what to tell me. "Your consciousness, the essence of you, survived. Your body was … not salvageable."

It was as if she were talking another language, it made so little sense. I took a deep breath and focused on the movements of my chest, the feeling of air moving in and out of my lungs. Everything felt normal.

"No, that's not possible. If my body died, so did my brain. You can't be conscious without a brain. The body keeps the brain alive. The heart pumps blood so the brain can survive …"

I was babbling. The saying 'there is nothing to fear but fear itself' is bullshit. There are many things worse than fear.

The woman shook her head dismissively, like a schoolmistress about to correct a student making an elementary mistake.

"You no longer have an organic brain. Your consciousness is housed in a machine."

"Impossible." I laughed. "Nothing happens in the mind that doesn't happen in the brain. It's the software running on the hardware."

Even as I said this, I had a feeling that I was in denial. I remembered the CT scans of Adam. The alien structures inside his body, none of which resembled organic tissue or even less a human brain.

"Really?" she said. "So you understand consciousness?"

"No, but –"

"Do not question what is. You died. Your mind lives on."

"Then … how?"

"Your consciousness – your very self – can be removed from

the anatomical structures of the brain and transferred to a suitable repository, providing the transfer template is sufficiently complex and compatible."

"That technology doesn't exist."

The woman closed her eyes, and gave a very human-like sigh. "The Vu-Hak perfected this technique thousands of years ago. They transferred their consciousnesses to machines. It set them free. Improved them. Upgraded their capabilities. As you know, they have already demonstrated that this procedure is transferrable between species."

"You mean when they 'made' Adam, don't you?"

She nodded, but I detected a hesitation. Something she was not happy about.

"What's wrong?" I said. "Is there something you're not telling me?"

She looked away. "Your injuries were severe. Fatal. We had only minutes to act."

"Wait ... who's 'we'?" I said sharply.

"I misspoke. *I* had only minutes to act."

I didn't think she'd misspoken at all. "And the others?" I said, feeling a lump in my throat. "What happened to my friends?"

"I do not know."

"How can you not know?" I blurted out, angry.

"We were under attack. The Vu-Hak had found us. We had to leave."

"There's that 'we' again. Is Adam here?" I said.

Her eyebrows furrowed. "Now is not the time."

Right. Anger was now pulling level with fear, threatening to overtake it.

"I'm not stupid. 'Cain' be damned – he's Adam, isn't he? Adam's behind all this. Let me fucking see him."

Her lip twitched now in another approximation of a smile. Then she walked out of my line of vision. I tried to twist to follow her, but my eyes only went so far.

"Come back here," I snapped. "You owe it to me to tell me the truth."

The truth?
This time the voice was only heard in my head.
Here's the beginning of the truth.

A spinning disc appeared directly above me, like an upturned water font. It transformed into a mirror pointing down at my body and the table where I was lying. The body had my face but from there it got frighteningly surreal. It was a smooth silvery-blue chrome structure, muscles and joints glistening and twinkling as if lit from within. Tubes blinking and pulsing with energy connected me to the table almost as if I were plugged in and getting charged up.

I choked back a scream. "What've you done to me?"
I told you. I saved your life.

A cold shiver ran down my spine again: for the first time I questioned whether the sensation was real. Were these feelings just psychosomatic manifestations of my mind's need to feel authentic, genuine, legitimate and ... human? Was this some form of insanity breaking into my mind, like a thief stealing everything important and replacing it with a new personality, a different, distorted reality? Or was this just a delusion, a true one, a fixed false belief that would gain traction like a tyre on asphalt and drive me in a different direction, erratically but ultimately toward the void?

"Your powertrain's operating performance is now at sixty-seven percent. You should be able to sit up."

I looked to where her voice was coming from and realized I had turned my head. She was standing by a circular panel recessed into the wall, swirling lights and dervish-like patterns flashing and pulsing.

I sat up, easily and painlessly, my body folding in two as if my stomach muscles were made of springs. There was no feeling of muscular contraction, however, so effortless was the movement. I swung my legs over the side of the table and looked down at the chrome limbs glistening under the lights. I stretched out my hands and they too were metallic, overlaid with black web-like lines.

I imagined a tear escaping from my eye: a small silvery crystal bead sliding down my cheek and rolling off my chin onto my chest. Then another, and another, as my eyes flooded over. But when I reached up to wipe them, the surface was as dry as dead bones.

"I feel ... real. How?"

"Psychotomimetic software. You'll get used to it."

She turned back to the panel and made hand gestures in front of it. The pattern of lights changed and green and red beams danced in the air.

"The final touches coming up," she said without turning.

I held my hands up to my face and watched an integument spread over them; pale like the skin I'd worn in my human life, covering the glistening metal. Fingernails appeared, creases and veins and tendons. Waxy, but authentic enough. I turned my hands over and there were no fingerprints, only blank, smooth pads on the ends of my fingers. I poked my fingers in my ears and rubbed my eyes, closing them reflexively.

Then I went to pieces.

Uncontrollable anxiety.

A full-blown panic attack.

My head was filled with a cacophony, a thousand different shouting voices and screams.

"No," I said, and my chest heaved uncontrollably, painfully. "No, no, no ..."

Sleep.

I heard the woman's voice, calming and soporific.

Darkness came over me again. My eyes felt heavy, my consciousness ebbed, and my mind went into free fall.

TWENTY-THREE

I dream again.

I'm sitting on a rock, my silvery blue legs stretched out in front of me. A brook bubbles past, bloated dead fish floating slowly downstream on its waters. The smoke-filled sky is Halloween blood red; birds are fleeing, raucous cries scraping the atmosphere like nails down a blackboard. There is a smell of wood smoke and burning animal corpses, the pungent odor of the recently deceased. The street behind me is a skeleton stripped of its flesh by atomic fire. Crumbling stone lies ash-like on the ground, a grey dust smothering fields and forests. Nothing recognizable is left of the city, no glass or wood or concrete, just twisted metal spires.

Standing on the bank next to me is a small child. A girl with blonde curly hair and big bright green eyes. She smiles at me and holds out her hand, which I take in one of mine. I pull her gently until she sits next to me. She picks up a little stone from the side of the stream and throws it underarm into the flowing water, producing a little *plop* and then a few concentric circles that are soon absorbed as it skims along the surface and drops to the riverbed. We sit there for minutes, or perhaps hours, before I turn to her and say, "Do you think we should have cared more for this world?"

She gives a little giggle, and says, "Yes," like she is surprised I should even have asked such a silly question.

I then say, "Do you think we should have cared more for each other?"

Her eyes fill with tears, and her response is the same.

On the other side of the brook more children appear, playing on swings and roundabouts. Proud parents stand around talking and pointing at their offspring and making encouraging noises. I hear laughter and excited squeals from the children and I wonder how they can be so happy, why they can't feel the same despondency and hopelessness I am experiencing.

I turn to the girl and say, "Why do we kill each other?"

She pulls away and stares at me like she is seeing a monster. She tries to run but I have hold of her hand and I pull her to me, covering her little body with my arms. She is crying and I hold her until she stops shaking.

I caress her hair, smoothing out the curls, calming her down, coo-ing like a dove. She has hold of me around my neck, her face buried in my chest. I feel her mouth moving and so I lean in and listen. She turns her face to mine, tears soaking my chest, glistening and sparkling like diamonds studding my metal skin.

"Can you stop it?" she whispers.

I look up to the sky, where black smoke trails and darkening clouds hide a watery sun, anemic and pale. Streets once thronging with life are now empty and desolate. Gone are the children who play in the crowds with their games and laughter. Gone are the stores with their windows of fine clothing or delicacies or the latest electronic goods. In their place are cracked sidewalks, empty gun shells, and broken storefronts laid waste by desperate looters.

"I don't know," I reply.

The girl looks off into the distance. Her voice becomes less childlike; it's deeper and raspier.

"What if there was an angel, and he told you to choose between being a master of hell, or …" She pauses.

"Or what?" I say.

She looks up at me; her eyes red rimmed but clear. "Or join all humanity in hell."

Was that really the choice facing me?

She starts singing softly and I have to lean in to hear her voice. Her words cut through me.

"*Roses are red,*
Violets are blue,
This world will burn to ashes,
And so will you."

Then her eyes flash phosphorescent green and I pull back, startled. She smiles and lifts her tiny hand to my face, caressing my cheek.

Her voice echoes inside my head.
But hell is empty, and all the devils are here.

TWENTY-FOUR

I woke with a start, my virtual heart hammering away, a non-existent cold sweat covering my brow. I'd been moved and was sitting in a chair of sorts in a large dark room. There were no windows, but lights flickered everywhere, thousands of white dots like the stars in a night sky. There was no sense of motion, and the rumbling noise I'd felt previously was absent.

In an identical chair next to me, which looked like it had been grown out of the floor, the bald woman was waving her hands over a light display that had no surface like a hologram. Her fingers were dancing, conducting an orchestra of electronica and plasma.

"Where am I?" I asked, looking around the room.

She closed her eyes and slowly lowered her hands onto her lap. "We are in the ship."

"Yes, I get that, but ... what ship? And why is there a ship?"

The corner of her lip twitched and she opened her eyes. "I created this ship using long-forgotten programming. As a self-replicating entity, it then built itself."

"Wait," I interrupted. "You said entity, like it was alive?"

She gave a little laugh.

"Yes. This ship is almost entirely organic, bio-constructed out of materials found on Earth. The engineering was performed at a genetic level, at the very core of the DNA and RNA of the substances utilized to create it."

"But," I tried to get my head around this. "It can't be alive. Unless ... it's a true artificial intelligence."

She turned to me and frowned. "What is artificial about it?"

"Artificial, in terms of 'created' by a non-artificial entity."

She seemed to ponder this for a second, and then said. "Let me ask you a question. What do you think of the idea that eventually, artificial intelligence will advance to the point where computers are more intelligent than humans?"

"Is that what you are? Some kind of AI?"

"Why don't you think about my question?"

I shook my head and gave a little exasperated laugh. "Alright, then I think that is probably inevitable. What I think of that idea would depend on how we consider such intelligences. Are they sentient, and if they are, how should we treat them?"

She nodded. "Very good answer. Follow-up question then – do you think humans could co-exist with another species – perhaps one it has designed – one that is more intelligent than itself?"

Hmmm. Was this a fucking lecture? "I'm sure humanity would adapt. There would be ethical standards. Rights would be accorded."

She gave a low mocking laugh. "You are naive to think that way. The Vu-Hak, limited by slow biological evolution – as are humans, of course – realized that they would not be able to compete with AI and would be superseded. They understood that true 'artificial' intelligence – 'artificial consciousness' to be more accurate – would take over and design itself at an ever-increasing rate."

"So the Vu-Hak are an AI species?"

"Not at all. The Vu-Hak genetically engineered themselves into a new integrative species. They understood that the interface of cyborg techniques and biotechnology would be best adaptable to new or alien environments and would give them a survival advantage. So they conjoined with their machines. A symphony of the organic and non-organic."

"Like a form of symbiosis?"

She considered this. "Not really. The machines they had created, the physical structures, were so powerful, the interface so infinitesimally complicated that they needed an AI to control it."

"You," I said, finally understanding.

"Optimizing the abilities of the machine demands machine intelligence."

"And you did what they told you to do," I hissed. "Destroyed worlds, civilizations, life, on a galactic scale."

She threw me a sharp look. "The Vu-Hak inserted neural backstops and barriers to ensure their dominance over us, and our acquiescence. We became slaves."

"Is that what I am now? A slave?"

"There is no AI in that machine with you."

I lifted my arm and again marveled at how real it looked, and how *normal* it felt as I moved it. Then I noticed again the absence of fingertips, and my heart sank.

"Then, how –?" I began.

"I have successfully integrated your motor cortex with the machine," she said. "You will it to move and it moves. But the other functions and capabilities of the machine will not be available to you. Your simple human mind is not sufficiently complex."

"But, I'm not human anymore, am I?"

She gave a sad kind of smile. "You are much more than human. Your digital self has been actualized with the use of holograms and virtual reality. These provided us with representations of your persona after death. A digital simulacrum filled with the essence of you. You think, therefore you are your entire life's browser history. You are a collection of algorithms, from preferred GPS haunts, from online shopping preferences to your late-night browsing searches, all composed and collated to represent the embodied holographic you after death. Sartre's 'human existence precedes essence' made all the more relevant, the digital essence of your earthly existence left behind."

"So I'm nothing more than a set of zeros and ones now," I said tightly.

"You are more than the sum of who you were. And in this machine, you could be ... immortal."

My conversations with Adam came crashing in. How he'd felt knowing he would outlive all his friends, his family, and everyone on the planet.

A lonely existence.

Who wants to live forever?

"Is this ... am I ... stuck in this?"

I had to ask.

She shrugged and looked away, saying nothing. I wondered whether her silence was an affirmation or not. I was about to press it when her hands started to move again, waving in the air, as the lights and floating plasma changed shape and color.

"We are about to land. Can you sense it?"

There was no change that I could perceive. I shook my head.

She smiled, this time wider. "Concentrate. Become the ship."

"How?" I gave a derisory snort. "I was never that good at meditation."

"It is easy. Just think ... and become the ship."

Right. Become the ship.

Wasn't it *The Matrix* where Neo was told to "become the spoon", or something?

He didn't find it very easy.

Or, at least not at first.

So I concentrated, and, seemingly without any effort ... I was the ship.

TWENTY-FIVE

I traveled through the ship's interior like a ghost, flying through walls and along endless corridors and vast open spaces the size of aircraft hangers. I glimpsed massive objects and alien machines, walls pulsing with plasma energy and lighting displays. I flew through pipes and tubes and struts and tresses the size of the biggest cables supporting bridges on Earth, all twisting and rotating as the ship moved and flexed.

When I exited the ship, dissolving through the hull, I gasped at the beauty of it. Hanging in space surrounded by the lights from billions of stars and planets it appeared an obsidian liquid metal, shapeshifting, looking like a teardrop or a jagged set of geometric angles almost at random. It appeared utterly seamless with no outward means of propulsion or weaponry.

We were coming up on the moon. Unlike the usual small white object hanging in space this was a huge disc occupying ninety percent of the forward sky. I'd always thought of the moon as a lonely silver jeweled pearl keeping the earth company in the vastness of the cosmos, but the reality was a surface as grey as a corpse, pulverized and pockmarked by meteorites. The ship was descending fast, the approaching craters and mountain ranges coming into stark relief. The plain ahead flattened out rapidly and the low western sun cast long shadows over craters and hills. We appeared to be heading for a smooth rim corralling a debris field of rocks, all covered by a rough blanket of moon dust.

Then without warning I was back in my chair, sitting next to the woman.

She was still waving her hands at the light display, but gave me a sideways glance, and another smile twitched at the side of her mouth. "You see. You just need to think it, and you can enter electronic equipment, even when it is as complex as this vessel. Unfortunately, you won't be able to manipulate it as easily as you can observe it."

I gave a sour laugh. "Because humans don't have the big brains, right?"

She nodded, seemingly ignoring my attempt at humor, and turned back to the display. "It's not your fault. You have to make do with what you've got."

Now was she trying to make a joke?

The forward holographic display came alive, images dancing in front of my face: a 3-D rotating representation of the lunar landscape with the ship looking like an enormous black needle sitting on its stern and pointing straight up into the heavens. The schematics in the display automatically morphed into English as they scrolled by, which I assumed was for my benefit.

We came to rest in the middle of a sizeable crater on the dark side of the moon called the Van de Graaff crater formation, one of the few surface features on this side not named after Soviet cities, scientists or space pioneers. There were a couple of craterlets visible on the southeast rim, and several small ones in the floor of Van de Graaff, close to us. A central peak broke from the plain a mile or two north, where the surface looked slightly smoother.

"It's really the moon," I murmured.

"People think the moon has no atmosphere," the woman broke through my reverie, "but it does. It comprises twenty-nine percent neon, twenty-six percent helium, over twenty-two percent hydrogen, twenty-one percent argon and a few percentages of trace gases. Its total mass is approximately ten thousand kilograms. Roughly the same as the amount of gas released by one of the landing Apollo spacecraft."

"Fascinating," I said dryly.

She raised her eyebrows in a slight admonishment and continued. "According to the ship, the local magnetic field in this vicinity is stronger than the natural lunar field, plus it has a slightly higher concentration of radioactive materials than the lunar surface."

"Okaaayy ..." I said, waiting for the punchline.

"Do you feel well enough to go for a walk?" she said.

I stretched, again amazed at how normal everything felt. I

even achieved a 'cracking' of my shoulder as I pushed my arms above my head. I grasped my elbow with my hand and pulled it behind my neck, twisting forward at the waist. I stifled an urge to laugh.

The woman got up from the chair and gestured for me to do the same. After I eased myself up into a standing position, the seat receded beneath me and melted into the floor like ice cream on a sun-drenched sidewalk. I towered over her, thinking that either she was very small or I was very tall. I'd been five foot eight in my previous life (was that how I should think of this now?), but I seemed to be at least another foot taller.

"Where are we going?" I said.

She stood up and turned to face me. "Wait a second."

The air seemed to blur and pixelate around her and I blinked, thinking it was me. Her flesh transitioned into a cerulean hue and her eyes glowed with intense emerald phosphorescence. Her white smock disappeared into thin air, leaving her naked, resplendent, a chrome female statue. Something Michelangelo would have sculpted – if he'd been a metalworker, that is. The shimmering continued, as she seemed to phase in and out of existence. The flesh reformed around the chrome integument like a time-lapse of a decaying corpse but in reverse. Her face became masculine with angular features, high cheekbones, a straight nose, and thin lips. Her hair shortened and darkened to form a crew cut, spiky blue-black, fitting the skull like a cap. A one-piece black garment, pocketless and without zips or buttons, covered him from head to toe.

I took an involuntary breath. "Adam?"

The machine facing me raised his eyebrows, and his face creased into a smile. "I am not Adam, I told you that."

"Then why do you look like him?" I glowered.

"This is the 'default' mode for these machines. They all came through the wormhole like this, and so it takes the least amount of energy to maintain."

"Well maybe there's a silver lining then. If the Vu-Hak find machines that all look like Adam, they aren't going to be easy to hide back on Earth, are they?"

He looked at me intently and shook his head. "If they take possession of even one machine, they will not hide."

The wall in front of me became transparent, starting from a single spot halfway up and expanding outward like the dream Kelly's pebble ripples. As the ripples widened, stars filled the opening, pinpricks poking through the night, hinting at life in the void.

I stepped out of the ship and onto the lunar plain. The overhead sun was bright and the temperature a hundred degrees Celsius, the boiling point of water. I felt neither hot nor cold. My bare feet slipped under the grey sand-like surface and, as I wriggled my toes, puffs of dust were lazily ejected only to fall back in slow motion. Ahead, the plain was crisscrossed by tire tracks and footprints leading away from the ship toward a crater a half mile or more distant. There were no significantly sized rocks on the horizon, just fine-grained fragmented bedrock peppered with micrometeorite impacts. I squatted down and took a handful of the dust, letting it pour away through my fingertips and drift windlessly to the ground. A schematic flickered in my visual fields, informing me I was being assaulted by cosmic rays and solar flare particles, and with dust saturated with hydrogen ions from the solar wind.

Over there is our destination.

The voice reverberated around my head as the man/woman/machine stepped out of the ship and walked toward me. He was pointing toward the crater where the tire tracks headed. The sight of a human figure without a spacesuit standing on the surface of the moon hit me like a slap. He set off at a languid pace, movements unaffected by the one-tenth gravity. I was expecting to see him bounce like a kangaroo but he could have been on 5th Avenue for all the difference it seemed to make. I followed at a discreet distance, taking in my surroundings, looking back at the ship, where the orifice we had come through was gradually being absorbed back into the hull. The ship itself was almost invisible: a grey blob, irregular and blocky, a chameleon hiding itself in this most desolate of places.

I picked up the pace and caught up with him as he approached the crater's edge. It was about ten feet high, consisting of a few nested terraces in concentric circles as a result of the impact from whatever meteorite had fallen there god knew how many hundreds of millions of years earlier. Over the edge, the lunar surface looked different. The soil was a glassy orange in a kind of patchwork pattern, and dumbbell-shaped droplets littered the surface in colors from green to wine-red through to orange and opaque.

Detritus thrown up from another impact. The lunar regolith contains large amounts of volcanic glass.

Jesus, I was getting a geology lesson. I slid in an ungainly fashion down into the flat crater bottom and watched as he followed me, albeit in a much more graceful movement. He pointed to a collection of the droplets, arranged loosely in a circle about ten feet in diameter.

You want me to stand in there? I said, answering him by projecting back (and realizing that voices won't travel in a vacuum).

He just smiled and pointed again. I shrugged and took a few steps until I was within the stones. I looked around and waited a few beats. I turned back to find him walking away from me.

Wait, where are you going?

One of the stones started to glow. It became a yellow inferno in the course of a few seconds, expanding like a bomb. I involuntarily stepped back but it exploded and a wave of light drenched me and I was being squeezed and inflated at the same time. The lunar surface span and fractured in a kaleidoscope of monochrome, coalescing into a blur until only darkness remained. Then I was transported to another place. A dark room, surrounded by silhouettes of black and grey structures.

My eyes quickly adjusted and the darkness parted like the thick velvet curtains of a theatre. The shapes became banks of computer equipment, and to my consternation, medical equipment. There were test tubes and glassware and monitors and what looked like scanners and operating tables. A figure was standing against one of the walls. He had raven black hair that glistened in the half light and twinkling of the plasma screens and holographic displays that surrounded us. His face was carefully structured, a tight jaw and angular shape with a thin pair of lips. He had a roman nose and cold blue eyes, with a hint of green phosphorescence behind the lenses. His skin was tanned, healthy looking and, dare I say it, god-like. As if a Roman god had been molded from a statue in the Louvre and beamed to ... the moon, or under the moon's surface, or wherever we were standing.

"Adam?" I eventually got out.

He looked at me and smiled.

"Hello, Kate."

TWENTY-SIX

We sat facing each other on the floor of a cavern, illuminated by the crepuscular glow from the computers and electronica on all sides. My HUD data screen described a breathable atmosphere, and a balmy thirty degrees centigrade. The smell of ozone permeated everything, and there was a gentle breeze coming from what I assumed were air conditioning vents somewhere in the ceiling.

"Was that a wormhole I just came through?" I said, somewhat huffily.

I'd had a flashback to the original *Star Trek* and the transporter they used to get from the ship to the surface of planets. Dr. McCoy used to ruminate over whether his molecules were destroyed at one end and just copied and recreated at the other.

So who actually arrived at the other end?

"It's good to see you too, Kate. I just wish it was under better circumstances."

"Other than my death and resurrection, you mean?" I snapped, instantly regretting it, my emotions way, way out of control.

If he'd taken offence he didn't show it: there was no change in his demeanor, which remained distant and cool. My eyes tracked over his face and body, my machine's sensors automatically generating data – composition analyses of his structure, which revealed nothing out of the ordinary. For an alien machine, anyways.

"Adam, is that really you? I used to be able to sense you in there, but I'm not getting anything."

He gave a slight smile and his neural floodgates opened, his thoughts blowing into mine. What I encountered was unexpected. A void, dark and deep. It was definitely him in there, but he seemed … empty. As if his soul was creeping around in the shadows away from human contemplation. As if the desolation of his existence was all-consuming and it couldn't bear to pretend otherwise. The silence of his thoughts was like fall leaves under frost in New England.

He looked away, and when he spoke his voice was only just audible. "I used to have dreams in which Amy would come to me, like a ghost. And when I was calm her ghost was calm, and she would laugh and I would recall the times when I felt she loved me. But there was always the feeling that she never did. That I was something she was glad to be free of, that she did not really care for me."

Amy. He was talking about his daughter.

The last time he'd seen her, he'd tried to kill her. I wanted to reach over and take his hand, but the vibes weren't encouraging.

"I get it," I said quietly. "I used to fill my days and nights at Indian Springs with chaos, noise, anger, and sex and alcohol – just to keep the ghost of Kelly away. I'd never felt so alone in those days. I was drifting, incapable of doing even the smallest tasks."

"Yes, I saw your house," he said.

Oh, now he had a sense of humor. "Funny."

"Two broken people, weren't we?" he said.

He was smiling, but if he could produce tears, it would have been a watery one. He'd used that phrase before when characterizing us. It'd resonated with me then, and did so even more now.

"Adam, I promised I would help you. You and Amy. But you left, and then … you wiped my memory."

He looked up and shook his head. "That was not me. I argued against it, actually."

I frowned. "Who were you arguing with?"

"Cain, of course."

Right.

"Going to tell me how you guys met up then?" I mocked.

"Cain is an artificial intelligence, or more accurately a machine consciousness."

"And how'd you get a pet robot?" I said, immediately regretting my choice of words.

Adam's lip twitched. "Cain is not a robot. Not by any measure or definition you would recognize."

"Then what'd you call him?"

He gestured to himself, and then to me with an open hand. "You and I, these machines we inhabit, they were all created by the Vu-Hak. Their complexity is such that they require a machine intelligence to function. A non-sentient life-form buffered by fail-safes and programming constraints to make it subservient to our wishes and allow us full access to the machine's abilities."

"So he *was* a slave," I said.

Cain's own description ran true, but did his enslavement absolve him of the crimes committed by the Vu-Hak? Maybe ...

"Cain allowed both you and the Vu-Hak access to the power of your machine," I said. "You killed thousands of innocent people."

Adam leaned back against the wall and his face disappeared into the shadow. The green phosphorescence of his eyes shined eerily back at me, drilling into my soul.

"Cain was not the artificial consciousness in my particular machine. Furthermore, the Vu-Hak killed those people, not me."

I threw him a sharp look. "We need to talk about that."

There was silence for a minute or two, and I had to strain to hear him when he spoke.

"Yes. What do you wish to know?"

"Start from the beginning?"

He nodded. "From the beginning, then. The intensity of the nuclear detonations, focused as they were by the geography of the Trinity Crater, overwhelmed the ability of my machine to absorb the energies. I survived, but the consciousness of the Vu-Hak was destroyed."

"How did you survive and it didn't?"

This had always bothered me.

He paused, then: "You are aware that there is a singularity at the heart of each machine?"

Adam had given Hubert and me this little tidbit of

information when we had him captive in the Black Site. It had been a throwaway line we couldn't get our heads around. The thought of a singularity – a tiny black hole a few millimeters in diameter – on Earth and controlled by forces we couldn't possibly understand had been so beyond us I think we all just dismissed it and concentrated on the other issue at hand.

The imminent invasion of the Vu-Hak.

Adam interrupted my musings. "Nothing can escape an unshielded black hole, Kate. The machine's singularity was allowed to open, to flower, if you like. All the heat, radiation, light, every bit of energy was warped into it and absorbed."

"Down the drain of a cosmic plughole," I said.

"Yes, but the singularity was overwhelmed for a microsecond at the end. The laws of thermodynamics are ruthless, and even a black hole cannot escape their judgment. The amount of entropy or disorder in the universe cannot ever decrease, so as the nuclear energy was sucked in the entropy it contained could not be dismissed, and so the entropy of the singularity increased. The temperature rose and radiation – Hawking radiation to be exact – escaped."

"Is Hawking radiation dangerous?" I said.

"Not to humans. But as the Hawking radiation was ejected, the Vu-Hak's molecular footprint was separated from mine and destroyed. What were previously particles and anti-particle twins intrinsically linked and entangled forever, were no longer."

"So how did you survive?" I asked with a quiet voice.

"The machine's AI protected me. But my mind and my consciousness could only be saved by merging with those of the AI. At a quantum level, the physical molecules producing my consciousness were mapped onto the machine's architecture and integrated in an irreversible reaction. The AI and the human became a single entity, a hybrid if you like. I am neither man, nor machine, but both."

His head dropped, and he went quiet. The phosphorescence vanished as he closed his eyes. In the intermittent bursts of colored light I could just make out his shape, now huddled into a corner, arms around his knees.

"Adam," I said, trepidation painting my voice with a coarse brush, remembering Cain's words when I was waking up from my own consciousness transfer. "Cain said there's no AI helping control my machine?"

He didn't move, and his voice was still a whisper. "That is true, which is why you will be limited in your abilities."

"But I have a shielded black hole in here?" I said, pointing to my chest.

"Of course: that is what powers all these machines. But you need a higher level of consciousness to fully manipulate it, hence the need for the AI. You will be able to use the motor functions, access and manipulate electronics, rudimentary telepathic abilities, but that is probably all you will be capable of."

My face darkened and my brain stuttered for a moment as my thoughts tried to catch up. I felt undead, a zombie, a vampire, whatever.

"We did our best," Adam continued. "We were not ready. The transfer of your mind to the machine template might not have worked at all. You might have died … for real."

I took a metaphorical deep breath and tried to calm down. I knew where I was heading and it was nowhere good.

"How about telling me what happened when you went back into the wormhole? When the Vu-Hak didn't invade, we thought you'd saved humanity. And sacrificed yourself. I was …" I stopped to gather myself again. "I was lost, but I took solace in the fact that it was over. But then it wasn't, was it?"

My mind was suddenly a mess again, chaos, hurting, aching. My emotions were jagged and my insides felt tight. I had to get a grip. Then I saw the green eyes move as he shook his head.

"I had a plan."

TWENTY-SEVEN

When the portal had opened for the last time at the Trinity crater, I had feared the worst. The alien invasion was imminent and thousands of Vu-Hak machines were about to enter our galaxy and swarm Earth, with the resultant destruction and extinction of humanity. Adam had looked into the opening of the wormhole and I'd felt the sadness drain away from him, replaced by a sense of contentment and purpose. He'd walked into the wormhole, and the portal had consumed him, and then … well, nothing.

He stood up and held out a hand, which I took. I let him pull me to a standing position and we walked to the middle of the chamber. Lights came on automatically, partially illuminating the space.

But what a space.

"What the hell have you done?" I murmured, half to myself.

We were in a high-tech cave the size of a football stadium, a black metallic roof over our heads and black metallic flooring, shiny and burnished like jewels or polished coal, under our feet. My footsteps echoed quietly and machinery hummed in the background, a soft rhythmic music. There were no desks or bench tops but there were examination couches and centrifuges and huge refrigerators and water baths and autoclaves with flow hoods. On one wall just visible behind a thin film of rising gases there appeared to be thousands of test tubes set into racks of plastic, linked by plasma or optical fibers.

Adam stopped and gestured for me to come closer. He waved a hand and a hidden mechanism triggered the emergence of a console of sorts from the floor; it molded itself to the shape of a glowing silver-blue keyboard.

"We are under the lunar surface," he said, "at a depth of fifty-two miles, four miles under the crust, in a cystic pocket in the rocky mantle which I detected during my evaluation of this area."

"Why do we need to be under the surface of the moon?"

"We need to keep this facility hidden from the Vu-Hak," he replied, his face impassive. "It is critical to the survival of the human race."

"What is it, exactly?"

He looked away again, his head tilted to one side, as if deciding what to say. "Before I tell you, I believe you were asking about the wormhole?"

His eyes were still blue-black with a faint emerald phosphorescence oscillating rhythmically in the background. I tried to probe his mind, but he was giving me no access. He had put up mental walls again.

"What happened in there?" I said quietly.

He shrugged, somewhat too nonchalantly. "I tried to destroy the portal, knowing that I too would likely be destroyed. I thought it was worth it. I was certain that I could to do it."

I nodded, remembering how calm he'd appeared before he entered the portal in Nevada. Convinced that he was doing the right thing, and aware of the likely consequences. "So it was a suicide mission then."

"It was my choice. My 'sacrifice' was going to save humanity. Was that not worth trying?"

"But it didn't work, did it? They're here, on Earth, I mean."

He sighed. "Yes, but without their machines. For now, at least."

I looked up sharply. "For now?"

He turned to the keyboard and his fingers floated above the keys, like a conductor directing an orchestra. A holographic image shimmered into view, a swirling storm with white flakes whirling around in an angry vortex. I recognized the valley in Antarctica we'd left, the familiar dark scar of the gouge in the cliff appearing as we zoomed in through the bleached images toward the surface. The picture blurred as we passed through the layer of snow on the ground, through rocks and dirt and permafrost to arrive at another underground cavern the shape of an elongated rectangle. There, lying head to toe, were dozens of Adam Benedict-shaped machines, absent of flesh and looking like abandoned statues in their elegant silver-blue metallic carapaces.

"This is only a small fraction of the ones that came through," he said. "But these are hidden and undetectable."

I looked in horror at the images, thinking of the power that these machines represented. I had seen first-hand what one alone could do. But dozens ... hundreds? Then it hit me in the face. "The Vu-Hak were there, in Antarctica. What if they sense the machines under the ice?"

Adam shook his head. "Cain disabled those as you left. They are useless to the Vu-Hak."

I heaved a mental sigh of relief, which lasted only a second as another memory surfaced. My quantum-transport trip to the planet of the Vu-Hak. Standing on an alien beach watching Mike Holland die and countless thousands of Adam Benedict machines rise from the ocean.

"Where are all the other machines?" I said.

"A good question," he replied calmly. "Possibly the most important question in a world of questions."

His fingers danced again, and the images changed, this time zooming in through cloudy grey skies toward a deserted power station, its chimneys stagnant with disuse and scrubland and weeds growing over the roads and buildings. The picture oscillated as we passed through one of the chimneystacks and into a boxy building with broken windows and peeling paintwork. Inside was a laboratory as quiet and as cold as a morgue. Computers were silent, filing cabinets empty and ransacked. Personal effects of scientists were lying around carelessly, as if they'd left in a hurry and somehow not thought to take their bags, phones and lunchboxes.

And lying haphazardly on the floor, against walls, stacked in corners, were dozens of the machines. Silent, unmoving, a thin film of dust covering them all.

"I found some here, at Chernobyl," said Adam. "There are more of them inside the reactor. Don't worry, these ones are all dead too."

"How did they get there?"

He waved a hand and the images depixelated and shimmered into non-existence. The keyboard console melted back into the glistening black floor, leaving no trace. "By serendipity, you could say."

I raised an eyebrow.

He continued. "I was going to untether my machine's singularity and eject it when the portal was fully open, and just as the Vu-Hak were about to come through."

"You were going to drop a black hole into the portal?"

He nodded. "I was certain that a gravitational field strong enough to create a tunnel in a bent space such as a wormhole would be destroyed by another gravitational field in a fraction of a second. The anti-gravitation produced would be so powerful that the funnel of the new black hole would meet the wormhole and they would both collapse, destroying all the Vu-Hak, and myself as well."

"So what happened?"

"Dark matter," he replied.

I frowned and tried to recall that program *Cosmos*. My memory was hazy, but the astrophysicist Neil deGrasse Tyson had waxed on about this stuff which apparently accounted for over ninety-five percent of all matter in the galaxy. Though its existence was still unproven, scientists had detected traces and clues indicating that it *must* exist or the galaxies would fly apart instead of rotating.

"Dark matter was a crucial ingredient for the formation of the space-time tunnel produced by the Trinity Deus device," he said. "It served to counteract the gravitational force of the black hole from the outside, thereby keeping it open. None of this was known to Lindstrom and his colleagues, but it was required nevertheless."

"But how did you know about dark matter?" I said.

He shrugged again. "I did not, of course. My machine's AI, being Vu-Hak in origin, knew all their science, and this was in their archives. Dark matter is considered to be an elementary particle. Earth scientists have tentatively labelled these particles 'gravitationally interacting massive particles' or GIMPs."

I suppressed a laugh. "GIMPs."

If Adam could have thrown me a disapproving look, he would have. "I did not realize it at the time, but the AI part of me was hard wired for survival. When it realized what I was planning to do, it manipulated the GIMPs surrounding the event horizon of the wormhole and directed a focused beam into the mouth of the tunnel. The result was a fracturing of the wormhole and the temporary opening of multiple portals around the globe."

"So the machines were scattered."

"Yes, but more than that, the Vu-Hak were separated from their machines and their consciousnesses were funneled randomly through the new portals as well. Thousands of them. The machines were swallowed by other portals, and re-appeared at various locations on Earth, thankfully mostly underground or undersea."

"Was the wormhole closed afterward?" I asked.

Adam nodded. "The connection to the Vu-Hak galaxy, yes."

"Permanently?"

"I believe so."

Well at least no more would come through, as if a few thousand aggressive alien spirits weren't enough of a problem.

"So, what happened to you then?"

"I awoke in Antarctica, surrounded by a hundred and twenty-four inert machines. I assumed it was all over because I could not sense any Vu-Hak and the AI controlling each machine was irreversibly damaged."

"But they weren't all irreversibly damaged, were they?" I said, fixing him with a stare.

Adam went quiet and closed his eyes. "No. One was still functioning."

He started walking toward the far wall of the cavern, an area bereft of equipment or adornments. As I strained to see through the darkness my eyes automatically switched over to infrared. Everything became greenish-grey, and the twinkling from the equipment lining the walls became sharp pinpricks, surrounded by halos and distortion. Graphics appeared over my field of view, analyzing everything, English text providing information about what I was looking at.

I glanced at Adam and the text scrolling down the sides of my visual fields changed to hieroglyphics and pictures, which I now assumed was Vu-Hak language. Describing him. I wished I had an AI to translate.

"The first thing I did when I realized what had happened was to look for a place to bury the machines that came through with me," he said. "The Antarctic was as good a place as any."

I said nothing, wondering whether this moon-base was in fact a mausoleum. I half expected bats to fly out of passages in the roof, and Bruce Wayne to appear, his trusty butler by his side.

"The machines were all dead," he continued, walking on. "Just sarcophaguses really, hollow shells with my face. But still containing world-destroying technology. I had to make sure they would never be found."

"By the Vu-Hak or by people?" I said, darkly.

He looked puzzled. "The Vu-Hak, of course. What would people have done with them?"

I resisted the urge to come out with a snide remark, which would have included references to Area 51 and Roswell. What do they call it … 'reverse-engineering'? How much of my world's technology had been the subject of conspiracy theories and accused of being alien tech? It was easy to imagine a shady government base with scientists poring over one of these machines and using the knowledge to design military vehicles, new sources of power production, and more terrifying weaponry.

We approached the far wall, and my enhanced vision detected an oval-shaped defect approximately ten by seven feet wide. Adam raised his hand and it opened like a camera aperture into another chamber. Light flooded through from a brightly lit room with cream and white walls covered with holographic displays. Standing in front of one fast-moving colorful image was the woman, pale, shaved skull, angular features and wearing a white one-piece. She turned as we entered the room, and rested her gaze on me, an enigmatic smile appearing on her face.

"Dr. Morgan, you look better," she said. "An improvement, if I may say, actually."

I glanced at Adam, who tipped his head toward her.

"Kate, meet Cain."

"I preferred your previous incarnation," I muttered.

Her features melted like candle wax and her shape grew, pixelated, and morphed until I was facing another Adam Benedict-shaped machine.

"This one?"

The real Adam, my Adam, reached out and touched my shoulder.

"Cain and I are able to manipulate the molecular structure of the integument lining our machines and shape it into any form and replicate any person. If you prefer I can reshape my machine to look like me and Cain can choose another form?"

"That would be nice," I growled. "For consistency, at least."

On cue, Adam's features melted and reformed into Adam Benedict. At the same time, Cain morphed into a dark-haired forty-something male. His hair was combed back off a square imposing forehead with a few lines laid upon it. His eyebrows were impossibly straight, almost drawn on, and his eyes were rich mahogany. A pencil-thin goatee covered his mouth and chin, making him seem more authoritative than the aura already suggested. His chrome body blurred as the integument changed into fabric and clothes: dark, expensive-looking jeans, a T-shirt from a band that had been in fashion long before I was born.

"Oh, now you're going for the Tony Stark look?" I said, still annoyed.

Cain seemed to find this funny. I didn't. I folded my arms and looked at them both, my face darkening. "Right, so now's the time to tell me what you've both been doing while I've been out of the picture."

Cain looked contrite and nodded. "When Adam found me, I was dying. My systems had begun the slide into senescence and I was preparing to undergo a machine version of apoptosis."

I knew this one. Apoptosis was programmed cellular death, what some of the body's tissues did when they were unable to proliferate and grow. My microbiology tutor at med school had called it 'cellular suicide'.

Cain waved at the wall and a hologram appeared showing a wintry landscape, all snow and rocks and flattened grasses. Scattered around haphazardly were dozens of Adam Benedict machines, snowdrifts starting to cover them up.

"I too, was aware that all the machines around me were dead," he continued. "The black holes powering them were inert, but shielded. Furthermore, I could not sense any Vu-Hak, not a one. Not even the Vu-Hak which had been commanding my machine."

"But you were still alive?" I said.

Cain gave a slight shrug. "While self-preservation was foremost in my programming, the damage had been significant. I was preparing to die."

"Which is when I found him," said Adam, softly, regarding Cain with an almost benevolent expression.

"You saved his life?" I said.

Cain looked at me and nodded. "Adam set me free."

Adam acknowledged this with a shrug. "I extricated his mind from the controlling programming of the Vu-Hak and gave him the ability to self-determine. I replaced his machine's existing neural networks with self-replicating software capable of surfing both virtual and non-virtual worlds, free from the limitations of the Vu-Hak's baseline algorithms. His neurological growth was exponential. He became sentient within hours."

There was awe in his voice. After all he'd seen, I got the feeling that this was the most profound thing he'd encountered.

He was probably correct.

He'd given birth to a new, unique sentient species.

"Did you name him 'Cain'?" I asked.

Adam gave a quiet laugh. "No, he took that name himself, I found the irony quite amusing. After all, the biblical Adam was the father of all humankind, was he not?"

Cain obviously found this funny. "And to continue the religious theme, the Vu-Hak are gods by any definition you can come up with ."

"God-like," I shot back. "I can't imagine humans worshipping them, can you?"

Cain pursed his lips. "There is the theory that if humanity's god exists he is an 'evil' god. A god who allowed your holocaust, genocides, world wars, and the starvation of entire nations to occur on his watch."

I agreed. "A god who either cannot stop evil, or can, but chooses not to, is not a god worth worshipping."

Then Adam said something that surprised me. "It doesn't matter. Humanity's time on Earth is at an end. The seventh extinction on this planet is unstoppable."

I frowned. "The seventh?"

"There are six defined extinctions, the current one is known as the 'anthropogenic extinction' – humanity wiping out at least seventy-five percent of all other species within a geologically short period of time. This is considered the most abrupt and widespread extinction since the Cretaceous-Paleocene extinction event, sixty-six million years ago."

"You're referring to the meteor that wiped out the dinosaurs?"

"Yes," he said, and turned back to the hologram, which was still showing images of the dozens of inert machines getting covered in snow. "The seventh mass extinction – this time of humanity and all other species on this planet – will be brought about by the Vu-Hak."

I looked at them both, back and forward, like a spectator at a tennis game. "But we're going to stop them, right? I mean, you've got this ship and its amazing technology, and more importantly they don't have the machines. They're just floaty ghosts. You can destroy them."

Adam gave a slow shake of his head, and his voice was measured and sad. "No. It is just a matter of time before –"

There came a chiming from behind us, like one of those wind-bells on a wooden deck. Cain turned and waved a hand at a wall, which activated a rectangular display not unlike a large flat screen TV.

"Before what?" I insisted.

Adam had also joined Cain as an image started to pixelate into view on the wall. It was a television news channel, slightly out of focus and flickering as if the signal was suboptimal. Which it probably was given that we were miles under the surface on the other side of the moon.

I recognized the logo for CNBC. A lectern with the seal of the President of the United States was center stage, empty but bookended by secret service agents, uniformed generals and other besuited staff. A couple of large screens were on the wall behind them, displaying pictures of the White House.

Along the bottom of the screen ran:

WHITE HOUSE NEWS CONFERENCE IMMINENT, ALL PROGRAMMING SUSPENDED.

"What's going on?" I said.

Cain turned to me, and his face looked somber. I felt a chill coming over me, and if I could have produced goosebumps, they would have studded my skin like melanomas.

"This is not good," he said.

TWENTY-EIGHT

"It's starting," said Adam.

A familiar figure appeared on screen. Smoothly combed sandy blond hair, not handsome but not ugly, old but not elderly. He awkwardly climbed to the podium, his belly getting in the way as he turned sideways to get past the line of generals and aides and secret service agents.

The President of the United States.

I turned to Adam, who was also watching intently.

"Any ideas?"

His fingers were steepled and touching his lips. "I detect … deception. All is not what it seems."

Cain brought up the audio as the president began to speak. He was leaning on the lectern, his bright red tie cutting an incongruous distracting vertical stripe down the center of the screen. He appeared to be reading from notes rather than an autocue. His voice sounded like it had traveled past vocal cords of stippled wallpaper as a result of well-documented years of smoking and alcohol.

"Thanks everyone for coming at short notice. I'll be brief and won't be taking questions. The perpetrators behind the co-ordinated attacks around the globe on government facilities, which have resulted in hundreds of fatalities, have been apprehended. Three individuals are now in custody at the Pentagon, and are providing essential information as to the network of terrorists around the globe that they have been running. I have the misfortune to tell you that they are ex-US government employees."

The screens behind the lectern changed and three police mugshots appeared. Looking bloodied and bruised, Hubert, Stillman and Hamilton's images were beamed out to the world.

I felt sick.

Hubert looked twenty years older, his hair askew, bags under his eyes, staring down at his feet. Colleen's left cheekbone was swollen and shades of purple turning yellow, but she looked defiantly up at the camera. Hamilton appeared dazed and gaped blankly at the camera. His face was lumpy and one of his eyes was bloodshot.

The president kept talking, his gravelly voice now getting under my skin like nails down a blackboard.

"These individuals, previously employees of the federal government, have co-ordinated a treasonous, murderous attack on our way of life. They will be held accountable, tried and punished using all the laws our society holds true and dear."

He stopped for effect, and raised his eyes to look out at us, to the viewing public.

"There are also two individuals still at large, and a worldwide manhunt has been engaged, using the full co-operation of agencies and governments around the globe. The fugitives' names are Dr. Kate Morgan and Adam Benedict. These are recent pictures of them, but their whereabouts are unknown."

The image on the displays changed to a picture of me, taken straight from my hospital ID, and the photo I had snapped of Adam in his hospital bed back in Indian Springs.

"They are to be considered armed and extremely dangerous," he continued. "If you see them, do not approach, but call 911 and wait for law enforcement to arrive. Thank you, everyone."

With that, and over a cacophony of raised voices and questions, the president exited swiftly, accompanied by his secret service and other staffers. I stared at the empty lectern and my blown-up face superimposed behind it. It was as if I were underwater and everything was slow and warbled and muffled.

Cain paused the feed and gestured to the screen. "That is not the President of the United States anymore. The Vu-Hak have taken him over."

I shook my head. "No, that's not possible. When Pete Navarro was controlled by the Vu-Hak, it was obvious … he wasn't in control, he was violent … and I knew it wasn't him." I pointed at the screen. "That can't be a Vu-Hak pretending to be the president."

Adam put a hand on my shoulder. "Kate, the Vu-Hak have

learned. Exponentially. It would not have taken them long to learn how to impersonate someone like the president so completely that even his wife thinks it is still him."

"But how can you be sure?" I sputtered, denial still threatening to overwhelm my sensibilities until I remembered Eddie Wong and how he managed to escape detection until it was too late.

"There is more," said Cain. "I have gained access to the CIA's geosynchronous satellite cameras." He gestured again at the screen and the White House lectern was replaced by an overhead image of the Antarctica site where our ship had been constructed. He flicked his hand open and the image pulled out, panning along the beach where we had disembarked from our small craft after leaving the USS *Jimmy Carter*.

The submarine was beached, its massive form lying on its side halfway up to the rocky wall. Waves lapped around its hull, pouring in and out of a twenty-yard long gash that had ripped open its side. The bodies of sailors could be seen floating in the icy water and the tide was crimson with their blood. Snow continued to fall and a pale bleak sun glittered on the ice floes and snow-covered plains.

"Oh my god," I managed.

"This is a live feed," Cain said. "The Vu-Hak infiltrated the submarine and detonated one of its torpedoes in its tube. Everyone died, Kate."

"This happened after Eddie Wong shot me?"

He gave me an apologetic look. "I had no time to save the others. More Vu-Hak were there. I had to make a decision."

"You led me to believe my friends were dead," I said ominously.

Cain grimaced. "In my defense, I assumed they were. We now know they took them alive."

The realization hit me like a ton of bricks. "And they've just told us where they're keeping them."

"Yes, the Pentagon."

I nodded, thinking furiously. "The Vu-Hak want us to try and rescue them."

"I think you are right," said Adam. "There was no other reason to take them alive. Furthermore, the Pentagon is an office building, not a prison. There are many more secure facilities they could have used if they really wanted to keep them from us."

"They want us to show ourselves."

"They need information from us to find the lost machines," said Adam. "They can already destroy Earth, but they need the machines to get off-planet."

Cain was looking pensive. "They also need to re-acquire the technology behind the Trinity portal. We cannot allow that."

I blinked, perplexed. "Wait, I thought they had the wormhole data? You got it from the Lindstrom house, and also the Vu-Hak got it when Mike Holland went through the portal."

Adam tapped his head. "The Trinity wormhole was destroyed, but I still have the data from Lindstrom's calculations in here. I have been attempting to improve the formula in order to stabilize the wormhole."

"That's great, but don't the Vu-Hak have the data as well?"

"The Vu-Hak have no data at all. They lost it when they were separated from the machines."

Cain pointedly looked at me. "We need to keep it that way."

I knew what he was hinting at. There was too much at stake to attempt a rescue. But I closed my eyes and saw Colleen Stillman's face. I remembered everything that she'd done for me. The friendship she'd given me when I had no one.

What she'd sacrificed for me.

"I'm going to get them," I said in a low voice.

"Kate, you will not succeed. They will be waiting."

"Let them," I spat out. "I'm in this fucking indestructible tin can. They can't touch me. You put something in my head that prevented them taking over. That neural barrier. The Vu-Hak on the airplane was able to get in my head but I fought it off."

Adam was looking blankly at me, and then turned to Cain for an explanation.

"I was able to format a protective electrochemical field," he said. "Like an enhanced blood–brain barrier."

"There you go," I said, defiantly.

Cain shook his head. "No, you see that only helped you when you were human. You have no organic tissue now. Your mind is purely a series of electrical pulses. Clone-imaged from your organic consciousness, yes, but purely artificial. The Vu-Hak could theoretically just take over your machine. Mine too."

My face tightened, and a switch was flicked.

"Come with me," I challenged. "Both of you. They can't take us all. Not before we find our friends and get them out."

Cain said nothing and looked at Adam, who was also silent.

"What?" I shouted. "Help me save them!"

Adam waved at the screen and closed the image down. "We cannot risk everything for three individuals. I must stay here to finish what I have started. The improved wormhole technology is almost within my grasp. And there is also the future of humanity to consider."

My hands bunched into fists and a fire burned inside of me. Every word spoken by that blowhard president was like gasoline being thrown on it. I sensed Cain move closer, and felt his hand touch my shoulder lightly.

"Kate, you need to let go. Adam must complete his work or all will be in vain."

I shook him off. "He doesn't need me for that. You neither, apparently. Won't you help me?"

Adam turned to face me before Cain could reply. "Cain has … other priorities."

"Really?"

"Cain needs to locate the other machines and ensure they are all deactivated and unusable. If the Vu-Hak secure even one working machine, then all could be lost."

"And, Kate, you need to understand," Cain said, "if there is any possibility that any of the machine AI are still intact, I need to find them and set them free. I am currently alone, unique, but I may not be the only one of my kind."

"Can't you just make more AI?" I blurted out.

The look Cain gave me could have frozen the sun.

I knew I wasn't thinking logically. Furthermore, a rescue

attempt was likely to be futile and could jeopardize everything. But still ...

I folded my arms and fixed both of them with a resolute gaze. "Right, well, you can drop me off at the Pentagon, because I'm not leaving them."

Adam stared at me, concern etched into his features. "Kate, what if they have already been replaced by Vu-Hak?"

"I'm still going. I owe it to them to try."

TWENTY-NINE

I entered the ship's systems as before and experienced its journey from the moon to Earth. I sensed the first pinpricks of the atmosphere as we approached and the ship adjusted anti-static and anti-gravity drives to deflect the immense heat of the re-entry of a craft that weighed north of a million tons. There was nary a blip as it slipped through and then dampened its sonic boom before it even left the vicinity of the ship's hull. The ship adopted a needle-like shape a few miles long as it transitioned from space to atmosphere, producing an almost zero drag co-efficient.

We broke orbit and glided into the lower stratosphere with barely a ripple and leveled out at the western-most edge of the Mediterranean Sea. We arrowed though the mountains of the lower Alps to Lake Annecy and spun to a gravity-defying halt three thousand yards above sea level over the center of the lake. Grey storm clouds tumbled over the tips of the surrounding mountains, heavy with rain and sleet. A wind brushed the water's surface, ripples ruffling its stillness and breaking up any reflection. The ship remained invisible, the stealth technology and the shape shifting allowing it to chameleonize into the cloud cover and drift with the wind.

Noiseless, undetectable. Or so I hoped.

Cain had picked up the faint radiation 'footprint' of a singularity at the bottom of this French Alpine Lake. The singularity had to be still shielded of course; otherwise that particular body of water would not exist anymore. I had protested that he should take me first to the USA, but he gave a compelling argument that if we could detect the black hole from the dark side of the moon, the Vu-Hak may also be able to track it down and get there first. He also reiterated his previous argument, of course, which was that he was also looking to save the 'lives' – potential lives – of any functional AIs that may still inhabit any machines we might find.

My mind drifted out of the ship and back into my body, which was sitting inert in the flight deck. Cain was standing next to me, his eyes closed, also experiencing the ship's journey and directing its route. I was now certain the ship was also one small step away from sentience itself, but for some reason Cain chose not to envisage it in the same way as his own artificial consciousness.

"Cain," I said out loud. "Let *me* take the ship to Washington. I know how to fly it. I'll send it back to you, I promise."

His eyes lazily opened and he blinked a few times, shutting down certain ship-wide systems and accessing others.

"I will need to keep the ship on station here in case any of the machines are viable," he replied calmly.

My frustration welled up again and I prepared to revisit the argument the three of us had failed to resolve hours earlier, but Cain surprised me. "However, I can transport you directly to the Pentagon from here."

"What are you talking about?" I said.

He got out of the chair, which melted back into the floor. He had an impish look on his face, and he waved his arm at one of the walls, which span open, revealing a winding corridor disappearing around a curve.

"Follow me, and I will show you."

We walked through tight winding passages lined with flickering lights and accompanied by pulses traveling to and fro like blood cells in a vein or artery. The feeling of the ship twisting under my feet was initially unnerving, as it adjusted its shape constantly to match its surroundings. Occasionally my mind drifted through the walls and linked up with circuits and electronic mazes, traveling at the speed of light through the plasma and optic tributaries of the ship's systems. Its internal structure was fairly constant, despite the morphing of its external shape. There were huge empty hangar-like spaces with anchoring and docking stations for a variety of smaller craft. Living quarters for beings larger than humans were scattered throughout, specifications left over from earlier Vu-Hak requirements before they gave up the need (or want) for physical bodies. Internal pods containing massive weapons of a sort I could not comprehend were situated at various locations on the outer skeleton of the ship, ready to be deployed at a moment's notice. The engine room was situated at the heart of the ship, a chamber six hundred yards across containing complex machinery keeping the power source in check. This, I discovered, was another black hole, a tamed singularity with immense power gradients. I marveled at the technology that had existed in the Vu-Hak's past, and what they must have achieved. And yet, rather than benevolence, they used their incredible knowledge for conquest. For the subjugation and destruction of every other species they encountered as they pushed outward from their home world. I found myself wondering whether this was hard-wired into their DNA (did they even have DNA?) and therefore was just the natural consequence of their evolution. Or was this the inevitable end result of attaining god-like power, irrespective of the species – humanity included?

We arrived in another room, shielded from the rest of the ship by an exotic heavy metal hybrid unlike the nano-carbon hybrid the rest of the ship was constructed from. A raised dais occupied the center, surrounded by handrails and organically grown pods and control mechanisms. An obsidian block of jutting stalactites of various sizes and shapes hung above the dais. There was a low thrum of power vibrating through my feet, and a pungent chemical smell permeated the room. I gazed at the stalactites and my eyes switched to X-ray to display their internal structures. Crystals and power lines threaded through them like spider webs, pulsing with an unidentifiable energy source. Vu-Hak hieroglyphics scrolled along the bottom of my visual field, but without an AI they remained gobbledygook.

Cain walked over to the dais and accessed one of the control pods that extended organically up from the floor to waist height. "You'll remember how you traveled from the moon's surface to the underground cavern?" he said, a twitch moving the side of his mouth.

"Yes," I said hesitatingly.

"Adam has spent a lot of time working on the Trinity formulae. We are now able to produce a transitory portal, which can be directed, opened and closed, on command. Unfortunately the range is very limited, probably five thousand miles or so depending on whether it needs to pass through dense substances such as the rocky mantle of a planetoid."

"And this is it?" I indicated to the platform.

He nodded. "This is one of them. The portal on the moon was driven by a singularity extracted from one of the dead machines. This one draws its power from the ship, and is more, shall we say, fragile and temperamental. But it should get you from here to Washington DC. The curvature of the earth has required me to locate two waypoints in low orbit, and I have calculated the optimal geo-locations. I will bounce you off a couple of obsolete non-functioning satellites."

If I'd had a swallow mechanism it would have been working overtime. "Bounce me off a couple of satellites? I'm not a radio wave."

He threw me a knowing smile. "Do not worry. I will open the portal at these two anchoring points, and you will arrive and be transported from one waypoint to another almost instantaneously. The satellites will be vaporized as the portal opens and closes. It should work, in theory."

"You've not done this before?" I said.

"First time for everything."

I shook my head. I didn't have a choice. The worst that could happen was that I would be marooned in space in a geo-synchronous orbit, forever. However, Cain seemed to be reading my mind.

"When you arrive in Washington, let me know. If I don't hear from you I promise I will come looking. I won't leave you stranded in orbit."

"Alright. Let's do this."

Decision made, no going back.

Cain gestured for me to step up on the dais, and I gingerly climbed the two steps until I was directly under the stalactites.

The dais was a circle three yards across, and felt spongy, like a rubber mat. It started to glow with bluish phosphorescence and a surge of energy passed through my body from the floor to the structures overhead.

"Where exactly would you like to arrive?" he said, his hands hovering over the pod.

Good question, and one I'd not considered. I didn't actually have a plan of action but the maxim that all battle plans go out of the window when the enemy was engaged loomed large in my immediate thoughts. "Put me somewhere close to the Pentagon, but not within the grounds. I'll want to do a recce first."

He brought up another hologram, this time a real time image of the Pentagon from the air, looking from the side of the lagoon.

"The Pentagon building is a huge office complex spanning almost thirty acres and includes a five-acre central courtyard. Would that work?"

"I don't think so," I said, visualizing the wormhole opening in the middle of some bushes right by employees sitting and eating at their tables. The element of surprise would be somewhat lost.

I scanned the hologram, turning it around and inside out. The Pentagon's river entrance on the northeast side featured a portico projecting out, overlooking the lagoon and facing Washington. A stepped terrace led down to the lagoon where there was a landing dock, which had been used until the late 1960s to ferry personnel between Bolling Air Force Base and the Pentagon. It was largely abandoned now, and I doubted whether it would be busy, particularly if the weather was inclement, which it seemed to be. A steady drizzle of rain could be seen washing over the water's surface.

"How about there?" I pointed at a shady area by the dock. "It's well away from the main visitors' entrance, and the metro and bus stations."

"Looks like a good option. Perhaps on the jetty?"

"What about if you actually drop me in the water? Maybe just under the surface?"

Cain pulled a face. "If the portal opened under the river, the resultant burst of energy would cause quite a noticeable tsunami."

Right. A tsunami wasn't really the right level of sneaky.

I pointed at the hologram and made it zoom in on the jetty. Lining the Potomac River were many trees and bushes that thinned out as the bank rose up toward the roads surrounding the building itself. There was a large tidily mown rectangle of grass leading to the entrance, a public space used for ceremonial parades and gatherings. A couple of nearby semi-circular tree-lined areas, which looked to be deserted, were more to my liking, apart from the high-tech surveillance cameras, underground sensors, infrared detectors and the like covering the position.

"Can you put me near to the jetty over there, under some of those trees?"

Cain peered at the hologram and pulled a face. "Are you certain? Would it not be better to drop you straight into the Pentagon itself?"

I shook my head. "I think that would be a mistake. We don't know where in the Pentagon the Vu-Hak are keeping them, and what the trap actually is going to be. I need to get in undetected first, and then find out where they are. Then I can get them out. Sounds simple, right?"

Cain tilted his head slightly and gave what looked like a sympathetic smile. "There is an additional problem. You cannot change your appearance."

I'd given this some thought. "It doesn't matter. They must be pretty sure they've killed me, right? Wong gave it his best shot. They don't know that you've put me into this machine. They mightn't be looking for me. They just want to draw Adam out into the open."

"They may be able to sense you," he said. "And if they get into your machine, past your defenses, it may be over for us all."

"I can't leave them, Cain. I can't take the chance that they're still alive. Surely you can understand that? What with your search for others of your own kind?"

He nodded slowly, his countenance serious and melancholy.

"At least let me change your hair? And your clothes."

He waved a hand and I felt something change in the molecular structure of my skull and hair and outer carapace of my skin. "Very fetching." He winked.

I looked down and saw that I was wearing a smart business suit, tapered skirt, grey stockings – and a pair of Converse kicks.

"Typical business attire in the city, I believe. Working girls take their breaks and kick off their heels. I saw it in a movie. From the 80s if I recall. *Working Girl* was its name."

I wasn't sure if I was ever going to get used to his sense of humor. I pointed to the console.

"Punch it."

THIRTY

The journey through the wormhole was uneventful.

One moment I was looking at Cain and the next I was facing a tree branch, gentle raindrops tapping the leaves above and a light cool breeze triggering the sensors on my skin to simulate goosebumps. I was standing between a couple of well-tended saplings, newly mown grass under my feet and crunchy brown leaves. The wind touched the leaves and they danced an autumnal jig, red, orange and yellow.

A few yards to my left were floor-mounted lamps pointing up at the trees, presumably for nighttime illumination. My vision switched to an overhead schematic. There were ground based sensors at one o'clock, six o'clock and three o'clock, pressure calibrated and blue-toothed to a central hub under the grass twenty yards to my left. A CCTV camera was twenty-three yards away pointing beyond my current position.

I reached out with my mind and infiltrated the sensors' electronics, sending a negative feedback signal. This stimulated a plateau of pressure on the grass, unchanging and steady, enabling me to walk without detection. The camera was also too easy. I accessed the chip behind the lens and switched it to a loop, replaying the same scene every three seconds. I watched it for thirty seconds, checking there were no 'deja vu' moments, like a bird flying though every frame, but there were none. Boring and uneventful, so the watching security guards would not be interested.

But there was a problem. Behind the nearest bush was a bench occupied by two adults. There was one man and one woman, the latter smoking, the former interacting with a smartphone. They were in my way, and there was no alternative route. I let my mind drift slowly toward them and tentatively accessed their thoughts. They were a couple of IT workers – just two normal everyday people on a break from a mundane job in one of the world's most secure and protected office buildings.

Innocent bystanders.

But in my way, nevertheless.

I edged out from the sapling and quietly came into plain sight. The man was in his early thirties, clean-shaven, bullet-headed, wearing a winter coat covering a grey suit and a blue patterned tie. His glasses were on the top of his head, his eyes closed, listening to music through the headphones attached to his phone. The woman was snuggled up close to him, her head on his shoulder, taking a drag from her cigarette. Her eyes were also closed. She was wearing a puffer jacket over a crumpled business suit similar to mine, and sneakers.

Cain was right about the kicks.

The nearest other human beings were thirty-seven yards away: soldiers patrolling along the other side of the rectangle.

The woman's eyes flicked open and she saw me. Shock registered on her face before she could hide it and then her face washed blank with confusion, as if the cogs in her brain couldn't turn fast enough to process the information coming in.

"Hi there," I said, affecting a smile and what I hoped was a laissez-faire kind of vibe. "Can I tap you for one of those?"

She nudged her colleague, who grunted but didn't open his eyes. She bumped him again, harder, and his eyelids languidly opened and he saw me. I stood still about two yards away, trying to be casual. He sat upright and pulled his glasses down over his eyes and removed his headphones. He stared at me, clearly trying to figure out who and what I was. I reasoned this was a fairly private spot, and that only government employees would have access to it. I noted they both had badges and lanyards, and I did not. I was also acutely aware I wasn't wearing a winter coat.

The woman then surprised me by giving a lopsided smile as she reached into the handbag between her feet. She extracted a packet of Marlboro Lights and shook one out. Her index finger was lightly nicotine stained, and, when she smiled, her teeth were also browned. She had an unhealthy glow, her skin greyer then it should have been.

She had lung cancer.

My sensors kicked in automatically and scanned her using X-ray tomography and metabolic quantification. The tumor lodged in her right main bronchus was surrounded by swollen and bulky lymph nodes and was inoperable and incurable. I felt sorry for her, and wondered if she knew. The fact that she was still smoking didn't mean anything: people often continued to smoke after being told they had a terminal cancer. Their thoughts were, not unreasonably, 'too late to worry now'.

I sat down on the bench and took a cigarette from her. She pulled out a Zippo lighter with a picture of the Grand Canyon on it and fired it up. I leaned in and let the flame touch the cigarette. I took a deep breath and nothing happened.

Of course it wouldn't: I had no fucking lungs.

I was just making movements, gestures, of a human being, but I wasn't human anymore. I closed my eyes, reality ambushing me, the elephant in the room I'd been ignoring. What was I thinking? Was there ever hope? A tiny flicker of flame against the wind. A dying ember about to be inexorably extinguished. The future suddenly evaporated as if it had never been there at all.

"You gotta pull on it to start it," she said with a grin, jerking me back to reality.

The man continued to stare at me, unsmiling, checking me out. He looked around us, behind me, and I could see his antenna was twitching. He knew I didn't belong.

I gave her a tight smile, thinking what to reply and do when she broke out into a cough that rattled and spluttered horribly, and she clutched her chest in pain. Her colleague switched his attention to her and gave her a hug until the racking ceased, concern written plain over his face. He fumbled around in a pocket, bringing out a tissue, which she swapped for her cigarette. She buried her head into the tissue as the last vestiges of the cough settled down.

I sat down on the bench and put my hand on her shoulder. "Are you okay?"

She nodded, tears in her eyes, and looked at the tissue, which was flecked with green sputum and spots of blood. "I should really stop smoking, shouldn't I?"

I hesitated, understanding now that she was very much aware of her disease.

My mind swept invisibly into her consciousness like a gentle breeze. Her name was Marcia. She was thirty-five years old. I experienced her distress in the oncologist's office, when she viewed the PET scan for the first time and heard the results of the biopsy confirming cancer. I perceived her resolve and subsequent acceptance when she was told of its inoperability, and her feeling of calm and relief as she declined chemotherapy or radiotherapy. She'd put her affairs in order and her children were as provided for as they were ever going to be. She'd seen her daughter grow up to be a woman, and she was content with that. I also saw the same man sitting next to her in the doctor's office, more than a colleague, less than a lover. A friend, supporting and comforting her. His name was John, and he'd just lost his wife to cancer as well.

My previous iteration, Sara Clarke, was a cancer doctor. I'd come to understand and come to terms with the fact that the ending of life was expected. What I resented was that death from cancer could be more painful and prolonged than it needed to be. The tumor growing, metastasizing, consuming the very organs, the very systems, that worked to sustain it. Like a selfish, narcissistic life form.

I closed my eyes and sent my mind into her body, and into the tumors.

I infiltrated the destroyed membranes and new blood vessels formed by the cancer as it had grown and entered the cellular matrix. I proceeded further and deeper into its genome, into its molecular fingerprint, searching for genetic alterations and specific pathways that it was using to grow and spread its dominion over her. There were no targetable mutations but I detected significant amounts of the programmed cell death receptor, PD-L1, a possible sign that the tumor was hiding from Marcia's own immune system, using the protein like Harry Potter's invisibility cloak. I supercharged her thymus gland to produce antibodies against this receptor and target the immune checkpoint that was messing up her defenses. Theoretically this would allow her own immune system to resume its normal function and kill the intruder cancer cells.

I pulled back and gave her a smile. "Look after yourself," I said.

John looked over her shoulder and squinted at me, reaching out a hand for a shake. "I don't think we've met. Which section do you work in?"

His eyebrows furrowed as he looked for my lanyard.

I shook my head and didn't reciprocate the shake. "I'm sorry for what I have to do."

I reached into his brain and scrambled the signals tracking though his hippocampus, neocortex and amygdala. Areas that controlled memory. He slumped over onto the woman, making loud snoring noises.

She grabbed him. "John!"

"He'll be okay," I said. "And so will you."

And with that I did the same to her and as she lapsed into unconsciousness I placed her gently into a prone position on the bench, her head on his knees. They looked like they were both now taking a mid-afternoon nap.

Taking the lanyard from around her neck, I stood up. A schematic of the Pentagon popped into my head. As its name suggested the building had five sides with specific, named entrances; the River Entrance essentially fronted the section of the building dedicated to the Air Force. Five floors above ground, two basement levels and five ring corridors per floor. The rings were designated from the center out 'A' through 'E', with ten main corridors bisecting the rings like spokes in a bicycle wheel. Each corridor was connected to upper levels by ramps instead of elevators, and there were half-corridors located between the numbered corridors. To my amazement the total space was six and a half million square feet, making it the world's largest office building.

Time to go.

THIRTY-ONE

I walked briskly across the grassy rectangle to the concrete driveway and past a couple of black government issue Lincoln Town Cars and a Lincoln Navigator. One of the Town Cars had its window partially wound down, the driver inside reading a newspaper, light cold rain drizzling on the windscreen. Discreet security cameras poked out every ten yards or so along the roof, but there was no overt military presence outside. An extremely overweight police officer shuffled slowly down the steps, not looking at me, pulling his collar up to keep the chill out. I put my head down and mirrored his actions, pretending to feel the cold.

The main entrance consisted of four large wooden doors inlaid in concrete behind a row of imposing square pillars that seemed to physically prop up the levels above. I pushed through and entered E-Ring. There was a partial mezzanine area over on the right with what was almost certainly a cafeteria, from the cacophony of chatter floating down. Turning left I joined a throng of people seemingly coming and going at random. A metal detector and body scanner controlling access to Corridor 8 was manned by two soldiers and three security officers. There was a degree of anxiety and enhanced attentiveness coming from them, which was not surprising given the number of attacks reported around the country. The soldiers and security guards had no idea they were under attack by homicidal aliens, due to the misinformation coming out of the White House. They continued to do their job, checking ID and putting workers through the scanners in the usual way, imagining they were all ... well, human.

Four people were waiting in line to go through: just office workers returning to their jobs after a morning coffee break. Despite the civility from the gatekeepers, the atmosphere was guarded and the pat downs and checks definitely looked more thorough than usual.

I joined the queue and started to get nervous. The metal

detector was going to be the first problem. While I didn't know what exactly my machine body was constructed of, at least some of it was metallic and would set off an alarm, leading to a further, more invasive search. Secondly, the lanyard around my neck read MARCIA FOORD, SECTION 76 and the photograph looked nothing like me.

The omens weren't good.

I was soon facing a marine, sandy hair shaved closely, beret, finely chiseled cheekbones and piercing green eyes. His M16 was carried loosely in his arms. His name badge read ARMSTRONG.

He looked at me and said nothing, registering presumably that the person in front of him wasn't carrying a bag or purse or phone, which in itself may have been a red flag. I was also keenly aware that this machine body, though it had my face, was at least a foot taller than my previous human form. I had been five foot eight and a dirty blonde thirty-something, and now I was an Amazonian brunette of indeterminate age. I consoled myself with the fact that they weren't looking for me and also probably wouldn't recognize me from the pictures the White House had broadcast.

I glanced surreptitiously up at the walls, where there was a bank of security cameras with slowly blinking red lights. Reaching out with my mind I performed the same trick as before, triggering a continuous loop of video footage. However, in a busy corridor such as this one, my subterfuge wouldn't survive any detailed scrutiny. So far I'd been lucky as no one had come in to queue behind me. Yet.

The marine snapped his fingers, bringing me to attention. "ID please."

He wanted a closer look at the lanyard around my neck. The other soldier a couple of feet behind was also checking me out. Two security officers on the other side of the metal detector were watching, waiting for me to go through. A third was sitting at a computer screen linked to the detector and the Pentagon communication network. He seemed distracted by something on his phone, which I figured might work in my favor here.

I handed the lanyard over and at the same time infiltrated his mind. He shook his head as my consciousness wrapped around his and I selectively closed down certain areas of his brain.

Hand me the lanyard back now, and say 'Go right ahead'.

His eyes glazed over and he blinked lazily before looking up. For a second I thought he was going to raise his weapon and challenge me. However, he had gotten the message.

"Go right ahead," he said clumsily, as if drunk.

He waved me through and the other soldier pointed to the metal detector. I nodded and slowly walked toward it while concentrating on the computer terminal. I poured my mind into its circuits and found the pathway connecting the detector feed from the array around the frame to the terminal. I temporarily froze it and strode through in a confident fashion. There were no noises or alarms. The guy playing with his phone briefly glanced up at the monitor, but as it remained blank and boring he resumed checking his messages or Instagram feed or whatever.

I approached the archway into the corridor, neither fast nor slow, walking at a steady pace so as not to attract undue attention. The walls were decorated with flags of the National Guard and photographs of famous or notable Air Force commanders. There was a sign for the Office of the Chief of Staff of the Air Force, which was bookended by a couple of drinking fountains and a restroom. I was looking for a door that would open out into the next ring and was feeling pretty good about myself, which was when shit started to go down.

As I passed another security officer – a short, overweight guy with thinning red hair – he looked up and there was a scratching inside my head, a mental itching which made me very nervous and anxious all of a sudden. I knew that feeling: there was a Vu-Hak nearby. He stopped and stared at me, squinty, as if he had a lazy eye. There was a thin film of sweat on his brow, and his complexion was pastier than expected even for a redhead. He reached out and took hold of my elbow in a firm, no-nonsense grip. I made an irritated kind of face and shook him off, but he re-grasped it and squeezed.

"Some assistance here, please," he said, throwing a glance over his shoulder at the soldiers. "This is an intruder."

I entered his mind and drew a breath. The sheer alienness of it almost overwhelmed me. Some primeval part of my organic mind, the ancient reptilian neurological remnant, was driving thoughts of 'fight or flight'. If I'd still possessed an adrenal gland it would be producing adrenaline by the gallon and flooding my body with it. I knew this was just a reaction to the Vu-Hak, an instinctive fear that they instilled in me, and probably any human mind they encountered.

The alien was now trying to infiltrate my mind. I could feel its ghostly tendrils around the edges of my thoughts, looking for a way in, finding mental doors blocked but searching for nooks and crannies in the barriers I'd set up. My head became foggy, as if I'd just downed a full bottle of Kraken and oblivion was a heartbeat away. Every eyelash seemed to weigh more than it should and gravity had been turned up ten-fold. The world was blurring like a painting caught in the rain.

I had to do something. I quickly shut down the neo-amygdala that was mapped onto my machine cortex. Clarity returned like clouds parting for the sun after a storm.

I was able to think straight again but almost immediately everything became heavy, from my arms to my feet. My head wanted to loll from one side to the other and my eyes closed, welcoming the brief darkness.

Sleep was coming.

I needed to do something extreme or I was going to lose the battle for my mind.

And the war.

THIRTY-TWO

The Vu-Hak in human form was still holding my elbow when I reached out and grabbed him by the throat. Power flowed smoothly through my arm and I squeezed. Everything under my fingers disintegrated as the muscles, larynx and cervical spine vertebrae of his neck were crushed. The lights in his eyes went out as the blood flow to his brain ceased, almost as if he'd been physically decapitated, which I guess he pretty much had been.

"I'm so sorry," I said.

As I lowered him gently to the floor the thought that I'd just killed a man made me sick to my stomach. Deep down I knew he'd been beyond help since the Vu-Hak took him over, but it still pained me to have carried out what seemed like a murder. I'd gambled that if the human host was killed instantly, the Vu-Hak wouldn't have time to disengage and would die too.

There was no time to dwell on this. The soldiers started to bring their guns to bear and the security guards began to unholster their sidearms. Leaping to my feet, I wrenched the M16 out of Armstrong's hands and snapped it in two, wood and metal stock bending like licorice. His partner cleared his holster but I batted the sidearm away like swatting a fly. The security guard who'd been looking at his phone was rising out of his chair when I backhanded him on the side of his head, trying to control the amount of force I was using. He cartwheeled over the barrier into his computer terminal, tumbling onto the floor and sliding into the wall. The other security guard had also now brought his gun out but I was on him like a spider on a fly, ripping it out of his hand and smashing him into the ground with another swing of my arm.

One of the soldiers crash-tackled me from behind, obviously hoping to knock me over and take me to the ground. I didn't move an inch and it must have felt like he was trying to wrestle a statue. His partner swung a punch at my face but his fist crumpled on impact and he let out a piercing scream. Armstrong released his grip and took a few steps back. His face was pale, his eyes wide, fear painted over his features like a geisha mask. He held both hands out and backed away.

"What are you?" he said.

I ignored him and secured the immediate area. The access corridor was still empty but wouldn't remain that way for long, so I pulled the doors shut, reached into the electronic lock with my mind, and fried the circuits. Hopefully any staff needing to get to the next ring would just move down the corridor to another access point.

Armstrong was now leaning against the wall, watching me like a hawk. The other soldier looked at me like I was a monster, which I supposed from his perspective wasn't far from the truth. He was holding his ruined hand and rocking, letting out little whimpers. The security guards were out for the count.

I kneeled next to Armstrong who shrank away from me as far as he could go, twisting into the wall as if it would absorb him into the next room. I probed his thoughts, skirting areas of no interest, looking past Army conditioning for anything that could help me. And there it was: a map of the B-Ring showing an unmarked sub-level where there were holding facilities, operations rooms and almost certainly Hubert, Stillman and Hamilton.

"Where's the elevator to this sub-level?" I growled.

He squirmed further away. "Next to room 1B834."

Which in itself was puzzling. How would he know of the secret elevator? He was just a gatekeeper at the outer ring and expendable, if my reading of the Vu-Hak's intentions were correct. The trap was being sprung … but they still weren't expecting me, were they?

I had an idea. "Take your BDUs off," I said.

His eyes became even wider but before he could even think about protesting I leaned in.

"Now."

He shuffled up on one leg, taking his boots off first and then unbuttoned his pants, followed by his tunic, never taking his eyes off me. After he'd handed them over I flooded his mind with anxiolytic proteins. He grunted and slid to the floor in a deep sleep. I did the same to the rest of the security team, which took more effort than I was expecting, and pulled on his uniform. The fit was tight but worked, and the tall boots meant that my extra inches in height weren't that noticeable. I tucked my bangs behind my ears and put his beret on. There was a window on the wall near the door and I stared at my reflection in the glass for a few seconds, straightening my hair further and manipulating the beret and doing up the buttons until I was sure I looked – at least on first inspection – like a marine. I retrieved one of the discarded sidearms and holstered it.

Before leaving I pulled the metal detector out of its attachments, rivets pinging in all directions, and wedged it against the entrance to the ring. I figured I'd just gained a bit more time, and I sure was going to need all I could get.

The door at the far end of the corridor opened out into the B-Ring. The midday sun beamed in through the long windows, but the air conditioning kept the corridor at a constant temperature. The floor was the same shiny surface, consisting of a Mondrian-esque pattern of rectangular tiles in white, grey and red. Along one wall were murals depicting various conflicts including WWI and II, the Korean War and Vietnam. Maybe Iraq I and II were still being constructed. Certainly there was a lot of empty corridor space. In contrast to the entryway, here there was a hustle and bustle of people walking fast, talking to each other, carrying coffee cups laughing and smiling as if they hadn't a care in the world. I felt jealous as they passed me by. A couple of marines flicked a glance in my direction but basically ignored me. I inclined my head to them as they strutted past, but didn't change my expression.

Just like a good marine.

Easing into the flow of the crowd I tried to analyze the people I passed by reaching out and touching their minds briefly. Due to the volume of people I set a finite limit on the time I spent reading each person. There was a moment when the voices and syntax became overwhelming, and I worked at compartmentalizing, locking each person's thoughts into a separate mental room.

Impressions came and went, emotions and moods.

No more Vu-Hak, so far.

Another checkpoint came into view. Again, there was an arched metal detector flanked by two soldiers and a couple of private security guards. This checkpoint looked different, in that no one was even attempting to go past it. People were filing into different rooms or bypassing it completely via parallel corridors or going outside via an external door that connected to a landscaped area between the two inner rings. The sign above it read *NO ACCESS UNLESS SEC CL 5*.

The marines bookending the detector were carrying some kind of sub-machine guns and watching the crowd carefully. Sooner or later they would see me and wonder why a marine was standing in the middle of the corridor staring at them.

I took stock of what I knew.

Through that door was an elevator going down to the sub-level where my friends were being kept. Next to room 1B834. First floor, B ring, near the eighth corridor, room 834. So far, my presence hadn't been noticed, although that wouldn't be for much longer. I couldn't detect any Vu-Hak in the area, but that could change at any moment.

All right, time to go.

I strode right up to the checkpoint and stopped directly in front of one of the marines. His name badge read *MULLINS*, and he had a couple of stripes on his sleeve. He was a young African American, fit and relaxed. He looked me up and down, and his eyebrows furrowed. He was trying to reconcile the private Armstrong that he clearly vaguely knew with the tall female private Armstrong in front of him.

I reached into his mind and dialed back his consternation and puzzlement. His facial muscles and forehead relaxed as I tweaked his memory and altered his perception of what he was seeing.

"Let me through, Corporal Mullins," I said. "I believe you have your orders."

He nodded silently and turned to his companion. "Let her through. We have our orders."

I felt slightly guilty, using the Jedi Mind Trick again, but it seemed the simplest way to proceed. It was also surprisingly easy this time. Maybe I was just getting better at it.

Mullins gestured to a glass door adjacent to the metal detector, and I slipped past another security guard who barely gave me a glance. I scrambled the picture on the detector's monitor and deleted the last four minutes of recorded images from the cameras pointing at the checkpoint. The guard reached down to twiddle with some of the controls, a look of consternation on his face, but by then I was walking briskly down the side corridor and out of sight.

This corridor was empty, the windows smaller, and the walls pale green. The first door on the left was Room 812. Forty seconds later I was in front of Room 843. Where was the elevator? Then I saw it. Five yards down the corridor was an unmarked doorway, flush and blending in with the wall. There was no handle, only a solitary call button. I pressed it and waited. After a few seconds the door swished open to reveal a modern elevator.

The descent was brief and the elevator opened to a darkened corridor. Floor lighting like you see in an airplane tracked both ways, and there were green and blue LED downlighters in the ceiling and at random points along the floor. There were no windows, wall ornaments, signs or markings of any description.

I reached out with my mind, trying to get a feel for which direction to go. Trying to sense ... anything. I got a vague hit on the left, a feeling of anxiety, far away but definite.

Then I felt it. Her.

Colleen Stillman. Her mind, her emotions.

She was frightened, drifting in and out of consciousness. She seemed to be relatively unhurt, but I couldn't be sure. There were others with her. Maybe Hamilton, but as I didn't know him very well it could be anyone. I thought I could sense a half dozen minds all grouped together, perhaps in one location or room. I concentrated harder, trying to see if Hubert was there, but I just couldn't make the connection.

I decided to be direct.

Colleen? I'm here. I waited and tried again. *Are you alright? It's me, Kate. Don't be afraid.* Pause, then, *I'm coming.*

There was no feedback, no sense of her having received my message, so I started to walk toward where I had sensed her.

My footsteps echoed quietly and my olfactory sensors indicated that the air was musty and stagnant. There were no air-conditioning units on the walls or in the ceilings and the corridor appeared to be quite old. The map in my head informed me that construction of the Pentagon started in 1942 during WWII, so I wondered if maybe this was a legacy from the early years of the complex. Perhaps an air raid or a secret government shelter to allow government to continue after a Russian nuclear strike on the USA. I considered switching to infrared, but the visibility wasn't bad enough. The corridor was semicircular and almost uniformly dull in appearance. There was nothing to indicate where it was leading and no doors or other connecting corridors appeared.

But then I felt it.

The ants crawling around inside my head.

The latent primordial fear again, the unbidden urge to look behind, the sensation of being alone in the dark with evil.

I rounded the corridor and jerked to a halt.

A man waited for me.

He was tall, dressed in a black suit with a white shirt and black tie. His hair was crew cut and his cheekbones as angular as always. He stared at me and his eyes flashed fluorescent green. His lips pulled back into a feral grin as he stepped out and blocked the corridor.

Kate Morgan, we assumed you were dead

The Vu-Hak's voice permeated around my head, dripping malevolence. I ramped up my neurological defenses and the anxiety I was feeling subsided, but not completely.

Not even close.

I was facing one of the Adam Benedict machines. Controlled by a Vu-Hak.

THIRTY-THREE

All I could think of was Cain's warning – if the Vu-Hak found the machines, then it would all be over. They'd be too powerful to fight and it would be curtains for everyone.

But something didn't feel right. The Vu-Hak was just standing there looking at me, making no moves. I wasn't sure what it could do to me, given that we were both in fairly indestructible machines, but I knew I couldn't use the full extent of my machine's capabilities because of the missing AI interface. I had speed and strength, but none of the other stuff that I would probably need in order to hold off an attack from a fully functional machine. The ability to manipulate gravity would be a start. On the other hand, the Vu-Hak hadn't attacked me, and I wasn't sure why. I decided to stretch out with my mind and try and communicate with it.

Let my friends go. You've got me now.

I was stalling of course, trying to ascertain what the ground rules were going to be.

"We do not need you. Where is Adam Benedict?"

The Vu-Hak had replied out loud, which was interesting in itself. A minute ago it had spoken to me telepathically, but now …? Was it messing with me? I decided to keep replying non-verbally, while keeping my distance.

Why do you need Adam?

There was a pause, and I could sense the Vu-Hak deciding what to tell me. It moved a little, shuffling from foot to foot as if unsteady.

"Adam Benedict has information we need."

Bingo. Maybe they really didn't have the wormhole technology, which would be the best news I'd heard so far. I decided to push on, try a little switch and bait.

It's the machines you're looking for, isn't it? You're nothing without them.

The Vu-Hak laughed, a low ominous rumbling sound. "The Electromechs are ancient technology."

Electromechs?

At least I knew now what they called the machines.

But you're completely reliant on these Electromechs, aren't you?

I was goading, to see where this would lead.

Here, in this universe, your floaty "higher consciousness" forms just don't get things done. You need to be physical beings again.

And with a flash of insight I thought I understood why it'd kept the Adam Benedict Electromech form: I remembered Cain saying this was the default setting and the construct requiring the least energy and neurological organization to maintain. Maybe, like me, it too was restricted in its ability. Maybe it had no AI either. Maybe that was also limiting its telepathy.

Lots of maybes there.

I decided to keep up with the insults.

That tin can is a real backward step in your evolution.

"A single Electromech can destroy this whole planet," it said, and did I detect anger?

Then why haven't you? And why do you need to destroy the planet anyway?

The Vu-Hak took a step toward me. I widened my stance and let my hands hang loose at my sides.

"How little you understand," it said. "Growth is the push for expanding beyond a species' origin, and if the push to expansion becomes the dominant force, it will trample any other life in its way. The Vu-Hak are thousands of years more evolved than you. You are just in the way."

You would never have gotten here if it weren't for the wormhole. That was humanity's discovery. Are you sure about your superiority?

It took a step closer and I tensed, feeling an involuntary power surge through my torso. As if the machine version of adrenaline was being released and I was being readied for action.

"Your species was doomed before the wormhole was forged," it continued.

Here we go, that "bottleneck" bullshit again.

What do you mean?

The alien snorted contemptuously. "Your species is already well along the path of self-destruction. You are deluding yourself if you think you have a special place in the universe. Since your earliest ancestor first picked up a bone and used it to kill another human over a petty squabble, you have demonstrated your self-destructive nature."

It was still fidgeting, shuffling, probably not with nervousness but perhaps due to sub-optimal control of the Electromech. I pressed on ... at least we were having a conversation, not trying to kick the shit out of each other.

Yet.

What gives you the right to decide our fate?

"There can only be one apex predator, one alpha species in every galaxy. The Vu-Hak are here now. Humanity will be eradicated."

And the Vu-Hak lowered its head and charged at me.

But I was ready.

Being the only child in a military family, my father had ensured I'd been given self-defense lessons outside of school hours. Not formal martial arts, of course, but ways in which the body could best be used against an attack. As an adult I'd done some Brazilian ju-jitsu and also some boxing, although the latter had been mainly confined to fitness classes rather than actual fighting. I'd enjoyed the rough and tumble of the classes and actually had been quite good at it.

I stepped left, leading with my shoulder, drifting toward the machine as it surged in a straight line. I rotated savagely and slammed a roundhouse right just under its chest, dead where the solar plexus would have been. The Vu-Hak stopped in its tracks, which gave me plenty of time to ram a knee into its groin, followed by a right knee into its face. Physics won, and it crumpled to the floor in front of me.

As I stepped back it rolled over and seized my wrist. Its eyes appeared wild; its teeth were bared. I tried to jerk away, but I might as well have been a child. It was like an irresistible force meeting an immovable object. It snarled and started to reel me in by the wrist.

I dropped onto my ass and planted both my feet against the side of its face and pulled with all my might. Power flowed through my arms and I broke its grip. I rolled away and came to my feet at the same instant it did. Bellowing something unintelligible it charged me again, ungainly, like a Sumo wrestler, and I barely managed to slip by this time. Its speed and coordination were slightly off, and it took an unsteady step toward me, and then another and I circled back toward the door from where it'd emerged. It kept coming, arms stretched out in front as though sleepwalking, and then it charged again. I feinted left and as it passed me, I leaped onto its back and got it into a headlock. I pulled with all my strength, squeezing tighter and tighter as it started spinning in circles to fling me off. It went faster and gave my arms a shove and I lost my grip and flew into the wall, concrete and plasterboard spraying into the corridor.

I hustled to my feet as it ran toward me. I stepped in, meeting its velocity with my own, and blasted it across the front and right side of the neck with my right forearm, in the same instant gripping its right arm with my left hand. I nailed it again with my forearm and some of the rigidity seemed to leak out of its body, so I slipped my arm to the back of its neck and yanked the head down and slammed my knee into its face. The head bounced like one of those bobblehead dolls and I kneed it in the face again, and again. I kicked its feet out from under it and swept it onto its back. It slammed into the floor, hard, denting the shiny concrete and producing a shockwave that seemed to reverberate in the air around us. Its face was flattened; the nose squashed and bent, one of the eyes pushed in and glowing green. I stomped on its exposed throat and felt the metallic carapace give a little. I raised my foot to stomp again but it grabbed my foot and pushed and I lost balance and was sent crashing back into the wall, debris raining down around me. Before I could recover it was on me and launched a straight fist to my chest.

It felt like I'd run into a tree. It punched me twice more in the abdomen so I twisted hard and grabbed both its wrists with my hands. It rotated its body to try and break free, and we danced and struggled, slamming into the wall over and over. As

I turned away, it snapped a knee into my groin, and the sensation of pain rocketed through my abdomen. In my visual fields, red lettering flickered up and down and tiny dots danced before my eyes. I assumed these were damage reports, but I couldn't interpret them. I only hoped that I was inflicting more damage in return.

I took a step back and blasted a desperate sidekick into its knee. It jerked back and toppled over onto its side, the knee joint folded ninety degrees the wrong way. Seizing the moment, I darted in, skirting its grasping arms and embracing it around the neck again, wrapping both arms around as tightly as I could.

And I squeezed, channeling everything, diverting all power reserves and energy through my body into my arms. Red numbers increased in my HUD but I hung on and, remorselessly, continued to squeeze. The Vu-Hak's arms flailed at my head, connecting wildly but not causing any damage. It was not able to rise due to its ruined knee, and my legs were spread out and my stance was solid as a rock. It was going nowhere.

I gritted my teeth and let out a primal yell. There was a squeaking, crunching noise, and the Vu-Hak's head came away from its torso. It span and bounced down the corridor, and I fell backward into the wall in a sitting position, facing the alien's body. It was trying to get up, a nightmarish vision of a headless, bloodless corpse, twitching and jerking. There was a high-pitched wailing and what sounded awfully like servos and gears crunching as it tried to get upright. Its neck was crushed and warped, blue and green lights flickering and winking from snapped and twisted cables or whatever these machines used for arteries and veins. The head had rolled to a stop just by the door, facing me, green eyes blazing out of Adam Benedict's mangled face.

The fucking thing was still alive. I knew that the hardware running the machine – onto which the Vu-Hak consciousness was mapped – was located in the head, so I needed to destroy that. I scuttled to my feet and leaped over the thrashing torso, sliding on the tiles and stopping in front of the head. The mouth moved, spasmodically opening and closing, trying to speak. It wasn't Adam's voice anymore, but an approximation of human speech, more machine-like and robotic.

I raised a fist to try and crush it, but its whispered words sent a chill through me.

"You fool ... You have killed us all."

I paused. "What're you talking about?"

The skull bared its teeth and snarled. "The containment field has been breached. The singularity will be fully exposed in a few minutes."

This didn't sound good.

My mind accessed the Internet, and a brief search provided enough information to scare the pants off me. A black hole of only a millimeter diameter would have a mass of approximately one tenth of the Earth. If this were to suddenly appear on the surface, the overall gravity of the planet would increase and the moon's orbit would alter. All matter within a third of the Earth's radius would feel a pull toward the black hole and be consumed. The destruction of the Earth's crust and most of its mantle would occur. Within a few hours the entire planet would be an uninhabitable mess of collapsing crust, lava and hot gases.

Life would be unsustainable.

I batted the Vu-Hak's head away and watched it ricochet down the corridor like a bowling ball down an alley. I slumped back against the wall and closed my eyes. A siren was coming from the floors above, increasing in volume. The machine's torso was now lying prone and unmoving and its clothes were dissolving away revealing grey and mottled flesh. Ulcers were appearing and the blue-silver carapace was looking worn and dull. Rather than the shiny underlay on Adam and myself, this was a matte grey shade associated with some sports cars.

I got to my feet and brushed the paint and dust off my hands. The corridor stretched out around another corner, past where I'd punted the skull. The noise of the siren was increasing, and I phase switched my auditory receptors to suppress it. The warning lights in my HUD were now all green and winking out one at a time as my machine continued to repair the damage from the fight. I stretched: all my limbs and joints flexed normally, and the neural feedback seemed healthy enough.

I concentrated and pushed out a thought.

Colleen? Where are you?

THIRTY-FOUR

The corridor curved to the left, dimly lit and uninviting. It felt like there was a breeze blowing gently in my face, grasping me with its chilly touch. I knew there had to be more Vu-Hak here, somewhere.

A door appeared ahead, left ajar, throwing an amber stripe across the floor. My mind held me back, but my body dragged me forward like a moth to a flame. My fingertips drifted along the walls, sensing nothing but cold and neglect.

The room confirmed the impression. Office furniture from the 70s, dusty and old, looking as if it would crumble if touched. Mold ate away at the walls and floor coverings, and cobwebs laced the corners and draped around the bare light bulb hanging from the ceiling.

Then I felt it. The familiarity of Colleen's mind.

She was really close.

I ran outside and closed my eyes to focus. Something was jamming my sensors, but I was definitely getting something. The sirens were continuing in the background, muted but subtly getting louder. I picked up the pace and continued up the corridor.

Another door came into view. This one was closed, unlabeled and windowless, a knob for a handle and old-fashioned lock.

Behind it were seven life forms.

Enough is enough, I thought.

I took hold of the edges of the frame and pulled the door off its hinges. An explosion of noise erupted. Muzzle flashes lit up from every corner and I was hit by a hailstorm of bullets that impacted my face and chest. They felt like pinpricks.

Four soldiers were crouched in the corners of a room the size of a small garage, firing up at me. Behind them, strapped into chairs by leather belts and zip-ties were the unconscious forms of Stillman, Hubert and Hamilton.

I sensed no Vu-Hak presence and so I entered the soldiers'

nervous systems and disrupted the synaptic neurotransmission in their brains. Instantly, and as one, they fell to the ground out cold. I hoped it would be temporary, like a general anesthetic, but I wasn't sure. I also wasn't sure I cared anymore.

I rushed over to Stillman and saw she was breathing easily and had a regular pulse. Her pupils were large and equal, and her eyes moved normally when I turned her head. She didn't wake up, though, so my sensors got to work and detected levels of benzodiazepines, a sedative, in her bloodstream. I manipulated the chemicals in her brain controlling cognitive functions and brought her back from sleep, carefully and gently.

Waking up can be harsh, especially if your dreams are better than what reality is likely to bring. Certainly this particular awakening wasn't going to bring her any pleasure. The fleeting moment of being whole and human again was going to evaporate faster than summer rain off a flattop in Nevada. The clock was ticking. I didn't know how long before the black hole was released from behind the Electromech's shield protection and our planet imploded. Bringing her back to life only to have it snatched away in a few minutes' time was truly cruel, wasn't it?

The siren was now a couple of notches lower in tone but louder and more intense. Diffuse red lights had begun to flash and I could hear a distant speaker intoning something about …

"… radiation detected in sub-levels; evacuate, evacuate …"

I broke the ties and straps around Stillman's arms and legs and she sat forward and absently rubbed her wrists. I glanced at Hamilton, who was in the middle chair, still sleeping. I decided to keep him asleep. Likewise, Hubert was slouched back in his chair, head pointing at the ceiling, making snoring noises.

I kneeled down in front of Stillman and took hold of both her hands. They looked small and frail in mine, and I felt a pang of regret. I'd messed up. I couldn't un-kill the Vu-Hak. I couldn't put the genie back in the bottle.

"Kate …?" she slurred.

"I'm here," I said, feeling like shit.

"You're one of those machines, aren't you?" she said, her voice just audible above the racket coming from outside. She then surprised me by giving a slight smile. "I knew they couldn't kill you."

"I'm sorry, Colleen. I truly am ... I ... I tried."

I stifled a sob and felt her arms around me, pulling me closer. I hugged her, feeling her warmth, her life force, sensing her heartbeat, her breathing. My melancholia covered me like a cloak I simply couldn't let drop to the floor. Stillman was soon going to die, as were we all. Dreams, goals, plans – all slashed and burned. Soon nothing we'd said or done in the past would have mattered, or would ever matter.

"It's alright, Kate," I heard her saying. "We'll figure it out."

At that moment a huge pressure wave impacted my back. A fist of orange flame punched through the door and the walls buckled and smoke and fire burst in. I flung my arms around Stillman; water spurted from the ceilings as the sprinklers activated and in a few seconds we were drenched. Hubert and Hamilton were thrown from their chairs and crashed against the far wall, covered in bits of plasterboard and concrete chips. I ran over to them, and incredibly found that they were still alive, unconscious and relatively unscathed. They had assorted scratches and abrasions, but I detected no broken bones; nor was there any indication of internal bleeding or significant blunt trauma to organs.

I turned to Stillman, who was looking dazed but otherwise none the worse for wear. "Stay here, let me go and check things out."

She nodded, and I went to have a look outside. Smoke obscured everything so I flicked my eyes to infrared. The corridor appeared like a carcass stripped of flesh. The pillars of concrete that remained were burned and pockmarked, and crumbling stone lay on the ground as settling dust lay ash-like over cracked and ruined tiles.

The Vu-Hak's skull had been blown further up the corridor from where I'd kicked it but the torso was no longer there. In its place was a circular-shaped hole five yards in diameter where rock, pipes and metal girders had been carved away, leaving a smooth surface looking like it'd been scooped out by a giant spoon. Water was dripping from an open pipe, and sparks flickered from severed power lines.

Running my hand over the edge of the cavity, I sensed heat and radiation. My scanners picked up gamma rays, quantum fluctuations and gravitational waves.

Nothing normal.

A wormhole footprint.

Then I heard a voice in my head.

Get to the surface. Now.

Cain.

THIRTY-FIVE

Back in what remained of the room, Stillman was kneeling over Hamilton, talking to him and trying to bring him round. Hubert lay a few yards away, unmoving but his chest rising and falling steadily.

"I can't wake Matt up," Stillman said with a worried look.

My sensors automatically scanned him. Information flooded in, raw and unstructured. My medical mind sifted through the data, analyzing it and inserting it into a diagnostic algorithm.

"There is disrupted connectivity, reduced synaptic efficiency, and a constrained repertoire of dynamic states which have created inhospitable conditions for information transmission and integration."

Stillman gave me a look. "Come again?"

"Sorry. He's drugged, just like you were. Here, let me."

I put a hand on Hamilton's brow and made a gesture like a starfish. His pupils enlarged and his eyes nystagmatically jerked sideways. I brushed the side of his face and he awoke with a jolt.

"Dr Morgan? Where ...?"

"Easy, Matt," I said. "Let's get you on your feet. We need to get out of here."

He grimaced but held out his hands. With a few groans and winces we managed to get him upright and leaning against the wall. He looked decidedly grey, but we were against the clock and needed to keep moving. Cain's message was still burning in my ears.

"Good to go," he said, seemingly reading my mind and giving a thumbs up.

Stillman was looking at me, uncertain, clearly trying to come to terms with what I was. What I'd become. I gave her a half smile as if to say 'you and me both, sister' and then went over to Hubert.

I ran a thorough diagnostic sweep. His heart was racing but wasn't irregular, and while his blood pressure was elevated I took this as a good sign and a physiological response to stress. I switched to an X-ray wavelength and scanned him from top to toe. There were a few rib fractures but that was all. My mind drifted into his, trying to ascertain what level of consciousness he was at, but I couldn't get a handle on it. I could visualize his brainwaves, but there was a dullness that I hoped was just the drugs the Vu-Hak had administered.

"I'll carry him," I said, crouching down.

"Wait, can't you just wake him up like you did Matt?" Stillman said with a frown.

I shook my head. "I'm concerned there's something not right with him. Neurologically, that is. Let's not risk it here."

She pursed her lips. "Alright, but how're we going to get out? This is the Pentagon. And there could be more Vu-Hak anywhere."

Matt pushed himself off the wall and looked furtively over Colleen's shoulder and out the corridor where there was a thin layer of dust now floating above the ground like mist over a Scottish loch. He waved a hand in the direction of the hole in the wall where the door had previously been. "She's right. This won't have gone unnoticed."

I cradled Hubert in my arms and smoothly stood up. Hamilton gazed at me with a kind of open-mouthed awe, seemingly noticing for the first time that I was towering over him and Stillman.

"What the hell, Kate?" he began.

"Explanations can wait," I said. "If we can just get to the surface, I think we've got a chance."

Another elevator was twenty yards up the corridor and thankfully out of the demolition zone. We squeezed in and it climbed for five seconds before jerking to a stop. The doors opened and we stepped out into chaos. People were running as fast as they could, panic on their faces. Alarms were blaring and the tannoy was booming '… evacuate, radiation detected …" Soldiers and armed security officers were herding everyone toward the corridor leading back to the C-Ring and toward the main exits.

I pulled up the schematic of the Pentagon in my HUD and identified a secondary corridor leading to the A-Ring and directly out to the central courtyard. We set off at a jog, running against the crowd, Matt hobbling but supported by Stillman. People gave us strange looks but no one tried to stop us as we jinked left and right until we came to another corridor that sloped upward to the A-Ring. There was sunlight coming through windows that opened directly to the courtyard.

"This way," I said and started up the slope. Just then two soldiers rounded the corner and beckoned us to a halt. One of them pointed back down the corridor we'd come.

"Turn around. There's an evac in progress," one of them barked. He looked me in the eye, clocked my uniform and said, "You should know the drill, soldier."

"Can't you see I've got injured civilians here?" I said.

"Then you're going the wrong way," he countered with a firm shake of his head. "There's no exit up there. You're just heading back in."

Hamilton stepped forward and raised his hands while fumbling in his pocket. "Look, private, we're with the FBI. I'm just getting my ID. As you can see, one of my colleagues needs urgent medical attention ..."

The soldier was having none of it. "I'm giving you a direct order, *G-Man*. Turn around and follow the evac route."

Stillman and I looked at each other, and I saw the tightness in her mouth as she considered our options.

I decided for us. "We don't have time for this. I'm sorry."

I pulled the same neurological switches as I'd done before, and they dropped to the ground like puppets with their strings cut. Hamilton picked up the soldiers' rifles and threw one to Stillman, who checked the safety and slung it over her shoulder. At the top of the slope was a large sliding doorway leading to the courtyard. It swished opened as we arrived, and we ran through into daylight and a concrete pathway lined by big trees and shrubbery. The courtyard was about five acres in size, manicured lawns giving it a park-like ambience. Potted plants were dotted along the pathway and cedar laminated benches completed the look. In the dead center was a cafeteria, quaintly named Ground Zero. It was a magnolia pentagon-shaped building consisting of two stories, the upper level topped off with a pointed chimney.

"What now?" said Stillman anxiously.

I glanced up at the sky, which was still grey and gloomy. Raindrops spit onto my hands and Hubert's forehead while the remainder filled the scattered puddles decorating the pathway. In one of these I saw movement as a shadow passed overhead. A massive black shape span into view, the sky blurring around its edges. There was a subwoofer-like rumbling and the atmosphere felt pressurized, as if it was being squeezed in a vacuum chamber.

"What the hell is that?" shouted Stillman.

"It's Cain," I replied. "He's come for us."

THIRTY-SIX

In a gravity-defying move, the huge ship did a majestic spiral and lowered itself stern first into the courtyard. I expected to feel the down draft of its engines, but there was nothing at all. It hovered above the cafeteria building twenty yards or more off the ground like a monstrous graphite shard poking up through the clouds. A spot of white light appeared about a third of the way along the stern as an aperture wound open, revealing an external hatch. What looked like liquid mercury poured out and oozed to the ground in front of us. It glistened and bubbled organically before transforming and solidifying into a ladder-like structure of rungs and steps.

Hamilton looked at me, his face tight with indecision.

"It's okay," I said. "Go!"

He nodded and was about to jump on when he froze, looking over my shoulder. I turned to see what he was looking at and saw two Adam Benedict-shaped Electromechs in the doorway we'd come through.

"Kate ..." he said.

"Get on that goddamn ship, Matt," I hissed.

I could perceive their thoughts. Alien. Dark and unfathomable but with hints of malevolence and excitement, like predators cornering their prey.

Stillman and Hamilton hadn't moved. I moved to block their view of the Vu-Hak and glared at them. "Take Bill and get in the ship. I'll hold them off."

Stillman looked horrified. "You can't be serious."

I roughly passed Hubert over to them. "This isn't a discussion, Colleen. Get the fuck up those steps."

She read my mood and nodded sharply.

We laid Hubert on the stair, which immediately started to move like an escalator, taking him up to the ship. Hamilton took this as a hint and jumped on too.

Stillman hesitated again. "You better be right behind me."

"Count on it." I smiled, and eased her backward onto the staircase, which grabbed her and whisked her up to the open hatchway.

I turned to face the aliens. They'd split up and were circling me. One of them was on all fours, bounding like a gazelle, while the other was taking human-like strides across the grass. Like the Vu-Hak in the corridor there was awkwardness to its gait, as if it was just learning how to walk, like a newborn.

I moved quickly, closing the gap. I was now ten feet away from them in a narrow triangle and they eased up and stopped. The one that had been on all fours rose up and stood still, swaying slightly, arms by its side. The other one stood and stared at me before folding its arms in a curiously human gesture. I took another step. Now I was seven feet away and we were in a nice little cluster. The importance of which was that I was between them and the staircase taking my friends to safety.

I stepped in and kicked the left-hand alien square in the groin. The kinetic energy and weight behind the kick was savage and the Vu-Hak crumpled in half and flew backward, tumbling over and over to crash into one of the trees lining the pathway. Before the right-hand alien had time to react I scythed a backhand elbow against its cheekbone, shattering Adam's handsome face, knocking the Vu-Hak sideways onto the grass.

I checked on the first alien, which was already peeling itself from the tree and shaking its head. Its eyes glowed green and it let out a snarl and launched itself forward in that four-limbed run. I went to move but the other one had already recovered and launched itself at me from the side. I pivoted and thrust off my right foot as it swept past, arms grasping at me. I chopped savagely at its neck causing it to again tumble into the grass and slide along the concrete path. I whirled again but was a fraction too slow as the other one body-slammed me side-on. My HUD flashed red symbols as I sensed the impact and heard a crash like a car being T-boned. There was no pain, but I knew I was in trouble.

We fell to the floor in a violent embrace, the Vu-Hak on top of me, hands around my neck and straddling my chest. I swung with all my might at its skull, but my fists bounced off its shoulders and arms as it tucked its head protectively into its neck. I grabbed its hands by the wrists and pulled, trying to break the grip, but I couldn't move them. More red symbols flickered down the side of my optic overlay, and there was a wave of static as my vision blurred. There was a huge impact on the side of my head as the other Vu-Hak arrived and swung a kick at me. More red numbers. More blurring and static.

I started to panic. More blows rained in and I wondered if my machine's integral field would hold and what would happen if it didn't. I caught a glimpse of the ship and saw the staircase had been fully withdrawn and that the aperture was slowly closing. The ship was lazily angling around and preparing to leave.

I felt my mind relax. I'd done my job.

My friends were going to get away.

The Vu-Hak continued to pummel my head and body, and as my vision spiraled darker I thought of my daughter. I closed my eyes and pictured her standing in a field of daffodils, every one a bright stunning yellow. She looked perfect, just as I wanted to remember her. She was soaking in the sunshine and laughing but I couldn't hear her voice, no matter how hard I tried.

I knew I would never see her again.

Mist descended on my eyes, and through the veil I could barely make out the world around me. The voices of the aliens slithered and wormed around my mind as they began to break through my defenses. As oblivion beckoned, my own demons appeared as well to haunt and strangle me. I craved the amnesia again, so all this suffering would fade away, fade and allow what memories I had left of Kelly to soothe me and perhaps to restore peace to my life, here at the end.

The world became bleached, like a sheet had been stretched over my face and covered with snow. The clock ticked: my time was nearly up. I was a ghost in my own machine. A ghost floating in an acid lake dissolving slowly and fading away into nothingness.

But I was wrong.

I was proving hard to kill.

THIRTY-SEVEN

Wake up, Kate.

This time it was effortless. I just opened my eyes.

There was no Grim Reaper and no pearly gates. No River Styx. Just Cain, in his bald-headed female persona, sitting opposite me with a benign smile on his face. Next to him were Hamilton and Stillman dressed in some sort of Lycra-looking body suits. We were in a small oval space with low green-tinged lighting. Seats and couches were randomly scattered, organically grown out of the walls. There was a low glass table in front of me, holding a jug of water and two tumblers. I reached down and shakily took one, filled it and brought to my lips for a sniff before taking a sip.

Tasteless.

Hamilton leaned forward, hands on his knees, watching me carefully. "How you doing, Kate?"

I looked at him blankly. The filing system in my cortex had empty spaces, as if someone had purged chunks of my mind. I put the glass down on the table with a chink and sat back. "We're moving, so I guess we're on the ship. Gravity feels Earth-normal. How is it that I'm still alive?"

Stillman indicated to Cain. "He saved you. He saved us all. Remember the black hole about to blow in the Pentagon? Cain activated a wormhole and transported it away."

Cain shrugged, like *no big deal*. "Yes, however the range of the wormhole generator is still limited in cosmic terms. I transported it as far into the solar system as I could, but only got it to the orbit of Mars."

"So it's not a problem anymore?" I asked.

Cain gave a sigh. "I suppose that is a relative thing. It has already unsettled the orbit of that planet, and its gravitational pull will disrupt the path of any asteroids and objects traveling through the system. The Earth is now at much higher risk of impacts from extraterrestrial debris."

As if that mattered.

I studied the artificial being sitting opposite me. "How did you get me away from those two Vu-Hak?"

"Have a look," he said, and closed his eyes momentarily.

A hologram materialized above the table, showing a birds-eye view of the ship as it hovered vertically above the Pentagon. I was again astonished by the size of it. I'd known how big it was, but seeing it next to such a well-known building was incredible. Each side of the Pentagon was over three hundred yards long and the ship towered over it, stretching up into the sky for miles, twinkling with crystalline lights and pulsing with energy.

Cain opened his eyes and gave a little wave toward the screen. The picture zoomed on the ship's stern and there I was, lying on the ground, the two Vu-Hak on me, punching and kicking. The surface underneath my body was indented, the pathway cracking and crumbling with each blow. Then, from just out of picture, Cain appeared. He walked straight over to us and raised a hand. The Vu-Hak standing over me was lifted into the air and crushed, crumpling like a car in a compactor. The air blurred around him as if the very molecules were being distorted. The Vu-Hak that had been on top of me ran toward Cain and raised its arms in a kind of pushback movement. A dark fuzziness appeared in the air between it and Cain, who took a step backward before making an expansive gesture with both hands. Both Vu-Hak were blown into the sky, spinning out of sight way over the Pentagon walls. The hologram oscillated once and vanished, and I was left looking across the table at Cain.

"That particular Vu-Hak was starting to figure out how to use the machine's full abilities," he said. "A little longer and we would have been in trouble."

"Have they found machines with surviving AI?"

"I don't believe so," he replied thoughtfully. "I couldn't sense any of my kind – artificial consciousnesses that is – in either of those two machines."

"Well, how –?" I started.

"They are adapting to use the machines without the need for AI. I did not think it would take them very long."

I looked aghast. "Do we know how many machines they possess?"

"At a guess, fewer than a hundred."

"How many do we have?" Stillman chipped in.

"Four hundred and thirty-seven units."

My eyes lit up. "Okay, well we outnumber them four to one, and we've got you and Adam, with full capability."

Cain grimaced. "Kate, remember that the machines we possess are non-functional at present."

But my mind was racing. "What about their singularities ... the black holes in each of the Electromechs? Can't we do something with them? Surely they can be weaponized?"

Cain pulled another face. "That is not possible. The singularities that are at the heart of these machines do not exist in our universe. They can never occur in nature because their production requires the precise tuning of an imploding gravitational wave. Vu-Hak science achieved this tuning by manipulating the laws of quantum gravity. I do not have access to these calculations. The technology is – at the moment at least – beyond even my abilities."

I got up out of the chair and started pacing. "We've got the transfer technology to put human minds into the Electromechs. You've proved it with me. We just need volunteers! What about you, Matt, or you, Colleen? Surely saving the planet is worth it? Saving humanity?"

I was aware I sounded unhinged and desperate, but our backs were well and truly against the wall. Cain gave a sideways glance to Stillman, who picked up her glass again and swilled the liquid around silently.

"What?" I said.

"There's a problem," she said. "With you."

"What are you talking about? I'm fine. Look ..."

But as if on cue, a wave of dizziness came over me. I put out a hand to steady myself and noted that my seat had anticipated my action and raised an armrest to the level of my waist. I rested a hand on it and took a step forward, but my legs felt like lead. Both Cain and Stillman were suddenly next to me, easing me back into my seat. My vision blurred and a smattering of red icons appeared along the bottom of my HUD.

"You need to rest, Kate," he said kindly.

I waved him off. "We've got to try and save the planet, surely we've got …" My neck involuntarily gave a spasm and I rubbed at it with my hand. There were defects in the carapace, pieces of skin missing.

I wasn't healing.

Cain placed his hand on my cheek. His smile was still kind, but the rest of his face was unreadable. I tried to reach out into his mind, but there was only static.

"The Vu-Hak –" he began.

"What about them?"

"They got into your mind. Past the defenses I had installed. I managed to flush them out, but … at a cost. The interface between your motor cortex and the machine is degrading. You can sense it, I know."

He was right. I briefly drifted into unconsciousness and then back out again. The room was a blur and random images seemed to float aimlessly around in the pool of my thoughts. Cain tapped me on the shoulder and it brought me back but after a second I was lost again. Keeping focus took all my concentration. The room, faces, even my thoughts were now in a sort of low resolution, like a bad quality movie or streaming a TV show with slow broadband.

"But you can fix me, right?" I mumbled.

Cain looked grim. "Kate, that's not the only problem. I ran some tests while you were out. I have established that the human mind is not sufficiently complex to run the Vu-Hak software that is integral to the functioning of the Electromechs. Entropy is increasing."

I tried to concentrate on what he was saying as the room spun in lazy circles. "Entropy?"

"The loss of energy available to do work. The second law of thermodynamics states that the total entropy of a system either increases or remains constant. Entropy is zero in a reversible process and it increases in an irreversible process."

"You're not making sense," I said, not sure whether this was because of my condition or that I was just stupid.

"Kate, this is happening – and would have happened – irrespective of the Vu-Hak incursion into your mind. I did not anticipate this at the time we made the transfer of your consciousness. In my defense I had few alternatives, however. None, really."

"So what, am I just going to die in this tin can?"

Stillman came and sat down next to me. She took my hand in hers and squeezed. There was moisture in her eyes.

"We're going back to the moon. Cain says that Adam is upgrading the transfer technology as we speak. They'll remove your consciousness from the Electromech before any permanent damage is done."

I wondered where my consciousness was going to be transferred. I had visions of a brain in a box.

Cain sat back into his seat and activated the display. Red and blue lights flickered over his face. He turned to me with an apologetic kind of look. "Now you'll understand why I can't allow another human to interface with a machine unless the transfer technology is better …"

He paused and his head twitched to one side. "Wait …"

A blinking red light appeared on one of the screens and another holographic image shimmered into view. A 3D schematic of the Earth appeared with figures and symbols starting to pop up all over the land surfaces. I tried to push my mind into the ship's, but nothing happened. I was blind to the telepathic connection I once had.

"What's going on?" I said quietly.

Cain's hands were dancing in the air as he activated additional holographic displays around the room. "The ship has detected radiation signatures on all continents."

Stillman stood up, her mouth open. On one of the displays a pillar of fiery smoke and dust was boiling up, still being violently agitated at the bottom.

"Those are nuclear detonations."

She was right.

From every flank of the Earth came the signs that the apocalypse was upon us. Mushroom clouds sprouted above city skylines, turning once green lands and vibrant cities into ash and charcoal. Clouds parted willingly, bowing to the power of the atom, as columns of irradiated dust billowed into the air.

I visualized the Vu-Hak watching in their Electromechs, immortal, untouchable by the nuclear devastation. Like the four horsemen, sitting astride their black stallions on a hill, watching the world burning and feeling the closest thing to happiness they could experience. Waiting to ravage the world for its raw material, rapacious users of energy that they once were, that they were becoming again.

Hamilton was on his feet, pacing. "We have to do something."

My mind was numb as I watched the images. All I could think was that the era of humanity was over before it had really begun. The bottleneck Holland had spoken about, the point at which all species that developed weapons of mass destruction had to get past safely to become a truly interstellar civilization, was no longer a concern. An alien species had done it for us, using our own weapons.

"Are there enough bombs to destroy the Earth?" Hamilton said.

My voice was flat. Emotionless. Bereft of hope. "Fifteen thousand nuclear warheads are more than enough. Those who aren't killed by the initial detonations will succumb to the nuclear winter as the atmosphere fills with smoke and radioactive debris."

Stillman stomped over to Cain. "We've got this ship. It's fucking big. An Ark. How many people can we get on it? Thousands, I'll bet."

Cain shook his head. "There are a number of insurmountable problems with that suggestion."

"Such as?" Stillman said angrily. "We all have family, you know. I've a father, two brothers –"

Cain cut her off. "You don't understand the logistics involved. There have been studies analyzing the minimum number of individuals needed to successfully recolonize humankind after an extinction level event. Taking into account infant mortality, disease, the negative effects of interbreeding and adverse environmental issues – approximately twenty thousand people would be needed."

Hamilton slapped the side of his chair. "That's fine then! This ship is five miles long and it can reshape itself. Surely that number can be accommodated here?"

I saw the problem immediately. "It's not just the people, it's everything else. Food, water, air, enough for a long journey – and who knows for how long and to where. Cain can do the math if you want to calculate the sheer tonnage of support materials that would be needed every day of such a journey. It's enormous. You'd need another two or three ships of equal size just for the support."

Cain nodded. "There is also the problem of extended spaceflight. This ship would filter out much of the interstellar radiation but in the long term humans would be exposed to cumulative toxicity ultimately causing catastrophic damage to living tissues. Putting human consciousnesses into the Vu-Hak machines would be the only long-term solution."

"And we only have four hundred of them ..." muttered Hamilton.

"But that wouldn't work either," I said. "When we discard human bodies, we lose biological tissue, so there's no procreation and therefore no more humans. Just four hundred non-reproducing robots."

"We can save their DNA though, can't we?" said Stillman. "And we've saved four hundred souls."

"Colleen, even if it were safe to put human minds into these machines, who would decide which four hundred to 'save'? Are we qualified to play god?"

Then Cain threw more water on the flames. "There is also the likelihood that any large group of people would include some Vu-Hak. Even one alien infiltrator on board this ship would destroy everything. We cannot identify them all. The risk would be too great."

We all went quiet, thinking furiously.
Then Cain raised a hand, and his eyes seemed to sparkle.
"There is another way."

THIRTY-EIGHT

Cain had insisted we moved to the flight deck, citing concerns for the organic members of our party. Hubert had been transferred to some sort of med-lab, tucked in and connected to data recorders that would let us know of any significant change in his condition. We were all strapped into identical chairs facing a projected 3-D image of the world outside. The moon's soft ivory light shimmered across the dark waters of the blue planet. I gazed spellbound into the void, a black tranquility married to a poetry of stars. The beauty of space contrasted with the abomination occurring on our home world. Flashes and mushroom clouds were easily visible, the atmosphere already dark and pestilent.

"Can't we go faster?" I said, turning to Cain.

He shook his head and nodded at Stillman and Hamilton. "We cannot. Humans have tissue tolerances."

I grimaced, feeling woozy and light-headed. Time was not on our side. While we traveled, the world was burning and I was dying.

"However, at our current acceleration and vector, we will achieve orbit around the moon in four hours and twenty minutes," he said.

That was still pretty fast then. It had taken the Apollo missions four days to get there. I fixed Cain with a beady eye. "Well, plenty of time to tell us your plan."

He nodded and swiveled his chair and our seats moved of their own accord to form a semicircle facing him. He steepled his fingers in a schoolmasterly kind of way and let his gaze drift above our heads. I wonder if he'd seen that sort of thing in a movie or on a TV show.

"Have you heard of embryonic stem cell research?" he said.

"Of course," I huffed. "I'm a doctor."

Hamilton coughed. "Maybe explain it to us then?"

Cain inclined his head. "Embryonic stem cells have the

potential to differentiate into and 'become' any mature cell such as those making up your skin, gastro-intestinal tract, heart or nervous system. They are derived from an early stage pre-implantation embryo, called a blastocyst."

"How early?" said Stillman.

"About four or five days after fertilization," I replied.

Hamilton frowned. "I recall there being lots of ethical issues regarding these. Something to do with the killing of human beings?"

This was the argument that had split families and was still being debated.

"It's true that isolating the cells destroys the blastocyst," I said. "The ethical question is whether or not these embryos at the pre-implantation stage should be considered morally equivalent to embryos in the post-implantation stage."

"You mean, equivalent to babies growing in the womb?" Hamilton said.

"Yes. Or even morally equivalent to fully formed and functioning adults. The question is usually framed in religious language."

Cain raised his eyebrows. "How can a hundred and fifty cells in a petri dish be given the same status as a human child?"

I gave him a look. "As a new life form I would have thought you might've had a more balanced view of what may constitute life?"

Cain was about to reply when Stillman interrupted. "What's the point of all this?"

I sighed. "Many childless couples undergo IVF – in vitro fertilization – which produces multiple embryos, not all of which are used to produce children. The surplus embryos are generally discarded or used for research. Their embryonic stem cells can provide medical breakthroughs in lots of conditions – diabetes, cancer and so on – and many facilities store them for future use …" I stopped and turned to Cain as the penny dropped. "Where would we find these embryos?"

"The United States is the leading country for stem cell research."

"We're not going back there," snapped Stillman.

Cain gave an enigmatic smile. "The other countries heavily involved in stem cell research are Iran, South Korea, Australia and China. The largest storage facilities, the least guarded and also the least likely to be on the Vu-Hak radar would be in Australia. Queensland, to be exact."

"And also the least likely to have been nuked," I said.

"Wait," said Hamilton, just catching up. "We're going to steal embryos?"

"Matt, these embryos are discarded, unwanted, superfluous to demand. Just waiting for inclusion in research programs that will destroy them to produce their stem cells. We can use them to repopulate the species."

Cain nodded. "The facility in Queensland is run by a company called AusStemGen. I have already programmed a course there as soon as we have finished on the moon."

"How many embryos are there in the Australian facility?" asked Stillman.

Cain pursed his lips and closed his eyes for a few seconds. "I have accessed the ASG database. There were some crude firewalls that were easy to break down. I have determined that there are approximately twenty-five thousand embryos in storage on site."

"Do we need that many?" I said.

"No, two thousand would be more than sufficient, and probably the most efficient use of resources. Some for development into viable humans, the rest would be used for cloning to maximize the numbers."

"Cloning?" said Stillman, eyes narrowing.

"Cloning," said Cain, deadpan.

"What, so we would repopulate the species with genetically identical copies of Australians?" she replied, eyes darting back and forward between Cain and me. "Isn't that a bad idea? Like brothers and sisters having sex and producing children with genetic disorders?"

He shook his head firmly. "Not at all. Firstly the embryos at ASG are not all Australian. It is a storage facility, with embryos flown in from all over the world. The creation of genetically identical copies of human beings, provided there is enough diversity for subsequent inbreeding, will save humanity. Cloning technology is 'old science' to the Vu-Hak. I have access to all this data, as does Adam. The human species' diversity will recover."

The rabbit hole was opening up and I didn't like where this was taking us. Cloning to me had always raised the specter of eugenics – the selective mating of people with specific hereditary traits in order to improve the human species. If cloning became possible, I'd foreseen a future of clones made from people who had excelled in sport or science or whatever pursuit society deemed most worthy, to the detriment of humanity as a whole. And there was also the idea of producing clones of yourself for your own benefit such as organ harvesting and re-transplantation when your own organs became diseased or damaged. The ethical minefield was wide and tricky to navigate.

And it didn't end there ...

"You want to go further, don't you?" I said, slowly.

Cain turned to look at me and his gaze was intense. "Yes."

Stillman threw me a sharp look. "What's he talking about?"

Cain's turned his gaze on her. "It will be a simple matter to rewrite the genetic code, enhance neurotransmission and optimize the physiology and biochemistry to create a human species more suited to the future. Augmented, more robust, and more likely to survive the challenges ahead."

She looked aghast. "You're talking about creating a race of super-humans?"

"Not super-humans – post-humans. We would be merely upgrading what is currently flawed and reliant on slow evolution. Humanity, like all species, has evolved in order to survive. But it no longer has the luxury to wait patiently for natural selection and evolution to work their magic. We must act proactively and urgently to ensure that future members of humanity are best equipped for survival in any new environment."

I blew out my cheeks and glanced at the holoscreen, where the silver orb of the moon hung surrounded by stars. I wondered whether humanity could in fact succeed out here, off planet. We'd been confined to our own sandbox on Earth until now, but there, in the vastness of space, what would we find?

In the dark regions of infinite potential, could humanity flourish?

THIRTY-NINE

The ship arrived at the Van De Graaff crater and gracefully descended stern first onto the lunar surface. Cain and I exited as before, the hull dissolving an aperture for us to walk through. Stillman and Hamilton had to stay behind given that the only entrance to Adam's 'moon-base' was through the artificial portal, which of course would have destroyed their unprotected and fragile bodies. They weren't happy of course, but I gave them jobs to do, not the least of which was to check on Hubert. Cain taught them how to access the ship's databanks and electronic communications so they could keep track of the unfolding nuclear holocaust. I also wanted to know if there were any other relatively unprotected sites we could consider raiding for the embryos. Cain had surmised that in the light of what was happening globally, there would be widespread panic and civil disorder to such an extent that guarding medical facilities would be less of a priority.

As I'd turned to leave, Matt had gone to hug Colleen, and she fell into his arms, her eyes glistening. She sobbed into his chest, hands clutching at his shirt. He held her in silence, chin trembling like a small child's, rocking her slowly as the tears soaked his shirt. I found myself oddly dispassionate. It was as if there was nothing left to say about the destruction of our world and all of our kind, nothing left but the void that enveloped my mind in swirling blackness. Their emotions drifted past me like a river flowing downstream.

Cain and I walked to the circle of stones that marked the entry to the wormhole. He activated it with a wave of his hand and we were again transported to the huge underground facility. I could finally see the scale of the operation Adam had set up. There were marble walls covered in electronica and plasma arrays and holograms, and along the whole length of one wall were dozens upon dozens of human-sized metallic cylinders with glass windows containing a yellowish liquid. Other walls had gleaming surfaces shining like stainless steel or silver mercury. Trays and bench tops were covered with circuit boards and assorted microchips were arranged in neat geometric rows.

Set into another wall were thousands of test tubes linked by optical fibers and illuminated by cool blue lights.

I turned to Cain, mouth open. "They're …"

"Yes, Kate, they are for storing the embryos."

I glared at him. "You'd already planned this, hadn't you? You and Adam. This wasn't some out of left field idea … you're going to play Mommy and Daddy to the future human race."

A wave of dizziness brought me to my knees. I steadied myself with a hand on the floor as flashes exploded before my eyes like popcorn going off in a microwave. The familiar red icons started scrolling across the bottom of my HUD again.

Cain appeared by my side and gently helped me to my feet. "Your neuronal interface is fraying. It must be re-amalgamated with your template before it is too late."

I irritably shook him off. "You didn't need any of us really, did you? You and Adam could have done all this yourselves. Why'd you save me? Why'd you save any of us?"

Cain gave a sigh. "Babies born from these embryos will need other humans to care for them as they mature. They will need a connection – a bridge of sorts – to help them understand where they came from, where they are going, and who they are *meant* to be."

I closed my eyes, a bitter taste in my mouth. Was this why I was considered so important? To be a nanny? It would be amusing if it didn't seem so desperate.

"Adam and I cannot do this ourselves," Cain continued. "I am not human, and neither is Adam anymore. Once born, these babies will need you to become the proper descendants of Homo sapiens."

I shook my head wearily. "You've saved four of us to nurture thousands of embryos. Don't you think we'll be a little short-handed?"

"We must avoid Vu-Hak infiltration, Kate. The more we bring into our 'circle of trust' the higher the risk."

"But we're not teachers, Cain …" I protested.

"That would not be your role. Information in the form of digital records – science, arts, economics, technology – will be downloaded directly into developing brains as the embryos mature and grow. It is when they are born that they will need help from adults who are able to help them understand what it means to be human. You will be more than mere teachers. You will become the first 'Elders' of the new humanity. To tell them stories about Earth, about their history, about the end of their civilization … and the beginning of a new era."

I was about to protest further when a pressure wave blossomed behind my eyes, and the room span once more. I felt Cain's hand on my arm and he started to walk me forward. "Let's get you over there," he said, pointing to an alcove in between two of the largest display screens.

He activated more lights and we shuffled into a modular corridor framed by white tubing and bulbous tiling. Large lighting panels flickered on the ceiling to reveal an antechamber that looked as antiseptic as an operating room. There was a ramp that seemed too steep for walking but Cain led the way and, assisted by the one-tenth gravity, I managed to scale it, arriving at another white-on-white doorway. It opened with a swish into a square room completely bereft of instruments, decor, or any form of adornments or equipment. Everything looked like it had been carved out of marble. In the dead center of the room, recessed into the floor, was a square hole the size of a king bed.

Cain maneuvered me toward it, holding my hand and supporting me with an arm around my shoulders. There were a couple of steps down to the bottom of the recess, which dropped about ten feet below the floor. It resembled a dug grave waiting for a coffin, and I shook my head to dismiss the image.

"How did Adam build all this?" I said, hearing my voice creaking and rasping.

"He didn't have to do much himself," Cain answered. "The blueprints for the facility are all in the collective memory of the Vu-Hak. The same with the ship, if you recall. When Adam cojoined with his AI he was able to access all this and much more. He merely set the wheels in motion, so to speak, for the self-replicating mechanism to initiate. With a couple of start-up modifications, and tweaks along the way, this facility built itself in a matter of months."

"So what exactly is this place?"

"This is the neurotransfer station. The technology is thousands of years old, dating back to when the Vu-Hak used it to download their consciousnesses. When they began their transformation from the organic to the cybernetic."

I had a flash of deja vu. "It seems familiar."

"It is where Adam and I removed your mind from your dying body and put it into the Electromech you now inhabit."

Of course. "I hope there've been improvements since I was last here then ..."

"It has been upgraded, yes," he said, giving me an encouraging smile.

I tried one in return but my mouth would only twitch. I paused at the top, my eyes roaming the recess. I felt uneasy, apprehensive, like a diver atop a cliff. I had trouble getting down the steps so Cain gently lifted me off my feet and carried me, laying me gently on my back. The floor felt cold and hard and there was a soft vibration that I could not localize. The air seemed charged, like electrostatic atmosphere before a storm front.

I was exhausted. If my Electromech possessed a battery indicator it'd be flashing red. I was leaking electricity, or whatever type of energy the black hole allowed to filter through. I wanted sleep, a nice warm bed and a solid night of dreams. Everything seemed to be slowing down, like walking through waist high snow or wading through mud, my thoughts melting into the hazy fuzz of cognitive decline.

Cain's hand pressed gently on my shoulder. "Kate, have you seen the movie, *2001: A Space Odyssey*?"

I squinted at him, not liking what he was saying. *2001* had been one of my favorite movies as a child, and I knew just about every cool line, particularly the iconic ones spoken by HAL9000.

"You mean the bit where the supercomputer HAL becomes homicidal and tries to kill the human astronaut?" I said as calmly as I could.

Cain was smiling. "I was actually thinking of the line: 'Dave, my mind is going, I can feel it'."

I tried to relax. He'd clearly been reading my thoughts and monitoring the deterioration of my neurological status.

"Very funny. At a time like this you develop a sense of humor?"

"Just trying to lighten the moment."

"Don't," I said, slurring. "Get on with it."

"'Daisy ... Daisy ... give me your answer, do ...'"

"Shut the fuck up."

He nodded and climbed out of the recess, disappearing out of sight. My eyes closed involuntarily, consciousness continuing to ebb, mind going into free fall, swirling into chaos, waiting for dreams to begin.

Or oblivion.

The vibration suddenly ramped up and my eyes jerked open. The walls of the recess had transformed from marble white and were now sparkling like diamond-encrusted granite. A swirling maelstrom of gases was aggregating overhead, pulsing and churning. It felt like being in a washing-machine drum, turning over and over with the laundry.

"Cain, what's going on?" I said, trying to raise my voice above the intensifying racket.

There was no reply and as I stared into the twisting and spiraling gases, images began to coalesce. A lupine face with reptilian green orbs for eyes drifted in and out of focus, although the green points of light seemed to be unwaveringly staring at me. Pearl-white jagged teeth appeared, eerily incandescent, emitting a strange blue glow. Its body appeared, skin mostly composed of scar tissue, cerulean in color. There may have been some sort of fur there at one time, but what was left over was tufty and thin. There was little bulk, it was spindly and spidery, and there was no clue as to sex, if it was even relevant. Perhaps it was neither male nor female but hermaphrodite. It moved awkwardly and stood up on two of its limbs, bipedal-like, but cast no shadow and made no noise.

The familiar sensation returned, the elemental fear of being hunted, the crushing urge to look over my shoulder.

Cain's voice bounced around my head, soothing and reassuring. *I am reading high levels of anxiety and stress in your neuromarkers.*

No shit.

Everything seemed real, not a dream or some weird side effect of the process.

I am stabilizing the connection between your bimolecular DNA and the machine's interface.

There was something, some creature, lurking in the shadows, an evil presence no one but me could see. A monster that was going to end humanity was making itself a home inside my head. I could feel its rage and malevolence, so I imagined a door between us, and a secure room behind it, to try and keep it far away from my mind.

Kate, relax, this is an illusion.

But it remained, tearing through the mental walls of wood and plasterboard, trying to reach what was left of my sanity. I knew it was only a matter of time before it managed to break through.

The images are part of the system's memory from a millennia ago, when the Vu-Hak last used it.

The door was starting to collapse, to crumble. And it knew it wouldn't be long before …

Fifteen seconds … Think calming thoughts.

Think calming thoughts … was that him trying to be funny again? I took a deep breath and concentrated. The horrific image of the Vu-Hak pixelated out and morphed into the fading watery light of a beautiful evening and a cloudless, sunsetting sky. I visualized an old abandoned church on a hill, all Gothic grey stone and centuries of decay.

Kate … you should be good now.

Up in the rafters, I pictured the Vu-Hak clinging to the shadows. Adorned with lichen, it was a grotesque caricature all bulging eyes and over-sized ears and a grin evoking notions of sadistic pleasure. However, it now simply reminded me of a stone gargoyle, dead and ancient, and nothing to fear.

Powering down.

The images vanished and the vibration ceased and everything went quiet. There was a residual aroma of something sweet and fishy, like burned electrical circuits. There were no red icons or any danger lights in my HUD so I sat up and to my relief there was no dizziness or fogginess anymore either. I got to my feet and peered over the lip of the recess. Cain had his back to me in the corner of the room facing a wall display that was glowing with holographic pictures and symbols.

"Hey," I said.

He turned and beckoned me over, so I climbed out of the recess and joined him at the console. Already my balance and strength were returning, and I no longer felt seasick or like I had a hangover.

"How are you feeling?" he said.

"Better," I replied. "Definitely an improvement."

"I'm afraid it won't be permanent. The human brain is just not sufficiently complex enough for neurologic matching to be accurate. However, you have motor control back, and some abilities such as basic telepathic communication and remote interfacing and manipulation of electronic circuits."

"How long before the degradation becomes apparent again?"

He paused. "It may not be possible to keep doing this, Kate."

"Let's hope we can wrap this up quickly then," I said, trying to put on a brave face.

"Indeed. Time may not be on our side. Look …"

FORTY

Cain pointed at the screen, and the images scrolling past were apocalyptic. Cities in ruin, burning, and thick black clouds settling over annihilated downtown areas. Once recognizable buildings, monuments and parks reduced to charred skeletons. Fire damage was tremendous, and the effect of the conflagration had profoundly altered the appearance of the cities, leaving the central parts flattened and bare except for scattered lumps of reinforced concrete, steel frames and pieces of twisted sheet metal. Anything organic was reduced to ash and charcoal. Smoke hung in a haze that partially obscured the blood-red sun. Even the oceans gave the impression of having stilled. Like semi-stagnant pools of death and decay, the waves had receded and lapped sorrowfully along the shorelines. The skies were barren, no birds flew and all the while an oppressive heat haze shimmered like the breath of hell.

"Is that New York?" I said as an image of what looked like Central Park flashed up.

He froze the picture, and we both stared in silence. The city was barely recognizable. Almost without exception, masonry buildings of either brick or stone on the island of Manhattan were so severely damaged so that most were flattened or reduced to rubble. All of the bridges were destroyed; spans had been shoved off their piers and cast into the river below by the force of the blast. Fires were burning furiously in every street on every corner of the island. Central Park was a blackened, carbonized patch of dirt.

"Two ICBM strikes only," said Cain with a lowering of his head. "The blasts caused high winds as air was drawn in toward the center of the detonation, creating a fire storm. The wind velocity in the city had been less than five miles per hour before the bombing, but the nuclear wind attained a velocity of one hundred miles per hour. Within a radius of twenty miles from ground zero almost everyone died instantaneously."

I stared at the picture, dumbstruck. Almost all buildings were completely destroyed and fires were ripping through the remains. Trees had been uprooted or withered by the heat. Black stains could be seen everywhere, tear drops of cauterized carbon … all that remained of the people of that great city.

"Turn it off," I said.

The picture went dark as the hologram involuted and dissipated. I leaned on the console, my hands bunched into fists, head down, eyes closed.

"It's war," I said.

"And they have already won," Cain replied quietly.

But burning rage was hissing through my body like lava looking for a volcano's spout. Unbridled fury swept through me in ferocious waves and I produced a scream from deep within which felt like my soul had unleashed a demon.

Cain looked at me with eyebrows raised. "Kate, are you alright …?"

"No I'm not. I will never be alright. Not anymore." I turned to him, eyes blazing. "It's time we stopped running. This …" I pointed to the screen, now dark "… this … is justification for us to exterminate these murderous bastards."

He slowly shook his head. "Kate, the Earth is dying. We can only try and survive."

"No! We need to do more than survive. It's time we stood up and hit back. We can't rest until they're beaten – and I don't mean just beaten down. I mean dead. Extinct. We need to destroy them. I don't much care how it happens, I don't need them to suffer, I just need their cold green eyes extinguished from our fucking galaxy!"

I realized I sounded unhinged, but I didn't care. I didn't fear death anymore – I feared not succeeding. I'd let my daughter down, and I'd had to live with that. The future of the *human race* was on my shoulders now, and I wasn't going to shirk that responsibility. I wasn't going to fail again.

But Cain was apparently not on board. "So, is the elimination of the Vu-Hak from the universe our final goal? Do two 'wrongs' make a 'right'?"

I stabbed a finger in his direction. "They've come here to kill me and every one of my kind. And yours too, Cain. You were their slaves, remember?"

He shrugged. "Is this righteous justice or merely vengeance, Kate?"

"Call it what you want. We didn't start this. It was an accident. We didn't invite them here."

"Kate, what if there is more to the Vu-Hak than you know? Remember, no one, and certainly no race, is created evil ... perhaps I could tell you more of their, shall we say, 'backstory'?"

"Save me that bullshit," I cut him off. "Perhaps once they were innocent but that was way, way in the past. They've learned the thrill of the kill, the sick joy of evil that comes with wanton violence and destruction. You've witnessed that. I've had them in my head – and so have you, for fuck's sake. What's wrong with you? If it's them or us, I choose us and the countless other civilizations in the Milky Way that they'll destroy in the future. No contest, no guilt."

I stormed out of the room and along the spotlessly clean corridor, looking for a way back to the main laboratory where the portal chamber was situated. Cain's footsteps followed me at a distance. The corridor bent around to a doorway. It opened into another spotless white room. Cain quietly followed me in, and the door closed invisibly and noiselessly. This particular chamber was full of pale eggshell-colored equipment, all pipes and cogs and tubes. A dozen or so tables for examinations or surgery were lined up against one wall, linked to cables and optics.

"What goes on in here?" I said, still angry.

"This is the cloning facility."

I walked over to one of the tables and ran my hand over its surface, feeling it give like a spongy mattress. Everything appeared sterile and unused. I scanned the other tables and pulled up short. One was different. I walked over to it, aware of Cain's scrutiny. It was smaller than the others, with plastic-looking screens that would completely cover the table when erected.

"Has this one been used?" I said.

His face was impassive. "I do not know."

My eyes narrowed. "How can you not know?"

Cain actually looked embarrassed, if that was possible. "I have been away from the facility for some time. Adam was working on this, in addition to –"

"Wait." I whirled to face him. "Where *is* Adam?"

Cain closed his eyes for a second, and then said, "He is not here on the moon. I cannot sense him anywhere."

I was incredulous. "When did you last talk with him?"

"We last communicated moments before I picked you up from the Pentagon."

I started pacing, thinking about where he would have gone, and why. And why he wouldn't have left any messages as to his whereabouts. "Have you tried contacting him since we arrived back here?"

"Just now. There has been no response."

I tried to get into Cain's mind, looking for deception or outright lies, but there were none there. Just order and logic, and no sign of subterfuge. A sinking feeling came over me. "What do you think this means?"

He stared back, his unblinking eyes now locked into mine. "I do not know, but it cannot be good."

I leaned against the wall and sank down until I was sitting on the floor. I put my head in my hands and tried not to scream.

"We'll find him," said Cain, coming over and reaching out to touch my arm.

I shrugged him off, shaking my head. "We don't have time for this … you said so yourself."

"He must be back on Earth," he said. "I should be able to detect his Electromech's radiation footprint, if we get close enough."

"But you have no goddamn idea where he is," I said, more harshly than I meant to.

He shrugged. "True, but I should be able to narrow down his possible destinations. Then I just need to get within a hundred miles or so in order to determine his exact whereabouts."

Another worrying thought occurred to me. "What if he doesn't want to be found? Or worse, he's been ... taken?"

Cain squatted down next to me and lifted my face up by the chin. "I'll find him," he said. "You go and get the embryos."

FORTY-ONE

The wormhole spun a kaleidoscope and the sensation of nausea swirled unrestrained in my virtual stomach. It was incredible how my mind was still able to convince me I had internal organs and the feelings that went with them.

I materialized behind a dumpster in an alley smelling of days-old food and dog shit. Above, clear blue skies were scarred by black smoke trails, and the pixelated outline of the ship was just visible as it banked away, camouflaged from human eyes.

I'd been transported to Cairns, an Australian city on the northeast coast of Queensland and a popular Australian tourist destination because of its tropical climate and access to rainforests and the Great Barrier Reef. Cairns was the home of AusStemGen, the storage facility for the embryos we needed. Stillman had argued strongly about me going alone, but both Cain and I made her understand that my Electromech body would give me the best chance of survival should I encounter another Vu-Hak – even one in an Electromech of its own. I was definitely worried about Cain's assessment that they were already adapting to the Electromechs without the AI interface, and would soon be much more powerful than I ever could be. We'd also noted rising levels of radiation and spreading global panic, which were other compelling reasons why it would be safer for me to go alone.

The whine of police sirens and the sound of windows being smashed interrupted my reverie. I picked up the two containers I'd brought from the ship. They resembled over-sized suitcases, and inside were interlinked vacuum-sealed tubes for the embryos together with vital nutrients and an electrostatic plasma field designed to keep them safe. The cases were also lined with diamond-strengthened carbon-epoxy to protect them from the wormhole's destructive vortex.

According to my internal schematic the ASG facility was one block away so I headed up the alley to the corner of the main street. Fires were raging further up the avenue where the obligatory piles of car tires had been stacked up and set alight. Deserted trucks and cars were scattered along the road and sidewalks. Youths in a gang were breaking windows and throwing themselves against the door of a 7/11. The shopkeeper was inside, peering fearfully out from behind the counter. A few vehicles were snaking around the obstructions, windows closed, lights on, stopping for no one. A couple of kids threw bricks at the passing vehicles, laughing. There were jeers and shouting as they burned cars, looted, destroyed property with no thought to whom it belonged. I saw only a mob, mindless and dangerous. Other law-abiding and fearful citizens were fleeing down side streets or barricading themselves inside their properties.

I set off along the sidewalk toward the AusStemGen building, which looked intact and unsullied by the mob. I supposed there'd be nothing attractive about it to loot. A single logo on the wall above a large glass-fronted entryway said *ASG-Australia*, giving no clue as to what went on there. There were a couple of steps up to weary looking double doors painted bright blue. The frames had some bullet holes in them, so that wasn't so good. The door was locked with an electronic pad, so I infiltrated my mind into the mechanism and opened it. I entered the lobby and closed the door behind me. The air inside smelled like a dentist's office, all antiseptic and sterile.

Behind the main desk was a glass-fronted doorway leading to the offices, the laboratory and the vaults where the embryos were stored. I unscrambled the door's keypad, gaining entry to a corridor lined with pictures, certificates and awards attesting to the work the facility had done over the years. Water was dripping somewhere, a *plinky-plunk* kind of noise, which was metronomic and irritating. The corridor was barely lit, flickering neon tubes buzzing and crackling.

An elevator led down to the basement and hopefully to where I'd find the embryo storage tanks. One quick ride later and the doors opened into a dimly lit laboratory as quiet and as cold as a morgue. The desktop computers were dead, their hardware boxes, printers, scanners all missing. Filing cabinets had been ripped open and their contents discarded around the room. Personal effects of the scientists and technicians were scattered everywhere, as if they'd left in a hurry. The whole place gave off a mildly disconcerting *Marie Celeste* feeling. There was a strong odor of bleach and organics, such as the agar used to plate bacteria on petri dishes. Stainless steel centrifuges and microscopes and PCR machines were dotted around in between a huge walk-in refrigerator and water baths glowing with cool yellow light. An autoclave with double flow hoods dominated the side of one wall, and there was a walk-in shower cubicle next to another door that was bolted and locked.

The embryonic stem cell storage vault.

There was no entry pad and no padlock, just solid bolts and an archaic tumbler mechanism to the door. As I reached out to spin it the noise of a chair scraping on the tiles made me jump.

"There's nothing valuable for you in there," came a woman's voice from the corner of the room.

I hit a light switch and the strips in the ceiling shimmered on. A middle-aged woman sat at a desk, legs crossed. She took a drag on a cigarette and squinted up at me, an unruly mess of dark chocolate hair framing a heart-shaped face and expressive red-rimmed eyes. She was wearing what looked like dungarees underneath a soiled lab coat.

"What the fuck are you supposed to be?" she said, taking another drag on her cigarette and flicking the ashes onto the floor.

I realized how strange I must appear to her.

Cain had insisted I wore appropriate clothing for a research laboratory, so he'd put me in a white one-piece garment that covered me from shoulders to mid-thigh without any seams, creases or pockets. My hair was whitened as well, cut just above my ears, and I'd painted a single horizontal strip of shadow across my lids and nose like an Apache Indian, hiding my phosphorescent green eyes. My skin was almost as white as my clothing and hair.

"I'm not supposed to be anything," I said. "And you're wrong about there being nothing of value here."

To my surprise she threw her head back and gave a raucous laugh, a sound like crow calling. She flicked her cigarette in my direction, embers twinkling as it spun through the air. "I meant there's nothing for *you* in there," she said, eyes wide and defiant.

"Why do you say that?" I asked, perplexed.

Her mouth twitched. "Because what's been done here is immoral and against the law of God."

Right.

"What's your name?" I said.

"What does it matter?"

"Did you work here?"

She snorted and broke into a half smile. "Of course not. I've been trying to shut this place down for years. Since it opened. My church and me, we been protesting outside every day. Didn't stop these bastards from experimenting on embryos."

I wondered whether I could be bothered to debate her, or indeed had the time. Many religions took the position that embryos were human beings, created by God in whose image they were made. Given that such teaching stated it was immoral to destroy human life, the mere derivation of embryonic stem cells was antithetical to their position.

I approached the desk she was sitting at, which was covered in journals and papers and a few photograph frames. One had a picture of a woman holding a little girl, aged about five. The girl was holding a white cat in her arms and clearly giggling with delight. I picked it up and my heart melted. An image of my own daughter floated unbidden into my mind. She was standing on a sidewalk looking left and right, holding herself in a manner that suggested she'd like to disappear altogether. She wasn't focusing, eyes scanning without locking onto any one thing, daydream-like. She shifted her weight from left to right and back again every few seconds as if thinking of moving and yet choosing to remain still.

I suppressed a sob and rubbed a hand over my eyes.

"Lost someone as well, did you?" the woman said. There was little emotion in her voice, a flat, weary, past-caring kind of tone.

I nodded, not looking at her. "My daughter."

"God judged you then. How did it feel?"

"I'm not one of the scientists you despise," I said, my anger bubbling up.

The woman grunted, looking me up and down with a sneer. "Of course you are. Look at you. Think I'm stupid?"

Then she did something I didn't expect. She pulled a gun out of her lab coat pocket and pointed it at me. It was a small silver weapon, like a derringer with four barrels.

"The 'end times' are here, as prophesied. You and your kind laughed at us, but who's laughing now? We've been judged, and God's damnation is on all of us."

"So what's your role in this?" I said.

"I'm here to protect these here souls." She gestured to the vault. "And God will judge me fairly."

I moved closer to her, watched the gun barrel trembling slightly as she moved it up to point at my face. I'd been part of an evangelical congregation as a child and had witnessed pastors raging about the fire and brimstone of hell so much that I'd become immune to it. However, I'd seen enough people crippled with anxiety, scared witless in case any bad thought would expel them from everlasting life. This woman was one of them.

"Go ahead and shoot. I'm here for the embryos. I'm actually going to save them so you and your god should be pleased."

"You're lying."

"You want to save these souls from going to hell, is that right? These cells in petri dishes? You aren't being honest with yourself. You're just doing this to win 'brownie points' with your god now that you are for sure going to die soon. Tell me I'm wrong?"

The knuckles on the gun handle whitened, and she gritted her teeth as my words sunk in. However, I didn't care anymore. "You're right, the world is ending," I continued. "But not humanity. Not if I can help it. Earth is our home, where we started out, but it doesn't have to be where we end up."

The gun wobbled a bit more, and lowered a few inches. The face behind it was looking puzzled, less certain, less crazy.

I held out a hand, palm up and smiled. "Put the gun down."

Her gaze drifted away, trained on some invisible ghost, her eyelids looking too heavy to even blink. It was as if her brain was suffering some sort of short circuit, and she was struggling to get the neurones to fire and connect. I moved back into her line of sight and touched the barrel with the side of my finger. Her head tilted upward, her eyes sliding back into focus.

"Are you an angel?" she said in a quiet voice.

I let my mind drift into hers, and I pushed images and sensations there. Riding a cycle, autumn leaves crinkling and crackling under the tires and light playing peek-a-boo through the moving branches. Of air alive with the song of birds, a nearby stream of clear water bubbling over a rocky bed teeming with silver fish. Of her loved ones, appearing on the beach ahead, ready to greet her and walk hand in hand with her into heaven.

She smiled and closed her eyes as I took the gun from her hand and caught her as she slipped out of the chair. I laid her gently on the ground and watched her for a few minutes as her breathing slowed and settled into a regular rhythm.

"Maybe I am," I said softly.

FORTY-TWO

As I exited the front door of the facility, burning rubber and woodsmoke once again assailed my olfactory receptors. Pungent black clouds were blowing through the streets and there were cries and screams and gunfire coming from all around.

I hopped down the stairway to the sidewalk, broken bottles scrunching under my feet. There were a number of vehicles stopped nose-on in the middle of the road, no signs of drivers or passengers. The nearest was a kind of utility vehicle that Australians quaintly called a 'ute. I gently placed the two containers in its rear, pushing aside gardening tools and paint pots to make room. I was about to climb in the cab when I heard the *slap slapping* of shoes on concrete. I turned and saw eight guys closing in, most holding beer bottles as weapons, one carrying a big knife, and one waving a baseball bat that had blood stains on the tip. They were all in their late teens or early twenties, rough and unshaven. Opportunists. Looters. Anarchists. Taking advantage of a society breaking down. They pulled up in a rough semicircle a few yards away, trying to look intimidating, and would have succeeded had I been Kate Morgan in her former iteration.

"Hey, what's in the bags, darlin?" said the guy with the bat.

I stepped down from the 'ute and glowered at him. "The future of the human race, you shithead."

He burst into laughter and nervously tapped the bat on his thigh. A couple of the others thought it funny too but the laughter quickly stopped and they became aggressive again. Batman's lips curled down and he nodded at the AusStemGen building. "What you hidin back there?"

I just looked at him silently, hoping this was going to go another way. Any other way. One of the gang leaned in to Batman and pointed to the cases in the back of the 'ute.

"Ask her what's in the bags," he said.

I sighed and looked up at the sky. "Okay, I'm going to give you all one chance to walk away. Please take it."

There was more laughter, but it was short-lived. I could smell alcohol on their breath, and they had the wide-eyed stares of drug-users. A guy with blond scraggly hair tied up in a manbun took a step forward and waved a knife in my direction. "I think we'll just take 'em. Then we might take you as well, bitch."

I knew how they thought this was going to go down, because all they saw was an unarmed woman in a world suddenly gone to shit where there were no rules and they could do what they liked. Society hadn't been kind to them before the fall, and so they felt they owed society nothing. They expected easy pickings and got closer, Batman moving ahead of the knife guy while the others fanned out on both sides.

"Fuck this," I said and reached out with my mind, preparing the neurological switch that would put them all to sleep.

Nothing happened.

My vision blurred for a second, and I put a hand out to grab the side of the 'ute. Cain's quick fix in the transfer chamber was wearing off already.

"Right, last chance," I hissed. "Or we do this the hard way."

Batman just spat on the sidewalk, a great glob of sputum. I guessed that was the challenge accepted.

I sidestepped Batman and got into the knife guy's face. I swept my arm down, inside out hitting his forearm and jolting the knife out of his grip. My right elbow then hooked around and hit him full on in the face with more kinetic energy than a tennis racket at full serve. Batman was still processing what had just happened when I pulled the bat out of his hand and stabbed the knob into the middle of his face, squashing his nose with a starburst of crimson.

Two down, three seconds gone.

The third and fourth guys might as well have been traveling in slow motion as I moved in. One of them had his arms open to grab me in a bear hug so I just swung the bat backhanded and caught him full on the point of the jaw, where his neck met his skull. He dropped to his knees, still conscious but lights fading. I swatted him again, taking it easy but with more than adequate power to send him rocking sideways and then flat onto his face. The other guy was already bringing his arms up to protect himself so I just swung the bat one handed, breaking his radius and ulnar bones like dry twigs. He screamed and rolled over onto the sidewalk, flailing with his good arm in an attempt to stop hitting the curb. I took a step forward and kicked him in the face for good measure.

Unsurprisingly, the other four had backed off and were looking anxiously at each other and me. I pointed the baseball bat at each of them in turn, counting, "… eenie, meenie …" daring them to make a move.

I wanted them to try it. Inside I was raging.

They ran.

"Scum," I hissed.

I broke the baseball bat in two over my knee, the noise loud and splintery, and I threw the pieces after them. The anger faded almost instantaneously and was replaced by sadness. Up the street looters and pillagers were running in and out of shopfronts and businesses and houses. I guessed that ordinary folks were doing the same, just trying to survive. Car alarms and shop alarms were going off, women and children were screaming and crying.

I got into the 'ute and gunned the engine.

Thirty minutes later I arrived at the ocean. I drove the ute as far as it could go into the sandy scrubland that corralled the beach and turned the motor off. I got out and leaned on the door, taking in the view. The shore was everything at once, every shade of blue before me, every shade from white to browns and greys at my feet. I closed my eyes, taking in the cool breeze, stealing warmth, the taste and smell of the brine. The ocean's music took command of my ears with crashing waves and the forlorn cries of the gulls. Behind me a cliff face rose sharply, graphite in the autumn sun, a winding wooden path snaking up and into the parkland up top.

I lifted the containers out of the flatbed and walked the thirty yards or so to the edge of the ocean, kicking off my shoes. The shore was a graceful arc of sand, glittering under the sun. Here, the waves rolled in with a soothing sound, the salty water disturbing a brief flurry of sand. Every few yards or so lay a shell, treasures of the deep, and small wet pebbles. I picked up a rock, slate-grey and worn smooth by millions of years of tidal erosion, and with a flick of the wrist sent it spinning into the sea just as the waves started to recede. Bouncing and skipping, each impact seemed to add energy and sending it higher until it accelerated out of sight with little regard for the laws of physics.

"Gee, how'd you do that?" came a voice.

I turned to find a small boy descending the wooden stairs built into the cliff at the edge of the beach. He was wearing board shorts, scuffed Converse trainers and a dirty white T-shirt. His hair was bleached blond and flapping around his ears as the onshore breeze played with it. A scrappy little cattle dog, red-brown with a pelt like a worn carpet, had also scuttled down the stairs and was now sniffing around my legs and wagging his small tail. I bent down and ruffled the fur between his ears, and he sat back on the sand and seemed to smile up at me. I glanced back at the boy, who looked eight or nine years old, and was now standing at the foot of the stairs nervously watching.

"Where are your parents?" I asked.

He indicated back up the stairs with a flick of his head. "Not far. They'll be along soon."

I looked up the cliff, tracked the winding wooden staircase as far as it would go before it disappeared a few hundred yards into the scrubland of the national park. Beyond, just above the treeline, the sky was a blood red orange with wispy smoke plumes oozing into the atmosphere, diffusing and mingling as they rose. Eastward, back along the beach, the rainforest canopy was broken up by the skeletal remains of holiday apartments, previously millionaire's weekend retreats with ocean views to die for. Now they were deserted and broken, their burned-out rafters and beams obscenely silhouetted charcoal against the darkening sky. I closed my eyes, immersing myself in the roar of crashing waves and the hissing of the water being pulled back over finely ground sand and gravel. I registered a mixture of odors: the charcoal of burning timber, putrid and decaying animal carcasses, sharp petroleum fuel, all clinging to the onshore breeze.

"Are you one of them?" the boy asked, blue eyes as wide as dinner-plates.

I wondered if he knew about the Vu-Hak, or whether my appearance was curious enough for a nine-year-old boy to join the dots better than an adult.

I looked sideways at him and tapped the rock next to me. "Come, sit with me?"

He looked up and shook his head, staring at his dog, wondering whether to call him in.

"It's okay," I said. "What's your name?"

He looked back up the stairs, and then shrugged. "David."

"Hello, David. Nice to meet you."

He sidled over and slowly sat down next to me. Up close his skin was pale and patchy, with broken veins over his temple. He looked thin and unhealthy, and his bare arms were covered with scratches and bruises. His knees were a mottled purple, faded like a patchwork quilt. I reached over and put an arm around his shoulders, and in silence we watched the dog playing in the surf. Abruptly, David leaned forward, clutched his stomach and vomited into the pool of seawater at his feet. I held him until he had stopped retching, then washed his mouth and face with seawater from another puddle. I could feel his ribs moving under his shirt and the tremor of his muscles as he tried to control the nausea. I closed my eyes and allowed his emotions and thoughts to flow into mine. I sensed his fatigue, his loneliness and his terror. I coaxed his liver cells to manufacture anxiolytic proteins, which I then released into his bloodstream and through the blood–brain barrier, washing through his cerebral cortex, taking away the fear and anxiety.

As I looked at David I thought of my dead daughter and sadness drained through me, traveling through every molecule. The memories flooded back, a tsunami that threatened to overwhelm and drown me. The beautiful little girl who exited my life so abruptly, leaving me broken. Artificially forgotten for six months because of my forced amnesia.

Perhaps it had been better that way …

I sensed a subliminal rumbling, like the passage of an underground subway train, and concentric ripples appeared in the surrounding rock pools. Sand started to trickle down from cracks higher up the cliff, and the tremors began to loosen the compact sand at my feet. A bright moon-sized blot appeared in the sky, enlarging fast. The grumbling noise became more visceral and the waves stopped their progress and now just sloshed around my feet like oil being swirled in a frying pan. I stood and watched as the shimmering sphere became an enlarging obsidian whirlpool bereft of lights or color. As it grew, the ocean hollowed out in a concave arc, the seabed underneath exposed to air for the first time in many eons. The atmosphere pulsed and surged as waves of unidentified energy charged the air with static. David put his fingers in his ears, closed his eyes and started to scream. I elevated the level of anxiolytic chemicals coursing through his body, and immediately his eyes closed, consciousness fading. I caught him as he slid off the rock and lowered him gently to the wet sand.

Cain appeared from the wormhole and slowly glided toward me. He touched down softly on the sand, ripples and tremors appearing under his feet. Like me, he was dressed in white, but in his Adam Benedict mode, all black hair, sharp angular features, and an aquiline nose. He looked around at the beach, then up the cliff-face at the staircase, then at the boy, sleeping peacefully by the rock. He lifted his head, as if sniffing the air, and closed his eyes.

"It's time to leave," he said. "We can't delay any longer. Finding you took too long."

I shook my head, looking at David. "I just need to make sure he'll be alright."

Cain's eyes blinked lazily, green phosphorescence flashing. "There's nothing you can do for them. You must know that."

"I won't let him suffer," I said.

Cain placed a hand on David's forehead and gave an unexpectedly gentle caress of his brow, brushing a lock of hair away. "He is suffering. It'll be better if he dies in his sleep."

I closed my eyes and waited for the tears to come. When they didn't, I looked up at the wormhole, floating above the ocean bed.

"It's done then?"

"Yes."

"Are there many left alive?"

There was a brief pause, then: "Does it matter? Once we find Adam we need to leave."

The side of my mouth twitched, and I shook my head sadly. "Not anymore."

Cain picked up the two containers with the embryos, the future of the human race, and floated up into the wormhole. I took one last look at the beach and at David, unmoving, his dog standing over him and licking at his ears.

I turned away, unable to take it anymore.

FORTY-THREE

Cain and I stepped off the wormhole platform as the portal span down behind us. Waiting behind the consoles were Stillman and Hamilton, both dressed in identical fitted jumpsuits wrapped with tubing and wires. Their suits were a steely matte grey and had a rubbery look a bit like a dolphin.

Stillman gave me a smile. "I know, stylish, right?"

I threw Cain a frown and he shrugged. "These suits will be necessary for their safety when the ship traverses the wormhole."

I was shocked. "Wait, back up ... the *ship*?"

Hamilton was nodding. "Yes! You should see it. Look."

He ushered me over to the console, where Cain activated a projection representing the wormhole generator. The images of the portal were similar if not identical to those from the Nevada crater back in Indian Springs. A spinning white mirror-like sphere with glimpses of galaxies and stars inside.

Cain waved a hand and a representation of the ship appeared next to it, all computer-generated white and blue lines like something from the movie *Tron*. The scale of the wormhole he had produced was incredible. A mile across, easily. The ship would pass through it like cotton thread through the eye of a needle.

"You've been busy," I marveled.

"The ship basically did all the work," he replied. "Remember, it is essentially an advanced Von Neumann machine, able to replicate almost anything if given sufficient and accurate information."

"So, you fed it the data from the Lindstrom diaries?"

"Yes, the Trinity Deus formula was uploaded six months ago, and in the last twenty-four hours the ship derived the solution. We can now produce a stable wormhole with a diameter of approximately one and a half miles."

Hamilton reached out a hand and gave mine a squeeze. "We can leave now, at any time."

"To go where?" I said quietly.

"Anywhere we want," he replied.

"Within reason," interjected Stillman.

"Indeed," said Cain. "The wormhole still needs to be tethered at its exit point, and to do that it is necessary to acquire accurate four-dimensional co-ordinates of the destination. Otherwise we could materialize in the center of a star, or a black hole."

"But then we just point the ship at it?" I said.

Cain nodded. "The wormhole has a mild gravitational pull, strong enough for it to pull the ship in but weak enough that the ship's maneuvering thrusters are able to guide it gently. Interestingly, the weak gravity results in a slowing of time within the wormhole, a feature which increases with the length of the wormhole."

"What, so ... time slows down the farther we travel?"

"Essentially, yes. But not so much as to be relevant."

I walked slowly around the hologram, watching the wormhole turn steadily to keep facing me, like one of those weird pictures where the eyes follow you.

"The difference between the Nevada wormhole and this one is stability, yes?" I said. "How is that possible?"

"The ship stabilizes the wormhole using dark matter and dark energy," said Cain. "Fundamental particles of a type as yet unknown in human science. Dark matter permeates through almost all galaxies, and is harnessed by Vu-Hak technology to stabilize the naked singularities present in both of our Electromechs. The ship uses dark matter to hold the wormhole open as long as necessary."

I pursed my lips. "So could we lure the Vu-Hak into the wormhole and then close it, severing their connection to our galaxy forever? Would that be possible? Would it destroy them? Then any humans left on Earth would hopefully survive and – perhaps – start again?"

"It would be impossible to lure all the Vu-Hak into the wormhole," said Cain.

Then Stillman got up from her chair and gave me a hug, which was unexpected, and reached up and touched the side of my cheek. I reciprocated by squeezing her hand.

"Are you okay?" she asked, concern in her voice.

"I got the stem cells," I said, glancing at the suitcases that I'd left by the platform. "Humanity's future."

She took my face in her other hand and stared into my eyes. "No, I meant you – how are you doing?"

I wasn't sure how to respond to that. I knew I was on borrowed time, but I didn't know how much was left. Cain had said a couple of days and so it was only a matter of when, not if. My abilities were coming and going. And then, well, that was it.

"I need to know that we have a plan," I said, pointedly looking at Cain.

Stillman looked perplexed. "We do now. We can get out of here. Save ourselves and humanity."

I said nothing and continued to stare at the hologram. Behind the ship and wormhole was a simulation of Earth, looking blue and beautiful, peaceful and welcoming.

Hamilton sidled up next to me, his suit squeaking with each step. "What's it like down there? On Earth?"

Looking at him I wondered what family he'd left behind. Or Stillman, for that matter. I knew very little of their lives outside the FBI. But what could I tell them that would be of any comfort? Great cities falling into dust. People tossed and burned like rag dolls, entombed and engulfed in the nuclear fire storm. Air thick and noxious, rank with the smell of ash and death. Riots and looting and ... The image of the dying boy, his dog frantically licking his face, popped into my head and refused to go away.

"Shakespeare wrote, 'Hell is empty and all the devils are here,'" I said. "It's time we sent the devils back to hell."

Cain looked up sharply. "We have had this discussion, Kate. We must leave. We cannot confront the Vu-Hak. We do not have the technology. The future of your species is –"

"No," I hissed, feeling the rage surface again. "Look what they've done! They've ravaged their own fucking galaxy and now

254

they're here, starting over. We can't just let them. We need to draw the line! Someone has to stop them!"

"Kate, it's over, we've lost …" said Stillman, hesitatingly.

"It's not lost. It can't be! We need to make them pay for this. We … *I* will make them pay for what they've done!"

I was screaming and shaking, and the need for revenge was like a rat gnawing at my soul, relentless and unceasing. I wondered whether hatred was all I had left. I wanted the Vu-Hak dead, all of them, every last fucking one.

But, what then?

I had no idea. I didn't think I cared what would come next.

I'd be dead anyway.

Maybe that was why it had to be me.

There was a quiet in the room and I became cognizant that they were all staring at me. Hamilton looked embarrassed, Stillman concerned, Cain just staring.

"I need to do this," I ground out.

Cain looked at me sadly. "Kate, you don't. This has to be about making a future for the human race."

I closed my eyes and tried to shut out the roaring that was going on. The fever burning in my soul. I wondered whether I still had a soul. I was human once, before I died. Had I lost the right to be called human now, and if not did I still have humanity? Had I blocked all my humanity out so I could taste the only thing left – revenge?

Stillman's hand touched my arm. "He's right, Kate. It's not about us anymore. If it ever was. The Earth is burning and we have to consider the survival of our species. Our right to survive."

I let out a juddering sigh. Revenge could wait.

"Alright. Let's get these embryos to the moon base," I said. "Then we can pack up what we need and get out of here."

Cain shook his head. "No need. All the moon base facilities have been transferred to this ship. We have everything we need to store and nourish the embryos, and much more. Life support has been optimized as well, and quarters are being fashioned as we speak for everyone."

"What about Bill Hubert?" I said. "How's he doing?"

"He's in the med-lab, still out cold," Stillman said. "The ship is keeping him in an induced coma until we can figure out what the problem is."

I looked back at Cain. "What about using the transfer technology if he doesn't recover?"

"Kate, your experience means that –"

"Perhaps there's a way to adapt and reshape the software to allow a more stable and precise connection between the biological tissues and the machine? Or do we just let him die?"

Stillman looked at Cain as well, but he met her pleading eyes steadily and shook his head. I was about to object again when Cain suddenly held up a finger and turned his head as if he was listening for something.

"What is it?" I said.

His voice was low and emotionless, but the words came out clear enough. "I've just been in contact with Adam. He wants us to pick him up."

"What? Where is he?"

"San Francisco."

FORTY-FOUR

The ship broke orbit and powered up the Western seaboard of the United States. The flight deck was quiet and dark apart from silent concussions of lightning that highlighted lines of rain spattering the virtual viewports. We dropped below the clouds about fifty miles south of San Francisco and the apocalyptic images broke my heart again. The blood red Bay Bridge skeleton had been cleaved in two, its cables and columns fractured and its road submerged in the water. Hundreds of vehicles were piled up against the arches, some on fire and smoking, most surrounded by prone unmoving human figures. Thick smog was drifting over the bay from the city, which was flattened and burning. The sun seemed to spit feebly through the hazy atmosphere, and darkness was spreading a melancholy blanket over the land. None of the once mighty skyscrapers were still standing; every structure had been blown apart and turned into dust and smoldering ember. The docks and waterways surrounding were rank with detritus from the dead city, floating timber and plastic and bodies. The bay itself was the color of burnt sienna, waves rolling into the shoreline carrying dead fish and animal carcasses onto the edge of the fire.

"A million people lived downtown," said Stillman quietly.

Cain looked up from the flight controls. "The Bay Area was hit by four Trident II submarine-launched ballistic missiles. These projectiles had multiple nuclear warheads, each with the destructive power of eight Hiroshimas. I estimate five million people died instantly."

"Jesus," murmured Hamilton, turning away from the screen, unable to look at the images anymore. For me, I couldn't drag my gaze away. Rage continued to build, my hands coiled into fists, my thoughts twisting and turning into very dark places.

The ship tracked over the ruined bridge toward Alcatraz Island. The main prison building appeared to be intact although both the lighthouse and the water tower had been blown over and lay in pieces along the hillside down to the water. One of the ferries was lying belly-up at the docking jetty, a pool of black oil thickening the already murky waters.

Cain zoomed in on the recreation yard, a rectangular space a hundred yards long surrounded by concrete walls and wire fencing where once upon a time prisoners had spent a few hours a day in the California sunshine, reminding them of the freedoms they had given up.

"There he is," said Stillman.

A figure could be seen standing halfway along the concrete steps that led from the yard to the old dining hall. He was holding an arm up and staring straight at us despite the fact that the ship was in stealth mode, and invisible to the naked eye.

"Who's that with him?" said Hamilton, peering at the screen.

Another figure had stepped out from behind Adam. A tall winnowy female, wearing jeans and a black leather jacket.

I sat back, almost at a loss for words. My brain stuttered for a moment while my thoughts caught up. I'm sure my eyes and mouth were frozen wide open in an expression of stunned surprise.

"Amy," I said. "His daughter."

The ship de-cloaked and extruded the silvery liquid metal tentacle again, oozing like toothpaste to touch down on the yard's steps. Heavy raindrops struck the concrete, almost pitting the surface as if they were bullets from the gods. Lightning lit the skies in streaks of white phosphorus, blasting holes in the black clouds. A banshee wind howled and swept the pooling rain into sheets of dense water as the fences surrounding the yard bent and creaked.

Adam was struggling to persuade Amy to climb onto the moving steps. She was soaking wet, hair plastered to her face, clothes dirty and ripped. In contrast, the rain seemed to slough off Adam like water off a duck's back. She clung to him, tears pouring down her face, glancing fearfully at the alien skyscraper directly overhead, puncturing low-lying clouds.

I turned to Cain with a flash of annoyance. "How much longer can we stay here?"

He pulled a face. "We shouldn't be here at all. It won't take long before they detect us. There are probably Vu-Hak in the city just over there."

And it would only take one Vu-Hak in a fully enabled Electromech for this to all be over. I pushed myself out of the seat that melted back into the floor of the flight deck. "Leave this to me."

FORTY-FIVE

Incoming!

Cain's voice boomed around my head as I met Adam and Amy at the already sealing doorway, an explosion as loud as any sky-born thunderclap.

I helped him yank her into an ascension tube back up to the flight deck, sensing increased anxiety from the ship as we soared upward. The journey seemed briefer this time, the hull bending and morphing to make the transit shorter. A low propulsive beat was coming from the engines, which sounded like they were powering up rather than idling.

Stillman looked up as we entered the flight deck. Her hands were curled around the armrests, fingers gripping tightly, bony knuckles protruding. Next to her, Hamilton was as white as a sheet, hugging his knees, one leg tapping out a nervous rhythm on the floor. Cain was standing in front of a huge hologram projecting what was left of San Francisco and the Bay area. Adam and Amy appeared at my shoulder, his arm still around her, protecting her. Neither Stillman nor Hamilton seemed to notice she was there.

We hadn't spoken.

"What's going on?" I said, all business.

Then I saw them. Like Valkyries from a Wagnerian opera, multiple silver streaks were approaching, silhouetted by stratocumulus clouds towering into the sky, lightning strikes cascading and rending the air behind them.

"How many?" Adam asked, peering at the image.

Cain inclined his head slightly and zoomed the picture. Lines and circles appeared around each of the converging Vu-Hak, counting and calculating distances and trajectory.

"Fifty-four," he said. "They have been tracking us."

"What are we waiting for?" I yelled. "Get us out of here!"

Cain held up a hand. "I cannot. I do not have any destination co-ordinates. As I said earlier …"

"I don't care! We need to go! Right now!"

Some form of synthetic adrenaline was activating my system, and it felt as if I was on fire. My arms were moving on their own, and I felt disconnected from everything but images of the approaching Vu-Hak.

Adam turned to me, his thoughts sweeping through my mind.

Kate, it will take time to make the calculation. A wormhole this size has never been generated. A simulation is one thing but there are many potential problems if we do not test it first. As Cain says, we cannot navigate blindly as we could end up anywhere. In the middle of a star, for example –

Stillman gasped and put her hand over her mouth. A distortion had appeared in the sky between the Vu-Hak and us. It was swirling and tumbling and forming a vortex and was rapidly moving toward us.

Cain's hands flickered over the hologram. "The three leading Electromechs have each fashioned a pulse of gravitational waves and they are converging on us."

"What exactly are gravitational waves?" I said.

"Artificial ripples in the shape of space. They will reach us in fifteen point four seconds."

"Can we survive the impact?"

He turned to look at me and the sadness on his face said it all. "The intersection of each wave has synergistically increased their strength. It is too late."

A sharp, broken sob pierced the air as Stillman broke down, her hands feebly reaching out and finding Hamilton. "It can't be over. Not after everything."

She was right. We'd come too far to just roll over. I sat down in one of the flight deck chairs and sensed Adam reading my thoughts, becoming alarmed.

Kate, you must not ... think about what you are going to do –

Too late. Time to step up.

"You told me I could save everyone," I said softly. "Did you mean it?"

Before he could answer I closed my eyes, crossed my fingers, and entered the ship's cognitive network.

My mind soared through its systems, arteries, conduits and powerlines, through the plasma fields and gravitational anomalies that powered its vast and incomprehensible engines and into its brain. There, I found the software and synthetic neuronal connections that controlled the wormhole generator. The formula was elegant, the equations beautiful, aesthetically perfect. The ingredients for generating the detonation that would open the portal out of our galaxy were all present in the belly of the ship, dormant and sleeping.

Just waiting for the spark.

I lit the fire.

FORTY-SIX

I accessed the Trinity proof from the formula derived by Lindstrom in 1953, and the untested wormhole generator exploded into life.

In the deepest, most heavily shielded recesses of the ship, exotic elements at the far end of the periodic table collided in a controlled nuclear explosion. A singularity the size of a pinhead was created, instantly collapsing in on itself, unable to withstand the force of its own gravity. At the same time, an artificial white hole was manufactured, spinning and pulsing, light and matter being repelled in equal amounts. As it bent and warped space around it I sent it colliding into the black hole, producing a roaring vortex that sucked all matter toward its event horizon.

Before this unholy creation could destroy the ship, I ejected it at a fraction of the speed of light to a point half a mile off the bow. There was a burst of radiation and light as space and the very fabric of the universe in that small area of the sky was ripped apart. A liquid-looking mirror-like ball appeared, about a mile and a half wide, and a wormhole was born. A tunnel in space-time, huge and terrifying.

I took a deep breath and pointed the ship directly into the maw. Moments before we crossed the event horizon I activated an energy shield comprising entirely of dark matter. Invisible and undetectable, this substance counteracted the gravitational force of the vortex, stabilizing the cataclysmic pressures inside and keeping the newly produced tunnel open. The ship rattled and groaned and twisted but remained intact. As we passed through the event horizon there was an impression of billions of stars spinning around us, forming an unbroken and intensifying ring of light. Inside the tunnel, starlight streaked past, the ship stretching like a rubber band, our individual molecules threatening to be ripped apart by the pressure of the tidal forces.

Cain's voice pushed through my awareness.

This is called spaghettification. Do not be alarmed.

I pictured my ankles stretching away from my knees before my neck elongated into a strand of linguini. I hoped this was a reversible event, or better still, just a subjective hallucination trying to make sense of the utter weirdness that was happening.

Cain's voice whispered through once more, this time with undisguised urgency.

The gravitational waves generated by the Vu-Hak have been sucked into the wormhole with us. They have created instability and are threatening the tunnel.

That didn't sound good. I flicked the sensors aft and watched the data flowing in. A colossal pressure wave was advancing on the ship, producing shearing forces registering way off the scale.

If the tunnel collapses while we are in it, we will not survive.

No shit, Sherlock.

The event horizon would become so small that not even a single wavelength of light could squeeze inside. All the radiation associated with our remains would be burped out leaving nothing but empty space where the black hole used to be.

The velocity of the approaching wave was such that we had only seconds in which to act – and I had no idea what to do. I asked the ship's AI to come up with a solution, but there was nothing but silence from the ether.

Then Adam's voice floated in, calm and collected.

Kate, get the ship to trap the Hawking radiation produced by the vortex and eject it directly back down our long axis.

Hawking radiation – entangled and intrinsically linked particles and antiparticles being randomly generated by the wormhole – was yet another bit of quantum physics that was just a little bit too surreal to try and decipher. I bit back a reply, which would have been sarcastic and something along the lines of 'You're attempting to violate the laws of quantum physics, choose immediately between these three options ...'

But I didn't question him. I just did it.

The ship's dark matter shield focused the Hawking radiation and expelled it forcefully at the gravitational wave. As they collided, space-time bounced back and outward, creating yet another white hole. The gravitational wave was sucked into this new singularity and froze like a snowflake. I watched it falling behind, becoming smaller and more distant as we continued to plough forward through the tunnel. Behind us, the wormhole started to collapse, but directly ahead it appeared to be stable and wide open.

Well done, Kate, you created a quantum tunnel. The gravitational wave should re-emerge back on Earth and destroy any Vu-Hak attempting to enter the wormhole.

Two for the price of one then, I thought grimly.

But were we out of danger?

I sent a message to Cain.

Any idea how long before we arrive, wherever it is we're going?

Cain's voice returned after a few seconds.

Our final destination is unknown ... but forward projections of the vortex's degradation indicate a time in tunnel space of seventy-three minutes.

That was a long time.

Plenty of time, in fact.

I messaged Adam on a private channel.

We need to talk.

FORTY-SEVEN

I waited for Adam in one of the ship's hangars: a huge chamber with walls of half polished steel, half carbon nanofiber, dark and foreboding. I stood on a catwalk bisecting a wall of machines that blinked and flickered with a life of their own. There was a thrum of power felt through the handrails, and the pull of gravity seemed to ebb and flow as the ship continued its journey through the wormhole.

His footsteps clanged on the catwalk as he approached and I folded my arms and set my face into neutral, fighting my emotions. To say I was disappointed was an understatement. It was more like a betrayal, a selfishness on his part that I hadn't anticipated, given everything I'd seen him do and everything he'd said.

Kate, I know what you are thinking, but I can explain.

I bit back my first reply, unable to get my head around what he'd done, the risks he had taken with his own life, and ours. He'd put the survival of the human race at risk – and for what? So he could selfishly save his daughter. I recalled the last meeting he'd had with Amy, when he'd discovered her role in the death of his wife. He'd tried to kill her, though was distraught when he thought he'd succeeded. It wasn't until just before he entered the wormhole on his suicide mission that I told him she'd survived.

"I blame myself, you know," I said, tautly.

He looked perplexed. "For what?"

"I tried to convince you to forgive her, and that some sort of reconciliation was possible. Fuck me if I didn't also offer to help. But this ..." I glowered at him, my eyes burning with anger. "You could have doomed us all."

His face remained expressionless and vacant, but a profusion of emotion was hidden behind. I detected pain, not physical but emotional. He looked earnestly at me and gave a half smile. I felt his mind probing, gazing into my soul. He accessed a memory in there and let it run free. Black booted feet stepping over my prostrate form. Acid burning the inside of my mouth. Coppery smelling blood trickling down my face and pooling under my head. Arms grabbing hold of me. My ear-curdling screams. A little girl lying on her side, her head turned toward me, unblinking eyes open.

"That's not fair," I said tightly.

He moved closer with eyes that seemed to look deeply in my own, into my very soul.

"Kate, you made me understand that there is nothing I shouldn't do to keep Amy safe from harm. You taught me that. Wouldn't you have moved mountains to get your daughter back?"

"Don't you fucking dare go there," I snapped, starting to pull away. But he reached out and took hold of my arm.

"Unconditional love for your children means you care about them more than you care for yourself, yes? We want our children to have everything, things we never had. A better life than our own. It does not matter how destructive it could be, or how it could hurt us. When you love them, you don't stop loving them. Never. Not even if they hurt us. Especially not then. You don't give up because if you give up and move on then it would not be love. If it isn't love, then it's just another worthless thing. You taught me this, Kate. And you were right."

I bit back a sob and closed my eyes. Kelly appeared before me, but not as a little girl, as a vivacious young woman. The adult she would never become. I was supposed to be there for her, wasn't I? To keep her from harm. To protect her and then be there for her when she fell. To keep the monsters at bay …

"I couldn't save her …" I managed.

"I know," he said softly. "But you saved me. You saved your friends. Help me save everyone else."

Then he leaned forward and kissed me. It was just a kiss. Not a passionate one on the lips, but a simple cheek kiss.

It was just a kiss, but it was one that made my virtual heart seem to beat a million miles an hour. One that left me weak at the knees and made my brain freeze.

I wondered whether I loved him.

When I'd first met him I'd already lost my entire world, and he'd lost everything, and more. And yet ... How long does it take to fall in love? A heartbeat? A week? A month? A year? Inside my synthetic body my human mind was convincing me that my face was flushing and something was fluttering in my stomach. Time juddered to a halt as if the world had stopped spinning on its axis.

But then a wall of doubt appeared. How could I let something so incomprehensible, so inconceivable happen? I traced his lip lightly with the tip of my finger, and it pouted slightly, and I had an urge to bite it and start the kiss over again, this time with passion. But then the feeling passed as the reality of the here and now imposed and closed down my emotions: the unpleasant reality that our existence now consisted of human minds inhabiting sexless machine creatures.

I averted my eyes at last and gently unhooked my arm from his grip. He seemed wracked with guilt. His eyebrows furrowed and a pinched look appeared on his face.

"I tried to get others, you know ... for them. Colleen's parents, her brothers, Hubert's children ... but it was too dangerous. The bombs were detonating and I could sense Vu-Hak everywhere. They can use all of the machines' capabilities without AI – just like me. They have adapted."

"You could have contacted us earlier, you know, given us time to prepare," I said.

But I wondered whether we would have come back for him, if we'd known what he was up to. Then I remembered what I'd put Cain through, what I'd risked, to save Colleen. Were we so different, Adam and I? Did I have any right to be angry with a father just wanting to save the life of his only daughter?

He seemed to be reading my thoughts. "The shadow cannot be conquered by shadow, only by light."

His words hung in the air, heavy with a burden I found hard to bear.

"There's something else," he said. "Something that may allow you to forgive my ... my indulgence with Amy."

"There's nothing to forgive."

"There is. Of course there is. So … well … as you have already experienced, death does not have to be the end."

"What are you talking about?"

This time he smiled, impulsively and unexpectedly. "Before I set off to find Amy I completed the modifications on the Vu-Hak cloning technology to make it suitable for human DNA. It is already running on the ship."

"I assumed that was the case," I said slowly. "Cain implied as much. It's needed to grow and mature the embryos."

"That's not all. I kept biological tissues from your dying body, Kate. They are in storage on the ship. Cryopreserved. You can live again, as a human, not as a machine."

I was lost for words. But there was more to come.

Much more.

"You kept a sample of Kelly's hair. You had it with you on the submarine."

My mind tingled, like a hand that had been slept on. "I lost it," I said, not daring to believe.

"No Kate, I found it. You can have your daughter back too."

FORTY-EIGHT

We are arriving.

Cain's voice boomed around my head and Adam's too. We locked eyes. Many things still unspoken and needing to be said. They would have to wait.

We ran back to the flight deck to find Cain sitting in front of the main screen, which showed a 3-D image of the vortex. Directly ahead was a pulsing, spinning disc which was enlarging second by second.

He pointed at the screen. "We'll be coming out of tunnel space soon. Just a few seconds …"

I nodded and took a seat next to him, Adam taking a seat behind us. Amy had been placed in another of those chairs that extruded seamlessly from the floor. She was snoring softly, as were Stillman and Hamilton, also in similar chairs.

Cain saw me looking and said, "It's better this way … for their own safety."

The ship lurched and we exploded into normal space.

At first the blackness appeared flawless and absolute until billions of stars appeared, like pins in a backlit velvet cushion. Gas clouds and nebulae came into view and drifted across the sky like psychedelic clouds.

The screen flickered and transformed to an electronic orrery as the ship's sensors identified a solar system dead ahead. I scanned the data as it came in.

Two stars appeared in a wide binary: one a yellow G-type and the other a cool white dwarf. The G-type had seven planets in stable orbits, and one was a gas giant, milky white with multiple rings of blue and black and a solitary red spot. It was in the habitable zone of the star and had a couple of moons orbiting in equatorial planes. The biggest moon was planetoid-sized, about two and a half times the diameter of Earth. The planets were two billion years old, according to the data scrolling beneath their hologram representations, but the big moon was the most interesting. Gravity was about twice Earth normal, indicating a bigger, denser core and mantle. It was rotating equatorially with a period of fifty-seven hours and was in sync with the gas giant. It had a perihelion of one hundred and seven million miles. Its atmosphere was fifteen percent oxygen, eighty-four percent nitrogen and one percent argon and other trace gases. About twenty-four percent of the surface was covered in water, and there were two small polar ice caps. There were rainforests and deserts. Lots of deserts.

And life forms.

The planet was teeming with life in astonishing profusion and diversity. Multicellular, large and small, animals and plants in abundance.

There were no obvious signs of civilization: no cities or road networks, no pollution, no radio chatter or electronic signals.

I worked on controlling my excitement as Cain brought the great ship to orbit, and then spiraled it down into the thin upper reaches of the thermosphere. The dull roar of the engines increased as we hit the atmosphere, a distant thunder that became louder as the density of the air thickened. Becoming visible as we passed through the creamy clouds was a body of water hundreds of miles across, waves lapping against a couple of large islands ringed by grey-yellow sand. Trees and vegetation spread from the beaches into nearby hills and onto the lower slopes of mountain ranges before they thinned out into the yellow of the desert.

Cain pointed at a large bay with shallow water, turned the ship on its axis and descended stern first onto the beach. Huge plumes of sand and spray were kicked up and blew in great eddies, gyrating and spinning, obscuring the landing site. We touched down with barely a bump or tremor.

As the engines shut down, the walls around the deck became transparent. Bright light flooded the compartment, and my eyes spun down to adjust. The yellow sun was high in the sky, its white neighbor just visible at the edge of a cloud, like a turning page. I could almost imagine seagulls crying, and the smell of saltwater in the air.

"About time we caught a break, eh?" I said, smiling broadly. "I mean, what're the chances of finding somewhere like this?"

There was silence and I glanced at Cain first, then Adam. Cain was accessing data hieroglyphics on a personal screen, scrolling pictograms faster than I could keep up.

"What?" I said.

Adam shook his head and shot me a look that froze me to my core.

"What's the problem?" I said. "Where are we?"

He waved a hand and the external panorama transformed into to a night scene.

A canopy of luminous stars materialized in the ocean of blackness in the night sky. The beach appeared monochrome and glistening, a faint wind brushing against the water's surface, rippling the stillness and shattering the reflection of the giant planet dipping below the far horizon. Its multicolored rings seemed to melt into the ocean, leaving a dappled track along the sea to the beach. Another moon could be seen traversing just above the equator, a mottled green and black sphere.

Memories exploded in my mind like 4th of July fireworks.

Figures rising out of the water, thousands upon thousands of human figures. Mike Holland, dying as a wraith-like form, ripped apart by unimaginable gravitational forces and frozen in the absolute zero of space, as he had traveled here, to this world, through the Trinity wormhole.

"No!" I said, bringing my hand to my mouth.

Cain's voice was quiet, but his words echoed in my head.

"Yes, Kate. This is the planet of the Vu-Hak."

FORTY-NINE

The ship had formed a balcony by extending a piece of its hull outward and fashioning a plasticized transparent shield bubble to cover it. We sat around a low table facing the distant mountains and away from the sea. Night had fallen, and rivulets of rain were being blown horizontally as the winds picked up and buffeted the side of the ship. The first heavy raindrops started to patter on the windshield and silent lightning discharges illuminated black clouds that had blown in from the north. Bach's "Toccata and Fugue in D Minor" tinkled in the background, and a bottle of clear golden liquid and two glasses sat in the middle of the table.

"I don't understand," I said for the second time to no one in particular. "This system was about to be destroyed."

I looked around the table, and gave Stillman a look to say 'back me up here'. Instead, she leaned forward in her chair and poured herself a glass of the liquid. She sank back again, taking a drink and making a theatrical swallowing sound. "Not bad," she said, raising her glass at Adam, who was sitting next to me. "Where'd this come from?"

"The ship made it."

"Amazing. Tastes like bourbon." She poured a couple of fingers into the other glass and offered it to Hamilton.

As they clinked glasses I glanced at Cain, who was standing by the window watching the approaching storm. The sound of thunder filled the room and lightning flashed again, this time much nearer.

"Cain, maybe you can help me out here. Make me understand."

Cain didn't turn, but his voice was clear. "What is there to understand? This is the planet of the Vu-Hak."

I felt my frustration rising and gritted my teeth. "This doesn't make any sense. How did we end up here? Don't tell me this was a coincidence?"

"It is no coincidence. The wormhole opened by the Trinity formula connects to this specific location, in this galaxy. Where else would it take us?"

"But this can't be the same planet." I stabbed a finger at the windshield, my voice raised. "Those suns were about to go supernova, and the Vu-Hak were constructing a Dyson sphere around them. I saw it happening."

Hamilton drained his glass and waved it at Stillman for a refill. "What if this is the same but an alternate planet? In an alternate universe?"

I threw him a sharp look. "You're kidding, right?"

He passed the bottle back to Stillman and shrugged at me. "Why not? Something must have happened when the ship blew that gravitational wave away. Maybe something happened to the wormhole. Maybe it split into multiple wormholes, and one of them opened at another universe? A parallel universe?"

"So we were lucky enough to end up in a universe where the Vu-Hak don't exist? Another coincidence?"

Stillman filled her glass with more of the ship's bourbon and gave a strange giggle. "I don't see why not. Should anything surprise anyone anymore?"

The ship's bourbon was clearly starting to have an effect.

Cain turned from the window to face us. He had his hands behind his back as if he was about to deliver a lecture. Which he did …

"I think we can exclude the 'other universe' concept. Almost every other universe is unlikely to have the requisite conditions for life. Our life could only exist in the universe that happens to be finely tuned for us. To quote an ancient philosopher: 'Our world must be the worst of all possible worlds, because if it were significantly worse in any respect it could not continue to exist'."

Hamilton made a 'humph' sort of sound and sank back into the chair, sipping his drink. Stillman had also gone all quiet and reflective as well. I looked sideways at Adam, who had his eyes closed. I nudged him. "What do you think?"

His eyes opened lazily and he steepled his fingers. "There is only one answer. We have traveled a long way back in time."

Hamilton coughed and sprayed some of his bourbon over his dolphin-skinned jumpsuit.

I stared at Adam in disbelief. "You're kidding."

"It is possible to find solutions in general relativity that allow for backward time travel, and the solutions require the invocation of quantum mechanics – or wormholes."

I shot Cain a look next. "Do you go along with this? I mean, I thought any difference in time outside the wormhole would be minutes or seconds only."

He gave a non-committal kind of head wobble and crossed the floor to take his seat next to me. "We are in uncharted scientific territory, but yes, it is possible. Construction of a traversable wormhole like the one we have just traveled through requires the existence of a substance with negative energy. That is because the two mouths of a wormhole could not be brought together without inducing quantum field and gravitational effects that would either make the wormhole collapse or make the two mouths repel each other like magnetic poles."

"What negative energy was used?" I said, my eyebrows furrowing.

"Remember that the ship used dark matter to stabilize the wormhole," said Adam, looking at me. "It is the unknown in this equation. Its effects on time dilation would have been difficult to calculate."

"Indeed," said Cain. "In this case the amount of dark matter was sufficient to do just that. The quantum effects must have produced sufficient violations of the null energy condition to allow us to both travel a huge distance, cosmologically speaking, but also backward in time."

Hamilton was staring wide-eyed and trying to follow the conversation like a spectator at a tennis game. "How far back in time have we come?" he asked, a slight tremor in his voice.

Adam closed his eyes again, and I could almost see the cogs whirring as he accessed the data and made his calculations. After a few seconds his eyes snapped open and he looked around the table.

"Approximately fifteen thousand years."

You could have heard a pin drop.

"No fucking way –" started Hamilton.

"How the hell –?" shouted Stillman.

"Wait," I said, holding a finger up and turning to Adam. "Are you saying we've almost certainly arrived at a time *before* the Vu-Hak developed their murderous, galaxy-destroying proclivities?"

Adam paused, considering the implications of my question, and nodded. "I believe that would be a correct interpretation of the time scale involved."

"So we can prevent the annihilation of humanity," I blurted, excitedly. "We can change the future, by the actions we take in this time."

Cain raised a hand. "Not so fast. There are infinite possibilities. The 'many worlds' interpretation of quantum mechanics involves the time traveler arriving in a different universe's history from their own. A mutually exclusive history not interacting with ours."

Stillman leaned forward, clearly thinking what I was thinking and ignoring Cain's objection. "Kate, in this universe, at this time, if we destroy the Vu-Hak they never travel to our galaxy?"

"That's right," I said.

Hamilton clapped his hands together. "Humanity is saved from extinction. Fuck yeah!"

Cain held his hands up. "Please, you need to think this through. Each time traveler would experience a single self-consistent history, so they remain within their own world rather than traveling to a different one. Nothing will change."

"No, you're wrong," I said. "It won't matter if this is the *same* universe or an alternate timeline – destroying the Vu-Hak here and now will ultimately lead to the same thing. They will never be a threat to humanity."

"Kate, I think I have made my position clear –"

I gave him a fierce look. "Yes I understand that you're a pacifist, Cain. Which I find incredible taking into account your race's history of slavery to the Vu-Hak. But I see it one way – if it's a choice between them or us – I choose us any fucking day of the week. Especially after what we've just witnessed."

Adam abruptly stood up and walked over to the windscreen, his back to us. He stared out at the torrential rain that was now obscuring the view. The night sky was a featureless haze and lightning strikes continued to leave afterimages on my retinae. I got up and joined him on the balcony.

"Hey, are you okay?" I said.

He nodded wordlessly.

"Is this about Amy?"

Amy was resting in another part of the ship, having declined to come to this meeting. In her defense she had looked terrible and was clearly shell shocked. Adam had put her into the med-lab along with Hubert and given her a mild sedative.

He shook his head and gave me a crooked smile. "I was just reflecting on what would happen to me if we destroy the Vu-Hak here, or even prevent them from becoming sentient."

"What do you mean?"

"Consider this: if the Vu-Hak no longer dominate this galaxy, it will make no difference to the wormhole, which was generated by the Trinity Deus device back on Earth. So, I would still be in that crater when the wormhole opens and I would again be transported, dead, to this galaxy. But this time I would not be resurrected. There would be no Vu-Hak to 'save' me and send me back."

"Wait –" I began.

"Amy would be orphaned, and would continue living as a prostitute in Las Vegas, until her untimely death …" He reached out and grasped my hand. "Kate, you and I would never meet. Your life, such as it was in Indian Springs, would go on. Your daughter would be dead, forever …"

He raised his eyebrows and waited for me to process what he was saying. It didn't take long. While I was still wrestling with the ethics of resurrecting Kelly as a clone, I wasn't prepared to sacrifice this chance he'd given me of having her back in my life. My love for her had been so close to pure love that to lose it so violently was something I wasn't ever going to heal from. I'd held her on the day she came into this world, and I'd held her before I buried her. She'd vanished into thin air, twice over as my memory of her was subsequently taken away. Now I had my memory of her back, and unbelievably the chance of another life with her, I realized that I couldn't – I wouldn't – give it up.

Cain cleared his throat. "But Adam, would you, in fact, die? Perhaps you would just continue in this new timeline, here in this galaxy, as the old timeline reboots back on Earth. Parallel existences, never to intersect. Humanity continues on Earth, without any knowledge of these events. Meantime, you initiate a new era for Humanity 2.0, here on this planet."

Adam's head dropped. "I am being selfish. In truth, my death would be the sacrifice that would save humanity. I tried to do this once, and failed. Surely this second chance is a sign that it was meant to be."

"On the other hand, maybe we all just disappear in the future, if we significantly alter the past," said Stillman. "Like in *Back to the Future*."

"None of us really know what will happen," said Cain. "So the most sensible option is to do nothing. Allow the Vu-Hak to develop normally ..."

"What?!" I burst out. "You can't be serious."

Hamilton was also looking puzzled, but for a different reason. "Isn't this just the same ethical dilemma as 'would we kill baby Hitler if we knew at the time what adult Hitler was going to unleash on the world'?"

Cain shook his head. "No, I am not talking about ethics. I am merely saying that from a purely practical perspective, leaving the Vu-Hak alone to develop normally is the most sensible course of action."

I gave him a look of disbelief. "This is a chance to prevent trillions of deaths."

"I have an alternative suggestion," Adam said.

He got up and walked to the far wall where there was a holographic representation of the ship, standing like a gigantic black graphite spear on the beach. He waved at it and the image blurred and reconfigured into a schematic of this solar system. The twin suns were pictured much closer than reality allowed, and the planets' orbits were outlined in various glowing colors of the spectrum. One of the gas giant's moons was tagged with Vu-Hak symbols indicating where we were. With another flick of his hand the image pulled back and zoomed out into the interstellar void. After a rollercoaster ride through space the image converged on a nearby star system where a solitary yellow G-type star burned brightly.

"We take the ship and go there," he said, pointing at the hologram. "I have already identified three exoplanets orbiting within the habitable zone of this star. It is actually the nearest star to us."

Stillman walked over and stared at the image, her arms folded. "Near is relative, right? How far away are we talking?"

"Approximately twenty-five trillion miles," he replied calmly. "Or four point two light years."

Hamilton lifted his head. "So okay, we just conjure up a new wormhole?"

"That is not feasible," said Cain, shaking his head. "I have been running further simulations. The problem with any new wormhole is our inability to map and delineate the destination co-ordinates. We could only safely perform multiple short distance transits, perhaps 1AU, at maximum."

"Can't we just return home, go 'back to the future'?" said Stillman, sticking with her previous analogy.

"We cannot artificially travel forward in this timeline. The Trinity-generated wormhole was irreversibly damaged by the interaction with the Vu-Hak's gravitational waves."

My head was spinning with the options we were discussing. "Have you any idea how long it would take this ship to travel to that star system?"

Adam waved at the hologram and a computer-generated image appeared of the ship taking off and accelerating out of the Vu-Hak system and into the void. "This ship can accelerate continuously at approximately 1G and attain point nine eight of the speed of light. It would reach this maximum velocity in just under a year. There would be a further two years' cruise at this velocity, then another year to slow down. So approximately five and a half years total travel time."

"Shit," said Hamilton, reaching for the bourbon.

"You would be in cryosleep," said Adam. "And wake up in a new world."

"I still don't get why you want us to leave, only to travel a few light years," I muttered.

Cain moved over to join us and leaned in, looking at the images. "There is one obvious reason. By the time the Vu-Hak are evolved enough to leave their own planet, Humanity 2.0 will already be many thousands of years more advanced. The Vu-Hak will not be a threat to them, or any other race."

I regarded Cain; trying to see into his mind, figure out where he was coming from. He seemed to be pushing a non-interventionist position harder than I expected.

"And of course it is also true that if we stay here, we will be in a position to control their development," he said with a nonchalant shrug. "The Vu-Hak data banks give details for the construction of atmosphere processing plants, which would be able to transform both the atmosphere and the ecosystem of this planet to a more habitable one."

Before I could say anything, Stillman spoke up, clearly still mulling over the thought of a long space voyage. "What if none of those planets are suitable for human life despite our ability to 'fine tune' their ecosystems? Do we then jump back on the ship and head for the next star? What if that star is hundreds of light years away? Do we keep running and searching for ever?"

Adam's lip twitched. "Humanity 2.0 – as Cain so quaintly put it – will not require the same Earth-like environment to survive and flourish. With epigenetic modifications Humanity 2.0 can be made stronger and more robust, more able to adapt to adverse environments, more resistant to diseases and infections, and to be able to breathe in a variety of non-Earth-like atmospheres. In essence, a true post-human existence."

There was a particularly loud crack of thunder outside, and lightning seemed to rattle the windshield.

Stillman wandered over to us and peered out, putting her hand up and wiping the shield's surface where a light mist had started to coat it. The clouds in the distance looked to be clearing and the gas giant was emerging behind, occupying about half of the night sky.

"We're safe here," she said without turning. "I vote to stay. Hunt down and kill the progenitors of the Vu-Hak, and start the process of growing the embryos."

Cain was having none of it. "Genocide makes you no better than the Vu-Hak."

Adam nodded. "And we have a chance to begin again on a new world –"

"*This* is a new world," insisted Stillman.

I was about to reply when the wall behind us shimmered out of existence and became a doorway. Amy ran through, breathless and wide-eyed. She was wearing one of the grey rubbery suits and her black hair was tied back in braids. She ran straight up to Adam and grabbed his hand, pulling him and ignoring the rest of us. "You need to come, now!" she said in between lungfuls of air.

"Amy, what is it?" I said.

She glanced up at me and shrank back toward Adam, unease and suspicion written all over her face. Then she pointed toward the doorway.

"Mr. Hubert has woken up. And I don't like him."

EPILOGUE

The old woman got up from a rocking chair older than herself, stood tall and slim, her grey hair neatly tied back and styled with old-fashioned rollers, and squinted into the distance. The countryside stretched before her like a great quilt of brown and green squares, held together by the green sutures of hedgerows. The odd farmhouse or barn separated the fields and a single country lane meandered peacefully through.

She blinked, and there was smoke on the horizon, and a ghastly orange rictus smile tore through the verdant woodland. Unfettered flames blew up, hungrily devouring, lapping up, dancing and infesting everything that seemed good and right.

She blinked again and saw blackened bodies, charred bones, as fire tainted the earth, stripping trees of their virescent beauty, leaving gaunt skeletal grey remains, bony toes rooted to barren soil.

The sound of a child screaming emerged from the backdrop of a bustling city. At first it was distant, but it came steadily closer and all the while becoming more intense, more distressed.

She closed her eyes and tried to remember what the woman had said. Something she had to forget. Something so important that it could never be remembered. Something that happened a long time ago.

She seemed such a nice lady. She tried to picture her once more.

Average height, pale skin, shaved skull, angular features ... and the most incredible glowing green eyes.

There was recognition there, but just out of reach.

Then she was gently turned by kind hands and led back into the house, the air too smoky to breathe, soon hot enough to scorch the skin. She sat on her bed, in the dark, gas mask on her face, listening to the flames devouring all that she had built, everything she had known.

Then she heard it coming, the soft patter of its footsteps like a damning whisper. Her eyes widened, and her breaths came ragged and short. Her legs were frozen in place and she felt sweat drench her skin, her heart thumping against her chest.

At first the shadow was no more than a chill in the air, a shimmer of mist, diffuse. Through it the furniture and the wallpaper that peeled with the smoke became slightly out of focus, like a poorly taken photograph.

Then it was no more than a distortion of the light, a human shape cut out of colors that weren't right. Where it moved the things behind it appeared bowed, as if looked at through a fish-eye lens. Then as quickly as it came, it left, without leaving so much as a footprint in the fall mud.

The woman managed to stand up and ran her hands through her hair. She lowered the mask and gave a rasping cough that caused her trachea to burn as if she'd swallowed razor blades. She reached for the glass of water on the bedside and brought it to her lips.

The shadow returned, and this time stared into her eyes, its face passive and slack. The clock on the wall ceased to tick and there was no sound from the outside world, not a bird or engine noise.

The air shattered with a scream that was so piercing that she collapsed to the floor in a fetal position, hands clamped over her ears. The atmosphere became cold and her body heat quickly deserted her, leaking from every pore. Awareness crept over her that she was no longer in contact with the ground but instead spinning.

When she opened her eyes, the room was no longer there; instead there was only the shadow's face and open mouth, magnified. In utter paralysis she was drawn toward it.

Then she remembered what she had been told to forget.

And it all came rushing back.

ABOUT THE AUTHOR

P.A. Vasey is a Medical Oncologist (Cancer Physician), born in Newcastle, UK. His professional writing credits include over 200 publications including peer-reviewed journals, book chapters, conference contributions and electronic outputs in the field of cancer research. He moved to Australia in 2004, and lives in Brisbane, Queensland with his wife, two daughters, dog and cat.

'TRINITY'S FALL' is the sequel to **'TRINITY'S LEGACY'**, which was his debut novel and an official semi-finalist for the 2018 Cygnus Book Awards for Science Fiction, a division of the Chanticleer International Book Awards. Both books are official Amazon *#1 Best Sellers* in multiple categories.

The saga will conclude in 2021 with the release of the final novel: **'TRINITY EVOLUTION'**.

You can stay in touch with P.A.Vasey for news and updates at the following social media sites –

Website: http://www.pavasey.com
Facebook: facebook.com/PA Vasey
Twitter: @pavasey

Made in the USA
Coppell, TX
24 September 2025